Spurred
Ambition

Also by the author
Heir Apparent
Family Claims

Spurred Ambition

A Pinnacle Peak Mystery

Twist Phelan

Poisoned Pen Press

Copyright © 2006 by Twist Phelan, Inc.
First Edition 2006
Large Print Edition 2006

10 9 8 7 6 5 4 3 2 1

Library of Congress Catalog Card Number: 2005928738
ISBN: 1-59058-174-1   Large Print

Poisoned Pen Press
6962 E. First Ave. Ste. 103
Scottsdale, AZ 85251
www.poisonedpenpress.com
info@poisonedpenpress.com
Printed in the United States of America

*for j
i forever do*

Acknowledgments

My heartfelt thanks to:

Barbara, Rob, and the rest of the terrific crew at Poisoned Pen Press. Another job well done!

Dr. Doug P. Lyle for his valuable information on hereditary diseases.

Kim—ice or rock, you never let me fall.

The two policemen who were nice enough not to arrest me. I haven't climbed any more buildings since that night. Honest.

I have no spur
To prick the sides of my intent, but only
Vaulting ambition, which o'erleaps itself
And falls on th' other—

Macbeth, ed. Sylvan Barnet (Signet 1963), act I, scene VII, lines 25-28

Chapter One

Sunday, September 13

Hannah Dain parked her Subaru behind a stand of sun-faded palo verde. She didn't know much about breaking and entering, but figured that hiding the getaway car was probably a good idea.

Dressed in black athletic tights and long-sleeved top, she reached into the rear seat for her rock-climbing shoes. The rubber soles would be quiet and provide good traction if she had to make a run for it. Slipping on her backpack and largest pair of sunglasses, Hannah checked out her reflection in the car's side mirror.

All I need is a balaclava to complete the burglar look. But a woolen hood would attract too much attention, especially in the middle of a hot Arizona afternoon.

Head down, she zigzagged through the chaparral toward the lone building. Two single-story wings stretched out from a high central section, stucco walls bright white against the sharp blue sky. The windows were covered with iron grilles that Hannah suspected were more functional than decorative. A pergola draped with vines led past well-groomed lawns to tennis courts and a lap pool.

Once in the parking lot, Hannah continued to work her way forward, using the cars as cover. Thirty feet from the building's main entrance, she crouched in the shade of an oversized SUV to survey the scene.

She had timed her visit for the afternoon, when the "guests"—Hannah thought the term ridiculous—were confined to their rooms and the staff spent more time in their offices. So far, the only person in sight was the security guard standing next to the front door.

White and in his mid-thirties, the guard wore mirrored sunglasses and a duty belt heavy with billy club, mace, and gun. He remained nearly as stationary as the building itself for the twenty minutes Hannah watched him.

Maybe he'll go to the bathroom soon. She toyed with the idea of plying him with a Coke from the gas station down the road.

Walking past the guard was Hannah's only

option. There were alternative means of entry—
climbing in through an air-conditioning vent,
prying open a window, picking a lock on a side
door. But they all required equipment and skills
that Hannah didn't have. She wondered if the penalty was less severe for *entering* sans *breaking*.

On the street side of the parking lot, Hannah
heard an engine rumble, then downshift. She squatted lower behind the SUV as a truck displaying a
nursery company's logo rolled up to the building's
main entrance. The driver's side window was down,
and Hannah heard the blare of mariachi music.

Two Hispanic men wearing dark green shirts and
matching baseball hats got out of the cab, slid open
the door in the back, and started unloading plants.
Hannah didn't know what kind they were, but it didn't
matter. They were tall and leafy and just the thing to
get her into the lobby past the security guard.

Keeping out of sight, Hannah crept up to the
truck and, standing on the running board, looked
through the open driver's window. A cap emblazoned with the nursery company's name, like the
ones the two delivery men wore, lay on the front
seat. Hannah reached in, snatched the cap, and
pulled it low on her head. Walking to the rear of the
truck, she picked up the closest plant—a four-foot-

tall specimen with thick fronds in a black plastic tub—and carried it toward the building entrance.

The two delivery men were already hauling tubs of their own. Hannah fell in line behind them, grateful for her dark hair and olive skin. If her fellow plant bearers noticed that their number had increased, they gave no sign.

As the two men passed the security guard, one turned to the other and spoke in rapid Spanish. The other laughed and answered. Hannah decided she better join the conversation.

"*Dé mis recuerdos a sus tíos,*" she said as she went by the guard, hoping he was as monolingual as he looked. Otherwise he might wonder why Hannah had just given her regards to his aunt and uncle. It was one of the few Spanish phrases she could recall from a summer course a few years ago—her East Coast prep school had emphasized French. Luckily, the guard ignored her.

The building's lobby was tastefully appointed with wood and leather furniture. Beautiful photographs of the Grand Canyon covered several walls. But despite the resort-hotel façade, Hannah wasn't fooled. Fully equipped gym, gourmet cuisine, and decorator-chosen color scheme aside, the place still had the air of a prison.

Holding the plant high in front of her, Hannah frog-marched across the tile floor. The plastic tub was starting to feel heavy—all told, her camouflage probably weighed forty pounds. At least it wasn't a cactus.

Eyes averted, she passed the reception desk, on course for the door that led to guest housing. Only when she got closer did she see the five-button keypad.

Now what? Hannah needed a free hand to work the lock, but didn't want to risk discovery by setting down the plant. In any event, it was a hypothetical dilemma. She didn't know the lock combination.

"Looks like you have your hands full. Let me help you."

A woman in a nurse's uniform reached around Hannah and tapped in a sequence on the keypad. There was a loud *click*. The woman grasped the handle and opened the door.

"*Muchas gracias,*" Hannah mumbled into the fronds.

As soon as the door shut behind her, Hannah put down the plant and rubbed her aching biceps. Her arms felt so stretched out, she almost expected her sleeves to be too short.

She was in a narrow corridor lined with closed

doors. Each one had a nameplate mounted beside it, and Hannah blew out a small sigh of relief. Finding the right room was going to be easier than she had thought.

Hannah read the first name.

Nope.

She crossed the hall and looked at the nameplate there.

Not this one.

She reached down, grabbed the rim of the plant, dragged it ten feet, then stopped and read the next name.

Uh-uh.

She checked the door across the way.

Not here either.

Hannah dragged the plant another ten feet, then paused, hands propped on her knees. Sweat dampened the bill of her cap.

Thirty seconds to check four doors. Thirty seconds wasn't very long. Unless you were hauling a heavy plant down a hallway where you didn't belong with another dozen doors to check—on each side. And when at any moment one of the doors might open, with the person behind it wanting to know just what in the heck you were up to.

On a hunch, Hannah jogged the length of the

corridor. From what she could tell, the rooms at the end were slightly larger, and so might be considered premium accommodations. She was pleased, and not altogether surprised, to find the name she was looking for on the last door on the right.

Hannah ran back to the plant and dragged it next to the main door again. In case she had to dash, she didn't want any obstacles in her way. And if someone else showed up, Hannah hoped that the plant would divert attention long enough for her to escape.

She returned to the room at the end of the corridor. Scarcely breathing, Hannah stood close to the door and pressed her ear against the metal, but couldn't hear anything—to be expected in a place where the insulation was thick enough to muffle the occasional scream.

Hannah reached for the knob. It turned under her hand, and she felt a surge of excitement. Heart pounding, she eased the door open about half an inch, unsure what she was going to find on the other side.

Just then, voices sounded at the other end of the corridor.

"What's this plant—"

Hannah pushed the door open wider and stepped into the room.

Chapter Two

She stood still, waiting for her pulse to slow, then cautiously looked around.

There wasn't much to see. It was a small room outfitted in dormitory-style furnishings—twin bed, four-drawer bureau, student desk. With bare floors and white walls, the space was decidedly spartan.

And occupied. A woman sat in a chair by the window, headphones over her ears. She wore blue cashmere sweats and her feet were bare. Gazing at the landscaped grounds on the other side of the glass, she absently stroked the stuffed animal on her lap.

"Hi," Hannah said.

There was no response. Hannah shut the door to the corridor.

"*Hi*," she repeated, louder this time.

The woman glanced over her shoulder, then did a double take. She yanked off the headphones.

"What are you doing here?" Shelby demanded.

Her blonde hair had lost some of its luster and her face looked thinner, but Hannah's older sister could still turn heads. Shelby's beauty was of the sort that made Hannah—and most other women— think that no matter how well they dressed, did their hair, or put on makeup, they still weren't playing in the same league.

"Visiting you," Hannah replied, trying to sound cheery.

"You know I don't want to see anyone. Go away!"

For the past three years Hannah had practiced law at Dain & Dain. Shelby, also an attorney with the family firm, was currently on leave of absence, having checked into rehab four weeks ago. Despite a lifetime of effort by Hannah, the sisters had never been close. But after the events of last month, Hannah was determined to keep trying.

So every week since Shelby's admission, she had come by to visit. And every week her sister had refused to see her. Leaving behind a five-pound bag of black jelly beans—the doctor said licorice could alleviate the craving for alcohol—Hannah would depart without pressing the issue.

The same traumatic events that had sent

Shelby back into rehab had also led to Hannah's uncovering of certain family secrets—a discovery that exposed as false the foundation upon which Hannah had built her life. A discovery that, for the moment, made it impossible for her to continue working at the firm.

Hannah wasn't about to reveal to Shelby the reason she was leaving—at this point, it would only worsen relations between them. But she didn't want to take a new job without first telling her sister. Already there had been too many unnecessary acts of unkindness within the Dain family.

Although Shelby was refusing all visitors and phone calls, Hannah thought leaving her a note would be too impersonal, cold even. But with a job interview tomorrow, Hannah was running out of time to break the news. Thus her plan to sneak into the rehab center. Unfortunately, her sister didn't seem all that impressed. Or pleased.

"Let me explain—" Hannah began as Shelby, her mouth set in a stubborn line, got up from her chair. She headed for the nightstand, where a thick ivory wire lay coiled next to a lamp and a clock/CD player. On the end of the wire was a plastic cylinder topped with a red knob.

A panic button. Hannah couldn't believe it—her

sister was calling Security. Launching herself across the bed, she grabbed Shelby around the waist in a low tackle. Both women crashed onto the floor.

"I just want to tell you something!" Hannah panted, pinning Shelby with her body weight. For someone thirty years old, her sister could be as bratty as a teenager.

"Let go!" Shelby squirmed and flailed her arms, trying to extricate herself.

"Just listen to me for a minute. After that, I'll leave."

Shelby struggled some more, then abruptly quit.

"Fine—you win. Now get off me!"

Hannah rolled onto her side and Shelby scrambled to her feet.

"I remembered your jelly beans," Hannah said in a conciliatory tone. Retrieving her backpack, she set it on the bed and unzipped it.

"You're just trying to get me fat," Shelby muttered.

Hannah found the bag of candy and undid the twist tie that held it closed. *This place must be doing some good.* In the past, her sister would never have given in so eas—

Shelby pounced on the panic button.

"Don't!" Hannah cried, lunging toward her.

But she was too late. Five pounds of jelly beans spilled across the bedspread as Shelby pressed the red knob with a triumphant smile. An alarm sounded outside in the corridor.

Leopards and their unchangeable spots, Hannah thought unhappily. She clambered off the bed, sending jelly beans cascading to the wooden floor. The pinging noise they made sounded like hail on pavement.

The door to the room flew open and a nurse rushed in.

"Ms. Dain, is everything all right?" the nurse asked, looking from Shelby to Hannah to the scattered black candies.

Shelby pointed at Hannah. "I want you to make her—"

Hannah spread her hands in a gesture of mute appeal and Shelby paused, chest heaving. The sisters stared at each other. Five seconds ticked by.

"Ms. Dain?" the nurse prompted.

Shelby lowered her arm to her side.

"Forget it," she said.

The nurse looked dubious. "But the panic button—"

"—was an accident. Can we have some privacy?"

"Of course." With the barest of head shakes,

the nurse left.

The stuffed animal that Shelby had been holding lay on the floor. She picked it up and reclaimed the chair by the window. After sweeping jelly beans out of the way, Hannah sat on a corner of the bed. Neither sister spoke.

"So…how's it going?" Hannah finally asked, unable to bear the silence any longer.

"How do you think?" Shelby snapped. "I've been here twenty-seven days, and every morning I still wake up craving a drink. So much for eight years sober."

Hannah twisted her mouth in sympathy. She wasn't the only one traumatized by last month's ordeal. Forced in the course of events to drink a fifth of hard liquor, Shelby—a recovering alcoholic—had barely escaped alcohol poisoning.

"It's not your fault. You didn't fall off the wagon—you were pushed."

"Doesn't make me want it any less." Shelby dug her fingers into the fake fur of what Hannah now recognized was a toy dog.

Must be a rehab thing. Her sister wasn't the stuffed-animal type.

"I know you're not here to find out how the family drunk is enjoying her"—Shelby pantomimed quotation marks with her fingers—"vacation." Her voice tightened. "Did something happen at the firm…or to Daddy?"

Hannah shook her head. "Richard's fine. The office has been pretty quiet since Olivia left."

Dain & Dain had been founded by Richard Dain and his wife, Elizabeth, after the latter's graduation from law school. They were joined a year later by Elizabeth's best friend, Olivia Parrish. Olivia became Shelby and Hannah's surrogate mother after Elizabeth died when the sisters were very young. Two weeks ago, she had departed on a six-month sabbatical to Africa.

"I don't understand Olivia and this Africa trip. And I still don't get why Daddy didn't take the judgeship." Shelby frowned. "What's going on that you're not telling me?"

Shelby didn't know? Hannah felt her muscles relax in relief. If Richard hadn't told her sister about Elizabeth, Hannah certainly wasn't going to say anything.

Hey, sis—or should I say half-sis? That's right— Mom had an affair, and you're looking at the result. But that's not all of it. When she was a lawyer…

Hannah curtailed her thoughts, reminding herself why she was there.

"I'm taking some time off from the firm, too. I wanted you to know before"—Hannah bit back *you got out of rehab*—"you came back to work," she added lamely.

Shelby stared at Hannah.

"You have *got* to be kidding. Olivia is off in Africa, I'm stuck in here, and you think it's a good time to leave Daddy? Who's going to handle the deals?" Hannah and Olivia were responsible for the transactions side of the practice, while Richard and Shelby concentrated on litigation.

"Once Olivia announced her plans, Richard cut back on accepting new business. And he farmed out some of the trial work to other firms." Hannah picked up a jelly bean and rolled it between her fingers, the candy leaving black streaks on her skin. Her sister's reaction wasn't at all what she had expected. Even though Richard's favorite—for reasons now obvious to Hannah—Shelby had always made it clear that she resented her sister's presence at the firm.

"I thought you'd like the idea of having the place to yourself," Hannah said.

Her sister made a sour face. "Even if you're not around, I'll still be the Dain who can't be trusted on her own. And this whole rehab thing will just make it worse."

Hannah was astonished. She never imagined Richard's nepotism had been hurtful to her sister, too.

Left largely to her own devices, Hannah had been forced to develop her legal skills quickly and mostly on her own. She had risen to the challenge, and was soon handling major transactions with little supervision. In contrast, while second-chairing many trials with Richard, her sister had yet to litigate a case by herself. What Hannah regarded as mentoring, Shelby had seen as lack of confidence in her abilities.

"That's not true—" Hannah began. But Shelby cut her off.

"Of course it is. Daddy's treated you differently since the moment you were born. He always said you were cut from a different cloth."

Hannah sucked in a breath. "Did he say anything else? About the cloth, I mean."

Shelby frowned in annoyance. "What are you talking about? It's just an expression."

"Right." Hannah plucked at a loose thread on the bedspread. Shelby studied her with narrowed eyes.

"Is there something you expected him to say?" she asked.

Hannah's hand tightened into a fist, crushing the jelly bean in her palm. She had forgotten how keen her sister's radar could be, especially when it came to detecting secrets.

"No!" She picked up her backpack. "I should get going. Nice dog, by the way."

"Gift from a friend," Shelby said, coloring slightly.

Hannah noticed the blush and was surprised. Not at the idea Shelby would meet someone—her sister never failed to attract admirers—but that she would be interested in a guy who would give a stuffed animal as a present. Jewelry and vacations were her sister's usual relationship booty.

"C'mon, tell me who he is," Hannah coaxed.

Shelby ignored her. "So what are you going to do?"

"Well, I thought I'd go to the rock-climbing park and—"

"I'm not talking about this afternoon! As if I care how you plan to get dirty and sweaty." Shelby thought sports a foolish expenditure of energy. "I meant for a *job*."

"Oh." Hannah wiped the palm of her hand on her pants, trying to get rid of the stickiness from the candy. "Actually, I don't have one yet. But I've got an interview tomorrow."

"Who with?"

"The Tohono O'odham Office of Tribal Affairs. They're looking for a contract lawyer to put together a real estate private placement."

"You're leaving the firm to do a no-frills deal for the *Indians*? The money better be good."

"It's just temporary," Hannah said, hoping Shelby wouldn't pursue it. She didn't want to admit the pay was as low-level as the project. At Dain & Dain Hannah had worked on far more complicated transactions for a monthly salary double that quoted in the ad for the Tohono O'odham position.

"Why are you doing this? After what happened last month, I thought you'd—"

"I better go, Shelby. It was good to see you." As Hannah said the words, she realized that she meant them.

"Just make sure it doesn't happen again."

"But I don't mind—"

Shelby hugged the stuffed dog, looking out the window again. "Makes it harder to be here," she said in a low voice.

Hannah felt the distance yawn between them, stretching beyond the confines of the small room. But she knew that now wasn't the time to try bridging the gap. Shelby had more imperative things to work through first.

Me, too. She slung her backpack over her shoulder.

"I'll drop off more jelly beans this week. Let me know if you need anything else."

Shelby didn't answer.

Hannah let herself out. She was halfway down the corridor when a door behind her opened.

"Some cinnamon flavor wouldn't hurt! And lose that stupid hat!" The door slammed shut again.

Maybe some leopards… Hannah kept walking, a small smile tugging at the corner of her mouth.

Chapter Three

The angry mob surged against Hannah's Subaru. Two men grabbed the roof rack and rocked the station wagon from side to side, while half a dozen others pummeled the car's hood. Crudely painted signs—*Save White Businesses, Boycott Indians*—waved back and forth above the crowd.

Inside the car it was eerily quiet, steel and plastic muffling the clamor. Hannah gripped the steering wheel and stared in shock at the crush of people. Twenty minutes ago she had left the rehab center, her conversation with Shelby and an afternoon of bouldering the only things on her mind. Now she was trapped in the middle of a near-riot.

The entrance to the rock-climbing park on the Tohono O'odham reservation—sanctuary, if Hannah could get there—was only a hundred yards away. But it might as well have been a hundred miles—the short strip of gravel in between the car and the park gates was overrun with protesters. Some had linked arms and were singing "We Shall Overcome." Hannah thought it an odd anthem choice for what appeared to be an all-white gathering.

"Go home!" shouted a man outside her driver-side window, speckling the glass with saliva. "Get out of here!"

Fine with me. Hannah shifted the car into reverse. But when the Subaru began to move backward, a collective howl went up, accompanied by a renewed assault of beating hands. Hannah slammed on the brakes and wondered what to do.

She had no idea what had the crowd so riled, or why so many people were there in the first place. A busy day at the climbing park usually meant a dozen visitors. Now ten times that number swarmed around her car.

Feeling a prickle of genuine worry, Hannah decided to call for help. She reached for the holster on the dash, but it was empty. *Of all the times…* In her hurry to get to the rehab center, she had left her cell phone at home.

A young woman in denim cut-offs and a trucker's cap slapped a flyer onto the Subaru's windshield, the sound of her hand against the glass making Hannah jump. The flyer featured a stick drawing of an Indian wearing a headdress overlaid with a red circle and a diagonal slash—the international *No* symbol. Across the bottom was printed *Boycott 9/13*.

Hannah knew Anglo-Indian tensions had been on the rise ever since the Tohono O'odham opened the new casino. Practically every issue of the local paper contained a guest editorial or letter to the editor railing against the slot machine/poker/ blackjack emporium. The complaints ranged from the evils of gambling to the Tohono O'odham's unwillingness to cover the added costs—road wear-and-tear, police overtime—the casino imposed on the town. Small business owners groused about being undersold by Indians not subject to sales tax. Environmentalists were alarmed because the tribe was exempt from regulation. Neighboring property owners feared losing their land to claims by Indians now able to afford top lawyers.

Boycott 9/13? Hannah vaguely recalled a news story several days ago. Something about a group of whites calling for a day-long boycott of Indian-owned businesses—the casino, the shopping mall, the—

The rock-climbing park. Hannah mentally kicked herself. If she hadn't been so preoccupied with getting in to see Shelby, she might have remembered.

A man clutching a longneck, *Share the Wealth* and *Indian Greed* bumper stickers glued to his clothing, tried to clamber onto the hood of the idling Subaru. Someone else's boot thudded against the tailgate and Hannah felt the metal give, along with what was left of her composure.

If similar demonstrations were happening elsewhere along the reservation's borders, Pinnacle Peak's small sheriff's department would be overwhelmed. Despite the air conditioning, her skin became clammy with sweat. She made sure the doors were locked.

A motorcycle engine snarled over the hubbub, and the throng parted like a biblical sea to let the rider through. A massive man on an equally massive bike coasted to a stop in front of the Subaru. The machine's chrome trim glittered so brightly in the sunlight, Hannah had to look away.

After a final rev of the engine, the man booted down the kickstand and swung his leg over the saddle. Folding ham-sized forearms adorned with tattoos across his chest, he glared at Hannah from under a dark shelf of brow. Printed on his t-shirt were the words *White Power*, the letters *te* and *Po* stretched wide by his overhanging belly.

Oh great. In Hannah's experience, anyone who

relied on the word *power* to express his viewpoint was a fanatic, an idiot, or both. She was pretty certain the man's arrival meant her situation was going to get worse—fast.

Just then a bald, slightly built man wearing glasses and a short-sleeved shirt pushed through the crowd and approached *White Power* man. His air of authority gave Hannah hope. *An off-duty cop? Tribal police?*

But instead of a badge, the smaller man brandished a pen and spiral-bound notebook. Hannah saw the laminated photo ID hanging from his shirt pocket and a sour taste filled her mouth.

Terrific—the press had arrived. Hannah knew she shouldn't be surprised—riots made good copy. She also knew the reporter wouldn't intercede, even if things got nasty. In fact, his presence would probably egg on the others.

Hannah scanned the milling protesters. Everywhere she looked she saw belligerence, the mob's hate radiating like heat. She doubted it mattered to most present whether she paid the Indians a buck to go rock climbing that day. More likely, it was the chance to engage in violence without repercussion that had so many people pumped.

Maybe she should abandon the car. When the

pack set upon it, she could slip away unnoticed. Hannah grasped the door handle, ready to run for it, when her eyes met those of a greasy-haired man in a stained t-shirt. He leered at her, grabbing his crotch and making humping movements with his hips. She shrank back from the door, no longer sure that outside the car would be safer than where she was.

Someone produced a metal trash barrel, which was turned upside down and planted about ten feet in front of the Subaru's bumper. *White Power* man climbed on top of it.

"What do we need to beat the Indians?" he shouted, pointing at his shirt.

"White power," called back a few people.

The man cupped his hand to his ear. "What's that?"

This time more voices joined in. "White power!"

"So let's do it!" With a rebel yell *White Power* man jumped off the trash barrel and headed straight for Hannah's car.

Let's do what? Fleetingly, Hannah considered driving through the mass of people, but the idea of running over someone—and the mob's certain retaliation—held her back. She remembered the news clips of the LA riots.

White Power man took up a position next to the Subaru's passenger side.

"What do we need?" he bellowed.

"White power!" the crowd answered. The chant quickly built to a roar. "White power! White power!"

Without warning, *White Power* man bent down out of Hannah's view. The next moment she felt the car begin to tilt. Her shoulder slammed into the doorframe.

The idiot is picking up my car! Hannah grabbed on to the steering wheel, her head nearly hitting the window. Seconds later, the Subaru dropped back to earth, whiplashing her against the seat back and spilling her sports gear into the footwell. A little bit higher, and the car would have rolled completely over.

Hannah struggled to disentangle herself from the seatbelt's stranglehold as two bodybuilding types, faces ugly with eagerness, emerged from the crowd to stand beside *White Power* man. Hannah had no doubt of their intentions. With three guys lifting, her car would end up like an overturned turtle for sure.

I've got to get out of here.

Fortunately, the Subaru's engine was still running. Hannah shifted into first and punched the gas pedal. The car lurched forward, scattering people right and left. Elbow jammed against the horn, Hannah steered as best she could, trying to see around the flyer that was still stuck to her windshield.

She was almost clear of the horde and starting to pick up speed when somebody threw the rock. The chunk of granite struck the driver-side window with a sharp crack. Instinctively Hannah ducked, wrenching the steering wheel to the right. She felt but didn't see the collision.

The Subaru ran up and over the obstacle with a horrific screech of metal scraping against metal. Hannah prayed the airbag wouldn't blow. When the car's four tires were on the ground again, she stomped on the gas, aiming for the park entrance and the refuge of tribal land.

In her rearview mirror, Hannah could see *White Power* man standing beside his mangled motorcycle—fists raised with middle fingers extended, mouth contorted in rage. She kept going, hoping her tires were churning up enough dust to hide her license plate.

Chapter Four

An hour after fleeing from *White Power* man, Hannah was on her way up a cliff face. Still amped on adrenaline, she grabbed a shallow pocket with her fingers—chalked to prevent slippage—and pulled herself across the vertical slab of granite. She planned to stay in the rock-climbing park until dark, hoping that by then police, fatigue, or boredom would have dispersed the mob.

At first, she had tried waiting in the Subaru but, still too jittery from her close escape, soon gave it up. From past experience she knew that nothing less than physical exertion would settle her mind. So she had decided to go climbing.

Even if the protesters dared to invade the reservation, Hannah wasn't overly worried about being found. The park was fairly large and crisscrossed by small canyons, like the one where she had parked her car. As a further precaution, Hannah had chosen to climb a formation that was well away from the road. If someone discovered the Subaru, she wouldn't be in the vicinity.

Unlike a traditional rock climber, Hannah wore no special gear other than a chalk bag and climbing shoes. Nothing attached her to the stone except for her feet and hands. A fall risked serious injury—or death. For safety's sake, she had left a crash pad—a six-by-four-foot chunk of foam sheathed in orange nylon—on the ground beneath her intended route.

As far as Hannah was concerned, the great thing about bouldering wasn't physical, but mental. The sport demanded just enough concentration to prevent her from thinking about anything else. Every hour spent on the rock was an hour away from the past and the future, white noise for her brain. Very different from road biking, her previous sport of choice. But lately cycling had lost some of its appeal, as had other activities conducive to contemplation. It wasn't that Hannah didn't have a lot of things to think about. She just didn't especially want to.

Pushing through her legs rather than pulling with her arms, Hannah reached for a sloper. Apparently not even climbing was going to keep her thoughts at bay this afternoon—she just couldn't get tomorrow's interview out of her head.

Shelby wasn't the only one surprised by Hannah's job choice. Her boyfriend, Cooper Smith, had also commented on the lousy pay and ordinary work. But Hannah knew that wasn't what was really bothering him. Cooper saw her reluctance to look for a permanent position as a lack of commitment to their renewed relationship.

Lately their discussions had intensified, culminating in a quarrel right before she had left for the rehab center. Hannah had made things worse by mentioning a job offer from a Boston law firm, extended before she and Cooper had started dating again. Cooper's ownership of a local ranch made his relocating back East impossible. Caught up in the heat of the moment, Hannah had wanted to take back the words as soon as she had said them.

She grabbed a rounded bulge, knowing the argument probably could have been avoided if she had just told Cooper the real reason she wanted the Tohono O'odham job—to buy time to find out the truth about her parents.

Because Elizabeth Dain had died two days after giving birth to Hannah, everything Hannah knew about her mother came from stories told by others—all of which painted Elizabeth as the ideal spouse, parent, and lawyer. So Hannah's discovery five weeks ago that her mother had not only committed malpractice to advance her legal career but also cheated on her husband—with Hannah the consequence of that affair—had rocked her world. Overnight she had gone from aspiring to follow her mother's example to not knowing who her birth father was.

Hannah's initial anger toward Elizabeth had yet to abate. And after a lifetime of idolatry, Hannah found herself wanting to get past the fiction, to find out the truth about her parents. Why had Elizabeth cheated on Richard? Was it a one-night stand or an extended affair? Who was her father?

She wondered if her desire to delve into family secrets would be so compelling if she enjoyed a better relationship with her sister and Richard. But as this afternoon had proved, she and Shelby were still far from reconciling their differences. Meanwhile, Richard remained as distant as ever. Part of Hannah couldn't blame him. After all, she was a walking, talking reminder of his wife's infidelity. Still, the rejection stung.

Family was Hannah's purchase on life—to her, biological connections mattered. She needed to know the stories that had merged to make her own narrative before she could continue the tale. That was why she had returned to Arizona after law school and joined Dain & Dain.

After three years of feeling like an outsider, Hannah had been on the verge of calling it quits and returning to Boston. Then the truth about Elizabeth had surfaced—and Cooper had come back into her life.

Hannah crimped onto an edge. If asked, she would say she was happy, maybe even in love, with him. And he seemed ready to make the commitment Hannah had always thought she wanted. For that reason alone, she would—happily—stay in Arizona.

But her family puzzle had to be solved first. Hannah thought of it as a clearing out of the old to make room for the new. Once the missing pieces to her parentage were in place, she would be able to give Cooper and their future her full attention. Until then, their relationship, along with her law career, would have to be on hold.

The sun declined over the mountains, throwing shadows across the splintered edges of rock. Hannah felt her back and legs beginning to tire, and she knew it was time to descend. She had climbed higher than she ever had before. The accomplishment should have made her feel better, but it didn't. *Carrying too much baggage.* Snugging her foot into a V-shaped crack, Hannah grabbed for the next hold.

Too late she realized that she should have re-chalked her fingers. Her right hand slipped, leaving her dangling from a flake of granite nearly four stories off the ground.

Hannah's lanky body hung in space for a few eternal moments before the weight became too much for her left arm. Her hold started to slide, and Hannah knew she had a second, maybe three, before she fell.

Sucking in her abs, she arched her back and heaved both feet onto a kernel. She then seized an edge and, taking advantage of momentum, scrabbled sideways. Four moves later, Hannah was again clinging to the cliff face.

She took a moment to catch her breath and tipped her head to one side, trying to loosen the knots that bunched in her left shoulder. The joint still hadn't recovered from the trauma of last month, and tweaks of pain warned that it was reaching its stress point.

A trickle of blood ran down the back of her hand from a cut on her finger. Hannah imagined she could see fragments of DNA floating in it, messages from her mother and father. *How much of her personality was self-determined, how much inherited?*

Catching sight of her orange crash pad through the brush jolted her back to reality. It was fifteen feet away from her fall line, useless in the event she peeled. For safety's sake, Hannah needed to maneuver back over the rectangle of foam before beginning her descent. Better yet would be if someone on the ground repositioned the pad and spotted her in the event she fell.

Hannah scanned the area where climbers usually parked. *I can't be the only person not to know about the boycott.* But she hadn't seen anyone else since she had arrived, and the roadside was empty.

Unlike traddies, who were more apt to value the spiritual aspects of climbing and take their time at it, boulder hounds tended to race up a chosen rock, top out, and head home. This section of the park closed at sunset, making new arrivals unlikely even if the protesters no longer blocked the entrance. And the large sign at the mountain's base—*This is a climber's access trail. Climbers only beyond this point. Technical equipment required*—kept the day hikers and mountain bikers away.

From her perch, Hannah raised her gaze to the low-slung town of Pinnacle Peak a few miles to the west. Behind her loomed El Piniculo, the thirty-four-hundred-foot granite spire that gave the town its name. In between were empty acres dotted with sage-green chaparral, the desert's signature monochrome.

Hannah scanned the arid landscape. People didn't travel much on foot in Arizona unless they were poor, jogging, or illegally crossing the border, and even then, they were rarely far from shade. No doubt about it—she was alone.

Her mind unexpectedly went to the lush trees and thick grass of the East Coast, to the memory of picnics with Cooper on the lawn in front of the law school. After they finished eating, she would push aside the blanket and fall back onto the cool grass, the blades caressing her cheek and tickling the backs of her bare knees.

Even after three years, Arizona still seemed hazardous and unforgiving. Harsh light, unrelenting heat, buildings as thick and unyielding as the earth. There was no reclining on its hard ground. Fall down there, and the scars could last forever.

Hannah studied the rock, looking for holds, trying not to think about how many of her bouldering instructor's rules she had disregarded. *Make sure you've got a spotter—you never know when you're going to peel. If you climb alone, tell someone where you're going. Don't go higher than your ability to descend easily.* The basics of bouldering safety. And Hannah had ignored every one.

Shadows edged up the granite, reminding her that a descent after dusk would be even more dangerous. *Time to move.* Hannah reached for a jug and began to sidepull toward the crash pad. Feet bridged over a gap, she leaned into her left arm, the other extended as counterbalance.

It happened in an instant—her left shoulder seized up. Pinwheels of light danced at the edge of her vision and she gasped in agony. Reflexively, she flattened herself against the cliff face, managing to grab a nubbin with her good arm.

More than a minute passed before the worst of the pain subsided. Hugging the sun-warmed stone, Hannah took stock of her situation.

If she weren't in trouble before, she was now. A descent she could barely manage using both arms would be impossible with just one. At the moment, five fingers were all that kept her from falling—five scraped-up, slick-with-sweat fingers holding on to a granite outcropping for all they were worth. She was over twenty feet up. Not far to run. Or to walk even. But very far to fall.

"Help! Can anybody hear me? Help!"

Hannah shouted the words over and over until she was hoarse. While she listened for a response, a stream of *if onlys* ran through her head. *If only she hadn't answered the ad for the job quarreled with Cooper stopped to see Shelby come by herself driven through the protesters moved off route...*

At this point, Hannah knew the best she could hope for was discovery by a deputy sheriff patrolling for breaches of park curfew. At worst, it was going to be a long night keeping herself awake and upright. She imagined time probably moved slowly when you were hanging by your fingertips.

A dark shape swooped low overhead—an owl getting an early start on the evening's hunt. Hannah's throat was dry from shouting, and she wished she had brought water. Her saliva barely moistened her mouth, and did nothing to slake her thirst. If anything, the liquid triggered a craving by every cell, overwhelming her senses until it was all she could think about.

Hannah pressed her cheek against the rough rock. She had never felt so isolated.

"Hello? Anybody there?"

Hannah looked up, certain she was imagining the voice until she saw the man's face peering at her over the top of the rock.

Chapter Five

"Down here!" Hannah shouted.

"You okay?" The man's voice was lightly accented—nearly Mexican, but not quite.

"I'm not sure about my shoulder. It might be dislocated."

"If I dropped you a harness, think you could get into it?"

Hannah tried to move her left arm. Pain shot through the joint and she bit back a yelp. Stepping into a harness while balanced on an outcrop was hard enough. Using only one arm made it out of the question.

"No," she said when the pain had receded.

"Hold on." The man's face disappeared.

What else does he think I'm going to do? Hannah nevertheless tightened her pinch on the rock.

Half a minute later a spray of pebbles rained down on her head, followed by a nylon rope skimming past her toward the ground.

"Ouch!" Hannah exclaimed as stones pelted her skin.

The face reappeared. "Look out—I'm coming down."

Now he tells me.

The face disappeared again, this time replaced by two legs and a posterior in tight blue shorts. A rather nice set of legs and posterior, Hannah couldn't help noticing.

The man rappelled down the cliff, his weight supported by a harness slung under his thighs. Drawing level with Hannah, he bounced to a stop and planted his feet on a ledge.

"You must be some highballer, way up here with no protection," he said.

Bright white teeth, curly black hair, and smooth brown skin—the man was beautiful in a thoroughly masculine way. His shirtless torso gleamed with sweat, and veins bulged in forearms braided with muscle. Hannah guessed him to be in his early thirties.

"I'm really just a newbie who got in over her head." Hannah glanced down at her crash pad, barely visible in the approaching twilight. "*Way* over."

The man followed her sightline. "Well, shift happens." He flashed her a grin. "Let's get back to *terra firma*. You a traddie climber?"

"No. I only started bouldering a month ago."

"Not a problem. I'm going to tap in a bolt to use as an anchor, then rig a sling to belay you down. It'll be a bumpy ride, but we should do okay."

"Sounds good." Hannah didn't have the faintest idea what he was talking about. But he had said the word *down*, and that was all that mattered.

"By the way, I'm Tony."

"Hannah."

"Okay, Hannah, let's do this." Enthusiasm lit up his dark eyes. At least that's what Hannah hoped it was.

She watched while he removed a bolt from the climbing bag around his waist and drove it into a crack in the rock face with a small hammer. He clipped a carabiner to the bolt and threaded the rope through it, then fed the rope through a small circle of wire cable attached to a piece of orange-painted metal and tied a loop in its end.

"What's that thing?" Hannah asked.

"Air Traffic Controller," Tony said. At Hannah's puzzled look, he added, "Brakes. Helps me make sure you don't exceed the speed limit on the way down."

Hannah felt a wave of vertigo, and swallowed hard.

Tony shook open the loop at the end of the

rope. "If I put this over your head, can you work it down under your arms?"

"I think so."

Tony dropped the loop onto her shoulders. Hannah managed to get her arms through it, one after another. Pain flared in her left shoulder with every movement.

"Lean into me so I can make sure the knot is tight around your chest."

Hesitantly, Hannah let her weight rest against his torso. Tony pulled her close and retied the knot. She was wearing a sports bra and climbing shorts, and his thatch of belly hair rubbed against her bare back. It felt rough, but in a nice way.

Too nice. Hannah jerked away, flustered by her body's reaction.

"Easy there." Tony tightened his arm around her waist. "I don't want to lose you."

"Sorry," Hannah replied, glad he couldn't see her flushed cheeks. She could feel his heart beating hard and strong against the back of her ribs, his pulse outracing hers.

Guess I'm not the only one getting some cardio out of this.

"Hold on to the rope and keep your feet on the wall." Tony wrapped her fingers into the correct grip. "Lean back and make sure your knees are bent—they're your shock absorbers. Ready?"

Hannah nodded. Tony moved sideways and braced his feet perpendicular to the rock.

"Belay," he said, and played out some rope. Hannah pushed away from the wall as she started to descend. She dropped about eight inches before coming to an abrupt stop.

"Walk your feet—don't bounce. Otherwise you'll pendulum back into the rock."

He adjusted the rope and Hannah felt herself drop again. Bottom lip jutted in concentration, she took smooth steps down the rock face. The rope chafed against her midriff, but she ignored it.

After what seemed a long time but was in reality just minutes, her feet touched sand. Hannah's knees went weak with relief.

"Untie the rope and watch out," Tony called.

Hannah worked the knot free and tottered sideways. She had barely regained her equilibrium when Tony touched down next to her.

"Great job!" He stepped out of his harness. "How's the shoulder?"

Hannah gingerly prodded the tender spot, her cut finger leaving a smear of blood on her skin. "I don't think it's dislocated. Hurts a lot, though."

"I've got some pain cream. Something to patch that finger, too."

Tony dug into the pouch around his waist. A patch sewn on the front of the bag read *Addicted to Crack*. It took Hannah a moment to understand it was a rock-climbing joke.

"Would you happen to have any water?" Her thirst had returned, stronger than ever.

"I left my water bottle on top, but I've got two of these." Tony held out an energy bar. "Hungry?"

Her need for liquid aside, Hannah realized she was ravenous. She tore off the first bar's wrapper and scarfed down the rubbery rectangle of vitamin-laced sugar. Normally not keen on "fake" food, she could have eaten half a dozen of the chewy snacks.

While Hannah ate, Tony took a small white tube from his bag. He unscrewed its cap and squeezed some ointment onto his fingertips.

"You should probably go to the ER. This will make you feel better until you get there."

With gentle strokes Tony worked the cream onto her sore shoulder, and Hannah got a whiff of eucalyptus. Notwithstanding his advice, she didn't plan on going to the doctor. The pain didn't feel like a permanent injury, and as a rule her body healed pretty well. *If only her psyche were as resilient.*

Tony paused to squirt out more cream, and Hannah remembered her manners. "Thank you so much for getting me down. I was in real trouble. Were you climbing on the other side?"

Tony nodded. "Cleaning up the rock."

"Cleaning?" Hannah repeated, unsure what he meant.

"Removing protection left by other climbers."

Hannah knew *protection* referred to the various types of metal devices that secured or guided ropes in traditional climbing, like the bolt Tony had used to anchor the carabiner. Mountain etiquette dictated they be removed except along dedicated routes, but the protocol wasn't always observed.

"Do you work for the park?" Hannah unconsciously leaned into the pressure of his hands as the medicated ointment began to blunt the pain.

"Nope. Strictly volunteer."

Hannah thought about being stranded—how scared she had felt, how close she had been to serious harm. Right now, she wasn't certain if she would ever climb again. Events of last month and now today had proved Nature to be quite uncontrollable, not to mention downright dangerous.

She peered up at the cliff face. "Do you ever think about falling?"

"Sure. The defining thing about climbing is that it can kill you."

"I'm starting to have second thoughts about the sport."

"Why? At the base of a mountain, all you have to ask is *Do I want to face life or death today?* Big questions like that are simple. It's the little ones that are complicated. *Do you stay at a crummy job to pay the bills? Do you spend the holidays with your family?* Much more difficult to answer compared with deciding whether to go up a mountain. Climbing is a break from the hard stuff."

Maybe he's right. At times, navigating the choices presented by an ordinary day seemed harder than tackling a V10 climb without the beta. Hannah wished life came with a route map.

"Besides, today the end justified the means," Tony added.

"Digging out other people's carabiners and bolts is worth the risk of a broken leg—or worse?"

Tony laughed. "I was talking about helping you. But I guess the equation is the same in either case. Sometimes taking risk as an individual is worth it for a greater good."

An avowed cynic, Hannah thought true self-lessness was rare, especially the sort practiced out of the public eye. All the same, it was rather nice to have her personal safety deemed *a greater good*.

Tony kneaded the base of her neck. "Do you usually climb alone?"

"Today was the first time. I know—pretty dumb."

"Not necessarily. Sometimes it's good to go by yourself. Gives you a chance to think."

Tony's thumbs smoothed out a knotted muscle and Hannah shut her eyes, now understanding why cats purred.

"Actually, that's what I was doing. I've got this job interview tomorrow…" Hannah's voice trailed off as Tony worked along the top of her spine.

"What kind of job?"

Hannah usually avoided discussing personal matters with strangers, barricading herself behind books on cross-country flights and abstaining from hair salon gab fests.

Perhaps it was the relief of escaping the protesters, or the intimacy created by their harrowing descent. Maybe it was no more than Tony's massage making her feel relaxed for the first time in weeks. In any event, she abandoned her usual reticence.

"A short-term thing for the Tohono O'odham. The tribe wants to put together a private offering, and they need a lawyer to do the paperwork."

"Sounds decent," Tony said.

"Actually the pay is lousy. At least it's easy work. And it might be interesting to spend some time on the rez."

Hannah stiffened in embarrassment at her use of the politically incorrect term, especially in non-white company. But when she was growing up in Pinnacle Peak, *the rez* was what the tribal lands abutting the desert town were called, even by the Tohono O'odham who lived there.

Tony didn't appear to notice her gaffe. "So you're a good lawyer?"

Harvard Law, three years at a top boutique firm, solo counsel on several multimillion-dollar deals…

"I am, actually." *Just don't ask about my people skills. Especially when it comes to boyfriends or family.*

"What's the toughest deal you've ever done?"

One last summer almost ruined my law firm and nearly got me and my sister killed. "A year ago I did a structured mortgage-backed security split into quality tranches…" Hannah went into a lengthy description while Tony rubbed her shoulders and occasionally interjected a question.

"Sounds like great work. Why are you leaving your current firm?" he asked when she had finished.

A sister who can't stand me, a father who lied to me... "I thought it was time for a change."

Tony gave her shoulder a final squeeze. "Let me see your finger."

Hannah held up her hand and Tony wiped away the dried blood with an antibacterial towelette from his waist bag.

"It's a pretty deep slice, and not in the best spot for stitches. The ER will probably butterfly it."

Hannah inspected the cut. "Do you have any superglue?"

She was new to bouldering, but not to the injuries it could inflict. Trashed tips and flappers—abraded fingertips and torn skin—were common byproducts of a climbing session. Having beat-up-looking hands didn't bother her. Twenty-eight years old, she had yet to get a manicure.

"Never leave home without it." Tony produced a roll of tape, another antibacterial wipe, small scissors, and a plastic syringe of medical-grade super-glue—field tools for repairing rock-torn skin.

"Why aren't you looking for something more permanent, like at a law firm or an investment bank?" Tony asked as he tore open the medicated wipe.

The same question Cooper had asked. "I've got some choices to make. A short-term job gives me breathing space." She flinched as Tony cleaned her wound.

"I know all about making choices—just did some of that myself." Tony picked up the syringe and snipped off the end, then grasped her wrist with his free hand. "Don't move."

"What do you do?" Hannah asked as Tony squeezed small dots of glue along the edge of the cut. He was careful not to get any in the wound itself.

"Investment banking—LA, mostly."

"Are you in AZ for a deal?"

Tony cut a piece of tape to size, pinched the edges of the gash together, then laid the tape on top and pressed down. "I've got family here. Bend your finger a little." He cut off two more pieces of tape and wound them around her finger, securing the first piece.

"There. Once it's healed, cut off the tape. Whatever glue is left will peel away if you soak your finger in warm water."

"Thanks—again."

"No worries." Tony put the glue, scissors, wipe, and tape back into his pouch and picked up his harness.

The sun slipped under the horizon, turning the cliff they had descended a deep purple-black.

Hannah knew that she should say good-bye, that her boyfriend was waiting and she had to get home. Her lips parted but no words came out. Instead, desire—more raw need than romantic longing—streamed through her. The feeling came on like a force of nature, all at once and inexplicable. Acting almost without thought, Hannah slipped a hand around Tony's neck, pulled him against her, and kissed him.

He kissed her back, with a fierceness that surprised her. Hannah didn't know how long they stood together, heartbeat to heartbeat, before he broke the clinch. Tony's dark eyes held hers for a moment, and Hannah felt something dangerous rise up in her.

"I should retrieve that top rope while there's still some light," he said.

Heat coursed through Hannah's cheeks, reddening them as though she were sitting too close to a fire.

"I better get my crash pad." She started toward the cliff base, twice almost stumbling over a granite outcropping in her haste. From behind a stand of creosote, she risked a look back.

Tony was gone.

To LA, she hoped, feeling a sudden chill.

Thanks to her uncharacteristic talkativeness, he now knew a lot about her—while she knew almost nothing about him. Unseen creatures rustled in the nearby chaparral, and Hannah's imagination amplified her unease.

Why hadn't he mentioned the protesters? Because of *White Power* man and his ruined motorcycle, Hannah had kept mum, but Tony must have seen the crowd. *So why not say something?*

And where was his car? The rock-climbing park was surrounded by the rez, off-limits to non-tribe members. The parking lot had been empty, and she hadn't seen any other vehicles since leaving the Subaru.

Visions of muggers and rapists ran through Hannah's head. Was Tony cruising the park, looking for prey? What if she had just kissed a serial killer? She felt incredibly stupid. Good thing she hadn't mentioned her last name.

But she had, Hannah realized a moment later, recalling her numerous references to Dain & Dain. A glance in the phone book or bar directory would confirm her identity.

By the time she found her crash pad, Hannah was nearly in a panic. Grabbing the rectangle of foam, she ran for her car.

Making it to the Subaru without incident, she hastily loaded her gear and slid behind the wheel. She sped toward the park entrance, oblivious to the ribbons of vermillion that trailed across the wide expanse of sky before fading into the encroaching dusk.

The protesters had dispersed, the only sign of their presence a few *Boycott* flyers scattered on the ground next to what looked like a smear of oil and some bits of glass and shiny metal. But it was Tony, not *White Power* man, who was on Hannah's mind as she pulled onto the highway.

A one-time mistake, she told herself, relieved she wouldn't be seeing him again.

And a bit disappointed, too.

Chapter Six

Monday, September 14

"Morning, beautiful." Cooper walked into the bedroom carrying two mugs and a white paper sack.

Hannah dragged the sheet over her head. "It can't be morning yet," she said in the slow vocabulary of near-sleep, the ends of her words drifting off.

"Does that mean you don't want a chipotle brownie?"

Hannah pushed the sheet away and sat up. "You went to Danny's?"

The *cantina* north of town was locally famous for its baked goods. Hannah scooted over so Cooper could sit next to her on the bed.

"Danny said to tell you these were baked this morning." Cooper squinted at her hand. "Hey, what happened to your finger?"

"I got a flapper climbing. No big deal." Hannah took the mug Cooper offered and blew on the hot tea inside. Her mouth tasted chalky from brushing her teeth extra long last night.

After leaving Tony and the rock-climbing park, Hannah had driven north, wanting to be alone with her thoughts—which had kept coming back to Cooper. The man she had loved but left during her second year at Harvard Law. The man who had stood by her this past summer, when her career, family, and life were at risk, and who afterward had opened his heart to her again.

Hannah had wanted a second chance with Cooper since she returned to Arizona after law school. While finding out about her parents was now uppermost in her mind, it didn't lessen her feelings for him. Hannah didn't want their relationship to end, just to slow down a bit while she dealt with her family issues.

As the miles sped by on the empty roads, she had thought about the kiss with Tony. *Irrelevant*, she had decided, a by-product of stress caused by her run-in with the protesters and near fall from the cliff. At worst, it was a temptation that she should have resisted. But at the time she had been tired, hurt…*and acting like her mother.*

The self-comparison to Elizabeth had ignited a hotness in Hannah's chest. When it came to nature versus nurture, Hannah was certain she bore Richard Dain's stamp—honest, responsible, rational.

Until I met Tony, she had said to herself, then pushed the thought from her mind.

The trauma of the past month—fraud, murder, her sister in rehab, her father's judgeship lost, all resulting from events set in motion by Elizabeth over a quarter of a century ago—would be enough to make any relationship vulnerable, especially a new one. Hannah had steered the car back toward the lights of town, realizing that even if she weren't yet ready to move forward, she could still give Cooper some of the reassurance he wanted. Starting with the Boston job. It may have been the best choice when she didn't have a reason to stay in Arizona, but things had changed, and she owed it to Cooper to let him know he was the reason why.

Hannah had turned onto the street that led to the condo, hoping Cooper would still be up. But days started early on his ranch, and by the time she had arrived home, he was already asleep. Now she cupped her hands around the mug of tea, more anxious than ever to set things straight.

"I'm sorry that I—"

"I'm the one who should be apologizing," Cooper interrupted. "You need to do what makes you happy. If that means working for the Tohono O'odham, I'm all for it."

His words pierced her heart, and she had to blink several times before answering.

"Maybe I should skip the interview. You're right— the pay *is* lousy, and the work will be pretty dull."

"But the job is only for six weeks. You may as well meet with them, listen to what they have to say."

Cooper took a brownie out of the bag, broke off a corner, and gave the piece to Hannah. She nibbled at it, the velvety taste of chocolate backed by a hint of fire from the chipotle.

"I saw Shelby yesterday," she said.

"I thought she didn't want visitors."

"She doesn't." Hannah sipped her tea. "I think she has a new boyfriend, but she wouldn't tell me anything about him."

"Shelby keeping a guy on the down-low? Could be serious."

"My sister, the serial dater, falling in love? I don't think so."

Cooper took a big bite of brownie and washed it down with a swig of coffee. "You never know— she might have changed. After all, rehab gives you a chance to think about who you are and who you want to be." His eyes met hers and his tone became serious. "Maybe the Tohono O'odham job would do the same for you."

Hannah drew in a startled breath. "What? I mean, I know what I want. I'm sorry about what I said about Boston yesterday. It's not even an option anymore, now that we're—"

Wordlessly, Cooper lifted Hannah's mug from her grasp and set it on the floor, then took her hands in his. Hannah felt his fingers trace along the freshly healed wounds, permanent reminders of her ordeal in the desert five weeks ago. Looking at the scars on her skin, Hannah remembered what it felt like to have a gun aimed at her, to believe she was going to die. Remembered it was Cooper who had been there for her when everyone else had turned their backs.

He squeezed her hands. "I don't want to lose you." His voice was raw.

Hannah winced. Exactly what Tony had said to her on the cliff face.

I'm sorry, Cooper—for leaving you the first time not sharing the secret about my mother and father Boston Tony...

The words welled up but she didn't say them, fearful of jeopardizing their future. Right now their potential felt fragile, as though the slightest pressure would crush it.

"You won't." Hannah gently pulled her hands from his grasp. "I better get in the shower if I'm going to be on time."

In truth, Hannah wanted to leave early for the interview. She had a stop to make on the way.

Chapter Seven

At sixty years old, Richard Dain was a handsome man. He had thick white hair, striking blue eyes, and a granite jaw with, Hannah knew, a will to match. Noosed in a power tie, he looked every inch the accomplished lawyer.

Hannah slipped her legal pad into her briefcase. It hadn't taken long to bring him up to date on the two deals she had pending.

Now for the hard part.

"If that's everything—" Richard reached for a file folder on the corner of his desk, the look on his face making plain he was ready to get on to something else.

Hannah leaned forward in the oversized guest chair. Even though her demeanor was calm, inside she felt as tense as an arrow poised in a bow.

"I'm thinking about taking some time off from the firm."

Richard paused, his hand on the unopened folder. "Are you accepting the contract position with the tribe?"

Hannah was stunned—she couldn't believe Shelby had called him. On second thought, she could. *Leopards and spots.* She was about to vent her outrage when Richard continued.

"Someone from the Tohono O'odham office called last week to confirm your credentials."

"Oh." Hannah was momentarily off balance. "I mean, I didn't intend for you to find out that way."

Richard made a dismissive gesture. "When do you start?"

"My interview's in an hour. If I get the job, I think right away."

"I'll close your last two transactions. Email me a status memo." Richard opened the file folder.

That's it? Hannah was hurt by his matter-of-factness. Even if they weren't blood relatives, had her three years at the firm meant nothing?

"I'm sure you'll be hired." Richard didn't lift his eyes from his reading. "I told whoever called that you're an excellent transactions lawyer."

Hannah felt herself warm with gratification—not so much because Richard thought she was a good lawyer, but because he had told her so.

Positive feedback on her work usually came from Olivia. When it came to praise, Richard had never been a spendthrift.

The early sun streamed through the window, highlighting his face. Hannah noticed new hollows in his cheeks, a more pronounced downward turn at the corners of his mouth.

Tiredness? Disappointment? Hannah thought of what her sister had said. With Olivia in Africa and Shelby in rehab, was this really the time for her to leave?

Her eyes went to the dark rectangle on the wall behind Richard's desk. As long as she could remember, a full-length portrait of Elizabeth Dain had hung there—a constant icon of beauty and wit, charm and intelligence, looming over Richard's shoulder.

But sometime during the last month the painting had been taken down, replaced by a collection of black-framed photographs. Shelby on a pony. Shelby eating an ice cream cone and laughing into the camera. Shelby and Hannah under a large Christmas tree. Group shots at various school graduations.

Only one photo featured Hannah by herself. Snapped by a freelancer—the kind who photographed people at events, then offered the print for sale minutes later—it showed Hannah in a green lace-collared dress slightly too short for her lanky preteen figure, her hair pinned back with flower barrettes. She stood stiffly on a red-patterned carpet in front of a gilt-trimmed wall.

The ballet. A Saturday matinee had been her and Richard's traditional outing during his annual visit to her boarding school. As part of parent-teacher conference week, each student was given an afternoon off to spend with family.

At first, eleven-year-old Hannah had suspected the excursion was only for appearances' sake. School personnel would have thought it strange if they didn't go someplace, and a trip to the ballet instead of lunch meant Richard wouldn't have to talk to her much. But his rapt attention during *Giselle* had made Hannah realize he was a true fan.

As the yearly ritual continued, Hannah grew to like ballet, too. For her, the enjoyment came not so much from the performances as the time spent with Richard. Even if only for an afternoon, it had made her feel as though they were truly father and daughter.

Was I wrong about that, Hannah thought, and pulled her mind back to the present. Her interview started in forty-five minutes, and she had yet to broach the real reason she was in his office that morning.

Hannah's relationship with Richard had moved into new territory since the events of last month. The revelations about Elizabeth, plus Richard's withdrawal as a judicial candidate, had changed the geography between them, put Hannah on more of an even footing. But now she was about to enter no-man's land.

"There's something else you need to know. I'm looking for my birth father."

Richard abruptly looked up, his expression not one Hannah had seen before. She felt a chill waft through the room, as palpable as the ice in the pitcher of water on the desk between them. Resisting the urge to shiver, she pressed on.

"I would appreciate your telling me what you know about him—his name, where he might be living, anything at all."

Hannah had made the same request of Olivia before she left for Africa. "I thought she might have been having an affair," Olivia had said. "But she never divulged any of the details." That had left Richard as Hannah's only source.

"I can't help you."

Hannah stared at him, speechless. Seconds passed, and an internal alchemy transformed her astonishment to anger.

It's his ego. Resentment of an alternative father figure, the lingering pain of Elizabeth's betrayal—regardless, it trumped her right to know her birth parent. *Unbelievable.*

"Can't?" Hannah spat the word. "Don't you mean *won't?*"

She blinked away a tear and summoned all her will to stop more from falling as she got to her feet. Unbidden, something Olivia had said during their last conversation came into her head, a quote from Oscar Wilde.

Children begin by loving their parents. After a time they judge them. Rarely, if ever, do they forgive them.

Make that never. Hannah stalked out the door, slamming it behind her.

Hannah finally found an empty space at the edge of the lot for her Subaru. Even at ten in the morning, parking near the front of the casino was hard to come by. She hurried across the pavement, already regretting her choice of skirt and new heels.

Usually Hannah wore pants and flat shoes to work. An interview, though, warranted something more formal. But fashion had come with a price. Two pairs of pantyhose had been sacrificed before she managed to get the toes pointed the right way, and already she could feel the beginnings of a blister on one heel.

The twenty-minute drive from the firm to the rez had given her a chance to calm down a little after her meeting with Richard. Now she wanted the Tohono O'odham job more than ever.

She stopped at the information kiosk in front of the casino entrance. It was hot. Not the hammer blows that stunned in the summer, but a heat that could still raise sweat within minutes. In spite of her status as a native Arizonan, Hannah still wasn't used to it. Plucking her blouse away from her damp skin, she studied the map in the center, then headed toward a detached office complex north of the casino.

The Office of Tribal Affairs—*OTA*, to locals— was a squat modern building, hard-edged in the glare of the sun. Satellite dishes hung like high-tech cobwebs under its eaves. Hannah pulled open the thick wooden door, feeling a rush of cool air that quickly dissipated when it slammed into the external inferno.

The reception area was furnished with dark wood furniture and rugs in earth tones. Hand-woven baskets—the Tohono O'odham's claim to handicraft fame—decorated shelves along the wall.

The two women seated at desks behind the low counter looked up from their computer terminals. *The latest model from Apple*, Hannah noticed as she introduced herself.

"Mr. Soto is expecting you," one of the women said. "Come with me."

Not trusting the slick soles of her new heels on the tile floor, Hannah gingerly followed the receptionist across the lobby and down a hallway. The woman indicated a pair of chairs in an alcove next to a closed door.

"Please have a seat. I'll tell Mr. Soto you're here."

The woman opened the door and spoke in what Hannah guessed was Tohono O'odham. A man's voice answered in the same language. The woman turned back to Hannah.

"Mr. Soto has to make a brief phone call. Then he'll be right with you."

"Thank you." Hannah leaned back in her chair and wriggled her toes, resisting the urge to rub her sore feet. She knew if she took off her shoes, she would never get them back on her swollen feet.

The hallway's only decoration was an antique-looking mirror hung on the wall across from where

Hannah sat. The receptionist had left the door to the office ajar, and Hannah could see a credenza with a phone and a stack of papers on top reflected in the glass.

As Hannah watched, a man came into view. He was facing away from her—all she could see was black hair and broad shoulders in a dark suit. He picked up the phone and punched in a number, then began speaking in what sounded like the same language the receptionist had used.

In short order, the conversation heated up. Hannah had never seen such emotion poured into an inanimate object. The man's voice filled his office, his words reverberating throughout the alcove. He shouted and begged, threatened and raged, oblivious of anything else. At one point, he sounded close to tears. Hannah tried to imagine who was on the other end. Only a brother or a deaf person wouldn't hang up.

Suddenly the man banged the phone down onto its cradle and swiveled his chair toward the front of the room before Hannah could look away. His eyes met hers in the mirror, and Hannah stifled a gasp.

It was Tony.

Chapter Eight

"Good to meet you, Ms. Dain." Tony's handshake was firm and dry.

"H-hello," Hannah stammered.

Good to meet me? Didn't he didn't recognize her?

After seating Hannah in one of the guest chairs, Tony reclaimed his seat behind the desk. The darkly handsome face was as Hannah remembered, except that this morning the razor-cut hair was swept back off his forehead. He wore suspenders but no tie, and his sleeves were rolled up to the elbow.

Hannah perched on the chair's edge, profoundly mortified. She affected a pleasant expression, determined to cut short the interview at the earliest possible moment, preferably before he realized who she was. Thank goodness it had been twilight, and that her hair and clothes were different. She slid her bandaged finger out of sight under a fold in her skirt.

Tony glanced at a sheet of paper on his desk. "I've read your résumé—quite a list of accomplishments. But I'm a little surprised."

"Oh?" Hannah didn't want to say much in the hopes her voice wouldn't ring any bells.

"I don't see any mention of bouldering."

So much for not knowing who I am. Her face hot, Hannah started to get up. *I've got to leave before he says anything about last night.*

"Thank you for your time—"

Tony interrupted her. "I talked to your firm about some of the deals you've done. Very impressive. The tribe's offering will be pretty straightforward, even easy, for someone with your experience."

Easy work…lousy pay… Hannah lowered herself back into the chair, ruing her lack of tact. The room felt like a crucible, and she resisted the urge to tug at her collar.

"Your only employment since law school has been with Dain & Dain?"

"That's correct."

"I presume a relation?"

"Yes." *Only to one of them.*

"So other than time away at school, you've lived in Arizona your whole life?"

"Desert born." *Though not necessarily bred.*

Hannah heard how clipped her responses were and told herself to stop it. She couldn't let her anger toward Richard derail her job prospects. *Not after I've done such a good job on my own at the rock-climbing park.*

Apparently oblivious to her turmoil, Tony leaned back in his chair and interlaced his fingers behind his head. An oval-shaped scar wrapped around the inside of his wrist. Hannah hadn't noticed it last night. It looked like the kind left after a tattoo was removed.

"I moved here a few months ago from LA." Tony's grin was wry. "Just in time for the summer heat. Before that, I was a junior partner with Leighton & Riegle."

The investment bank was the biggest on the West Coast. Given Tony's age, a junior partnership meant he was the real deal when it came to finance.

"Big change," Hannah said.

"It was time to reconnect with my family and my people. The Indian half, that is. My father is Mexican-American and my mother's Tohono O'odham."

That explains the accent, and how he got into the rock-climbing park via the rez. "The tribe must be glad to have you."

"In fact, I work for Peña & Moreno, a private

equity firm that's also investing in the offering. We're a small outfit—two partners, plus me. I'm sure the only reason P&M got a piece of this deal is because I'm part Tohono O'odham." He grinned and started rolling down his sleeves. "For once, being a half-breed paid off."

His cuffs buttoned, Tony got to his feet and put on the jacket that had been hanging on the coat rack next to his desk. Taking his cue, Hannah stood as well, glad the embarrassing encounter was almost over.

All that's left is the Thank-you-for-coming-I'll-be-in-touch spiel and then I'm out of here. She picked up her purse.

"Do you have lunch plans?" he said.

Lunch? Hannah had a terrible thought. *Was he asking her out?*

"Um—"

Tony looked chagrined. "I'm sorry, I should have been clearer. The job is yours, has been since you showed up this morning. I thought we could go over the specifics of the deal while we ate."

"You knew before this morning you were going to hire me?" *Because of what happened at the park?* Hannah was horrified at the possibility.

Tony picked up a pair of sunglasses from the

desk and slipped them into a pocket. "You were the only non-Indian who applied, and I couldn't resist the idea of a white sidekick. Since Tonto, Indians—you can call us that, by the way—have always been in the Number Two slot. I thought it was time for some affirmative action."

Hannah didn't know how to respond—she couldn't tell whether he was kidding or if she should be insulted. Tony waited a beat, then cracked a smile.

"I decided to offer you the job because of your résumé and experience. No other candidate came close to having your qualifications."

As Tony opened the door, his eyes met Hannah's.

"And that's the *only* reason. How's that cut finger?"

Tony took a detour on the way to the lobby to show Hannah her office. It was nothing special—two plain desks and a file cabinet in an otherwise empty room.

"Your computer should be delivered tomorrow," he said. "You know, five years ago, *boot up* to an Indian meant pulling on his Tony Llamas. Now every new house built on rez is wired for the Internet."

There was a secretary's desk across the hall from her office door. The chair behind the desk was empty, and dingy-looking ivy sulked in a pot next to a dark computer monitor.

Tony looked puzzled. "I thought Wendi was supposed to be here today."

A note was on the desktop. Hannah leaned over the partition and read it aloud.

"I had to leave early today for personal reasons. Wendi." The *i* in *Wendi* had a smiley face instead of a dot. Hannah hated it when females older than sixteen did that.

"Well, you'll meet her tomorrow." Tony walked Hannah through the rest of the floor—coffee room, file storage, more offices—then led her out the front entrance.

"There's a small breakfast-lunch place next to the casino," he said, walking briskly across the crushed granite. "Okay with you?"

"Fine." Hannah could barely keep up without limping. New or not, her shoes were going into the trash the moment she got home.

They passed the main entrance to the casino, threading through the bovine flow of patrons, most dressed in the middle-class uniform of shorts, t-shirts, and baseball hats. On the other side of the glass doors, Hannah could see rows of slot machines trimmed in neon tubing and topped with blinking lights. Nearly each one had a customer staring at its screen with a devotion not unlike a true believer's at the altar.

Hannah noticed only a few of the machines had handles. Most were played by pushing a button after tokens were inserted. She watched a middle-aged woman near the door alternate between feeding tokens and pushing the *Play* button with amazing speed. *Anything to expedite the process of separating people from their money.*

"Two thousand machines under one roof, as many as Caesars Palace in Vegas. Some retro, most electronic. Fifty poker and blackjack tables in the back, with more on the drawing board. We've come a long way from bingo in a smoke-filled double-wide trailer." Tony's pride was obvious in his voice. "You ever been inside?"

"Not really my scene."

Tony looked thoughtful. "I'd like you to see where the money comes from and, more importantly, where it goes. How about a tour of the casino and the private section of the rez?"

Even though Hannah was not into gambling, seeing the rez was a different story. Access to the majority of the tribe's lands was restricted to Tohono O'odham or authorized visitors only. "I'd like that."

They came to a log-sided building with *Trading Post Café and Junque Shoppe* stenciled on a sign over the door. At first Hannah thought its weathered look was the result of expert painting rather than age. Yet according to the plaque out front, most of the structure was authentically old, the remains of the original trading post from frontier days.

Paddles of prickly pear cactus extended over the edges of the path to the door. Hannah rubbed a finger along the scars on her palm, thinking about last month, and circled wide to avoid the plant's reach. She and Tony arrived the café's front door just as another patron was leaving, and they stepped aside to let him pass. The man glanced at Tony, then looked again.

"Antoñio? Antoñio Soto?" he said eagerly. Slender, with a nose a bit too prominent for his face and a goatee that was largely wishful thinking, he wore wire-rimmed glasses and a short-sleeved shirt stuffed into pants but no belt. His head was shaved, perhaps in concession to a retreating hairline.

Tony raised his eyebrows. "Have we met?"

"I'm Zel Kassif, reporter for the *Pinnacle Peak*

Express." He whipped out a small notebook and pen from his shirt pocket, the movement slightly geeky. Hannah started in recognition.

He's the reporter who was talking to White Power *man at the protest.* First Tony, and now Kassif. *I am never going to that rock-climbing park again.*

"Do you have a response to concerns that the casino is being used as a conduit for money-laundering?" Kassif asked.

"The tribe has appointed a gaming commission to make sure that doesn't happen." Tony seemed unruffled, but Hannah thought she heard an undercurrent of tension in his voice.

"But if the tribe isn't subject to the federal cash-transaction reporting laws—"

"The commissioners still do their job." Tony reached for the restaurant's front door handle. "If you don't mind…"

Kassif ignored the brush-off. "How about a comment on the tribe's refusal to revenue-share with the town or contribute to improvements on non-reservation land affected by casino traffic?"

"All this was discussed at last week's town hall meeting. The Tohono O'odham have complied with all state and federal regulations. Revenue-sharing and infrastructure support are requests, not requirements. The tribe has chosen to contribute to Pinnacle Peak's economy in other ways. In fact, this is Hannah Dain, who will be our legal counsel on our upcoming real estate private placement. Now you'll really have to excuse us, Mr. Kassif."

Hannah managed a nod in the reporter's direction before Tony took her arm and started to usher her into the restaurant. She was relieved to go. Although it was unlikely that Kassif would recognize her, she didn't want to chance it.

Kassif raised his voice. "Even if the law doesn't require it, as a matter of principle shouldn't the tribe be funding gambling addiction programs?"

"The answer to alcoholism wasn't Prohibition," Tony said over his shoulder.

"Why not open your books to the public? What are you—"

The door swung shut, cutting off the rest of the reporter's question.

"Should we eat somewhere else?" Hannah asked, expecting Kassif to reappear momentarily.

Tony shook his head. "He won't bother us in here. The press knows the Trading Post is off-limits when it comes to interviews."

With a wave at the waitress, he picked up two menus from the lectern and led Hannah to one of the tables. The décor was Southwestern—Anglo and Indian—with an emphasis on antiques, mostly farm and food-preparation implements. Ox yokes and wagon wheels hung next to flat bowls shaped for grinding grain and sticks used to harvest saguaro fruit. Hannah had a vision of patrons a hundred years hence dining under dangling Cuisinart parts and tire jacks.

"The usual, Tony?" the waitress asked as she set down silverware and water.

"You bet. Hannah?"

She opened her menu. *Trading Post Café— Native-American Nouvelle Cuisine. Bon Appétit!* proclaimed the first page. *Somebody got hold of a French dictionary,* Hannah said to herself as she scanned the entrées.

"The sage, fig, and butternut squash pizza without cheese. And a bottle of mineral water."

"You vegetarian?" Tony asked after the waitress had left.

"Vegan. Since high school."

Tony cocked an eyebrow. "So you wear 'em but don't eat 'em?" At Hannah's questioning look, he added, "Hard to miss those red leather shoes."

Suddenly Hannah's toes didn't hurt so much. *This is a business meeting, not a date,* she reminded herself, choosing a safer topic.

"What was it like growing up on the rez—erva-tion?" She belatedly tacked on the syllables after *rez*.

"*Rez* is just fine." Tony propped his elbows on the table. "After my dad split, my mom and I moved in with my grandmother. The first time her brothers came to visit, I got out of bed to eavesdrop. I wanted to know if they talked in that weird staccato way Indians did in the old Westerns." Tony shook his head. "I didn't know any better. There weren't any role models, at least none who looked like me." He rapped his knuckles on the table. "Bet you never heard of Ira Hayes."

"Who?"

"My point, exactly. He's full Tohono O'odham—and one of the GIs in that famous photograph of the American flag being raised on Iwo Jima. Won the Congressional Medal of Honor." Tony paused. "He couldn't find a job after he got out of the military, and ended up drinking himself to death."

"That's terrible!"

Tony shrugged. "That's the way it was. Before the casino, I mean."

"It's changed things that much?"

"Before, over half the tribe was on government assistance. Today, no one is. Diabetes was crippling our population, but thanks to the new hospital's prevention program, the number of new cases has been halved. The education fund is putting a dozen kids through college. We've built an airfield and Lake Lagunita, and launched a telecommunications company that will bring cell service everywhere on the rez. Adequate housing, expansion into other businesses, political power through donations—and that is just for starters." Tony paused, looking rueful. "Sorry. It doesn't take much to get me going on my spiel."

He had one of those faces, Hannah realized. *Bright with dreams.* Rare on someone over thirty—she was almost envious.

"Sounds like this is more than just a job to you."

"If money was all that mattered, I would have stayed in LA. I did good as a banker—now I want to do good, period. Give something back to my people."

The waitress arrived with their order. She set down Hannah's pizza, then placed a stack of pancakes and a small pitcher in front of Tony. "Let me know if you need more saguaro syrup."

"Late breakfast?" Hannah asked as Tony drenched his pancakes in red liquid.

"Favorite lunch. These are the best pancakes in

the world." He took a bite. "Mmmm."

Hannah couldn't see how something made of a few basic ingredients could be proclaimed better than the thousands of other recipes for the same thing. But she was beginning to understand that to Tony, good things weren't just good, they were the best. On a certain level, his enthusiasm was appealing.

She cut into her pizza. "The *Express* doesn't seem to be a fan of the casino."

Tony grimaced. "You got that right. The tribe expected some resentment in the community. But what started out as angry letters has progressed to graffiti and other vandalism. Last week a Tohono O'odham casino worker was jumped by two white guys in the parking lot. The cops dismissed it as an isolated incident—sore losers venting their frustration—but I'm not so sure. That's one of the reasons we decided to hire outside counsel for the real estate deal. Everything has to be by the book. Which reminds me—don't talk to the media. Any inquires should be referred to the tribe's PR office."

"No problem." After the press and TV attention surrounding the traumatic events of last month, Hannah would be happy to never speak to another reporter again.

Tony took another bite of pancake. "In 1853, the white man held all the cards. That's when the United States bought a tract of land from Mexico and five thousand Tohono O'odham came with the deal. We never fought the Anglos, yet for over a hundred years we were cold-shouldered onto the edge of the economy, left to scrape a living off the sidewalk as best we could." He made a sweeping gesture with his arm, nearly toppling Hannah's water glass. "Now it's our turn. We've won every lawsuit aimed at taxing our wealth or limiting our growth. History is finally reversing itself—the Indian is buying up the white man's land, while the Anglos beg us to be reasonable."

Hannah found herself warming to Tony's idealism. *Part Don Quixote, part Don Corleone.* Her life with Cooper was largely a temperature-controlled environment, providing a coolness that was soothing. Tony's heat made for a nice contrast.

Careful, girl—you don't want to get burned, she reminded herself as a ruler-thin man folded himself into an unoccupied chair at their table.

"So how much land is enough, Tony?" he asked.

Dressed in a white suit—vest included—the newcomer had the tall forehead, somewhat protruding ears, and small chin of an English aristocrat. If he were photographed unsmiling, the applicable adjective would be *austere*.

Tony grinned at the man. "You know my answer, Osborne. The Tohono O'odham used to occupy twenty-four thousand square miles, from northern Mexico to southern Arizona. I wouldn't mind having it all back."

"Just remember where ambition got Custer." The man swiveled in his chair and offered Hannah an ingratiating smile. "I don't think we've met. Osborne Hepworth."

"Hannah Dain."

"Osborne's a sole practitioner who does immigration and small business law," Tony said.

Hepworth studied her. "Richard's daughter?"

A question that used to be easy to answer. Hannah pressed her lips together and nodded.

Tony forked up more pancake. "Hannah's just taken the job as offering attorney for the tribe's real estate private placement."

Hepworth's eyebrows circumflexed. "Dain & Dain is doing the deal?"

Hannah had the feeling his incredulity was bogus. "No. I'm working for the tribe."

"I see." He drew out the *ee*, stopping just sort of insulting.

Hannah couldn't tell if Hepworth's condescension was directed toward her abilities or the project itself. Whether it was his words or his presence that made her uncomfortable, she was already well down the road of dislike for the man.

"Looking for more work?" Hepworth asked. "I could use some help putting together out-of-state corporations. Bare-bones package; twenty-five hundred a company. Interested?"

Hannah was surprised at the overture, given his apparent disdain for her. Also, the fee he had quoted was about five times the going rate.

"I think a firm geared toward that sort of thing would be more reasonably priced. You wouldn't necessarily need to use a lawyer." Hannah knew registered agents hawked Nevada corporate packages for several hundred dollars on the Internet.

"I prefer that a lawyer sign the affidavits for the visa forms. Looks better when an attorney is a corporate officer."

"Visa forms?"

"Certifying employment offers. Seasonal jobs and offers to professionals. We'd only hire one or two people per company, so when they don't go back to Mexico the State Department doesn't get pissy."

When they don't go back to Mexico… All of a

sudden, Hannah got it. Hepworth wanted her help to run an immigration scam. She would create companies solely for the purpose of offering non-existent temporary jobs to Mexican nationals, while he prepared the visa applications. Once the foreigners were in the United States, both they and the companies would vanish.

Clever. Obviously lucrative, too, given the fee he had offered. And nothing she wanted any part of.

"Not interested," she said through barely parted teeth.

"It's easy work, a few hours—"

"Not interested," she repeated. *Didn't he understand they could get disbarred?* Hannah felt a rush of anger. *Serious time for multiple felonies was more like it.*

"You should go," she said to Hepworth, not caring if her rudeness made Tony angry. If this was the type of person he did business with, Hannah didn't want the position with the tribe. In fact, she almost wished Tony would tell her that *she* was the one who should leave. Then the whole mess—the kiss, the temporary job, Hepworth—would be behind her.

But he didn't. Instead, he relaxed in his chair with his arms crossed, his expression that of uninterested observer. It was Hepworth who glared at

Hannah in an unpleasant, boiled sort of way—lips tight, eyes bulging in their sockets, red creeping up the sides of his neck.

"Tony, it's a good thing your brothers taught you about guns." The lawyer's tone was as sour as an unripe orange. "Because this one's a loose cannon." Hepworth got up from his chair and walked stiff-backed to the exit.

Hannah hacked at a piece of cold pizza with her knife. In less than three hours, she had quit one job and was about to be fired from another. No wonder she was hungry.

But again, Tony surprised her.

"Don't worry about turning him down. Osborne will have no problem finding someone else for his scheme."

"Have you worked with him directly?" Hannah wanted to know just how close the relationship was between Tony and the lawyer.

"No. When he does immigration work for P&M clients, Mr. Peña is his contact."

"How does a private equity firm get involved in immigration issues?"

"Our business base is Hispanic. As long as there's a border, there will be Mexicans who want to cross it. Not just the illegals who walk over with a *coyote*, but people with money. If they can't come—or once they get here, if they can't stay—neither does their money. That means less business for P&M. Even though Hepworth may not be on your shortlist of dinner party guests, he gets the job done—from what my bosses tell me, better and faster than any other lawyer they've ever used." Tony gave her a funny look. "Too bad you couldn't help him."

Hannah raised her eyebrows. "You didn't want me to take his business!"

Tony spread his hands. "I said Hepworth was friends with Mr. Peña. I didn't say I liked him."

"Is there anything else you're not telling me?" Hannah crossed her arms. "About your bosses, perhaps?"

Tony quickly shook his head. "I didn't mean to give you a bad impression of Mr. Peña or Mr. Moreno. They've been really supportive of my work for the tribe, cutting their usual fee on the real estate deal and letting me log a lot of unbillable time. When you meet them, you'll see they really are good guys." He swiped at his mouth with a napkin, leaving a smear of syrup near the corner of his mouth.

What would kissing him taste like now? Hannah quickly banished the thought, irked where her mind had taken her.

"Let me tell you about the real estate project," Tony said. "It's pretty straightforward. Tough talk aside, we'd rather not have the town mad at us. As one of the few tribes who never fought the whites, we don't want to start now. The council's decision to let non-tribe members invest in the shopping center we're building next year was a public relations move. The first phase is done. Three million was raised to fund the development company—buy construction equipment, set up the office, and so on. You'll be putting together the offering documents for the construction phase."

"Couldn't the tribe just pay for the whole development and save itself a lot of hassle?"

Tony nodded. "We thought if we gave the community a chance to share the profits from an Indian project, it might ease tensions a bit. Pave the way for next year's election."

"Are you putting up a candidate?"

"A proposition. We're going to begin gathering signatures as soon as the private placement closes. It would allow the casino to increase the number of slots and poker tables, as well as add craps, roulette, and other big-money games. In return, the state gets to collect corporate income tax on casino profits."

So that's what this is about. The real estate offering

was supposed to show that the tribe could play nice, paving the way for the big-money-casino-games-in-exchange-for-tax-on-profits deal.

"It's a win-win for everyone," he added.

Hannah thought the environmentalists and morality police would probably take a different view.

"Are you on board?" Tony's eyes crinkled in the corners. "Even if the work is ordinary and the pay lousy?"

Hannah knew if she passed on this job, she would probably have to take a more time-intensive position, narrowing her opportunities to look for her father. And Tony did have a certain appeal, in a bad-boy kind of way.

"The work and the pay are fine. When would you like me to start?"

Tony beamed at her. "How about tomorrow morning?" He glanced at his watch. "I better get back to the office. There's a conference call coming in."

On the way back to the OTA building, Tony walked as swiftly as before. Her feet hurting more than ever, Hannah tried not to hobble. When they were almost at the casino entrance, his cell phone rang. Hannah recognized the opening bars from the Lone Ranger theme. *Maybe his sidekick comment wasn't a joke after all.*

Tony glanced at the screen to check the Caller ID, then opened the phone. "Hold on a minute," he said, then pressed the *Mute* button and looked apologetically at Hannah.

"I'm sorry, but this is the call I was expecting."

"That's okay. You can show me the casino some other time."

"It's best at night anyway. How about if I pick you up this evening, say around eight?"

"I'll meet you here," Hannah said quickly. "Main entrance okay?"

"It's a date," he said, raising the phone to his ear.

Hannah watched him walk away. After two hours together, she could already tell he was glib, self-involved, and a little too charming—not at all her type. And even in flat shoes, she was a good inch taller.

It's a date. Something inside her thrilled to the word.

Chapter Nine

Hannah let the Subaru cruise down Ocotillo, the road that connected the rez to downtown. Sliding a CD into the player, she tried to think of some errands to run. The afternoon was still early, and she didn't feel like going home to an empty condominium.

Or an occupied one, either. Her guilty conscience wasn't quite yet ready to face Cooper.

How did the interview go, honey?

Great. I'll be working for the guy I made a pass at Sunday night. At least now I know his last name.

Hannah turned down the volume, no longer in the mood for music. *It was a one-time lapse in judgment, not at all like what Elizabeth had done.* She tightened her grip on the steering wheel, unsure whether she was stating a fact or making an argument.

All her life, Hannah had assumed certain things about herself because of who she thought her parents were, literally and as people. The discovery that her self-understanding had been shaped by a fiction brought with it a determination to reconstruct it anew—this time, based on the truth.

Unfortunately, her sources of information were dwindling. Hannah's birth certificate had Richard's name on it, and snooping through what was left of her mother's personal papers hadn't yielded any clues. With Olivia in the dark and Richard refusing to help, she didn't know where to look next.

The Subaru neared the cross street that led to her condo. By habit, Hannah slowed and prepared to turn, braking when she saw a pedestrian in the crosswalk. The woman walked in front of her car, noticeably pregnant. A memory surfaced as Hannah watched the woman's slow progress across the street. *Maybe I'm not out of options after all.*

Hannah continued through the intersection, driving for another block before pulling to the curb. She gazed at the three-story building on the corner. With its rough stone exterior and narrow windows, it looked innocuous enough. Take away the *Ambulance Entrance* sign next to the driveway, and Pinnacle Peak Hospital wasn't that different from any other office building.

Olivia hadn't been able to answer any questions

about Elizabeth's out-of-town trips or male friends of thirty years ago. But she had remembered Elizabeth's concerns about her second child's health toward the end of the pregnancy. Specifically, she had been worried that the new baby might inherit a certain disease—something that hadn't been an issue when Shelby was born two years earlier. Olivia couldn't remember the name of the disease or any other details. When Hannah had been born healthy, apparently no one gave the potential crisis another thought.

If Hannah's birth father had been the parent with the potential for passing on the mystery disease, perhaps he had been contacted for testing or possible match as a donor. If so, his name should be in Elizabeth's hospital records.

Hannah knew she could get a court order for the documents—that is, if she wanted to broadcast the facts of her parentage all over town. She hoped a personal appeal to a hospital employee's sympathy, amplified by deceit as necessary, would yield the same information while otherwise keeping it private. Hannah got out of the Subaru.

The hospital's lack of color hadn't changed since her last visit—same white walls, same white-coated medical workers, same white-faced family members in the waiting room. Hannah passed the elevator that served the patient rooms, her pace faltering at the unavoidable memory of another tragedy, also indirectly caused by Elizabeth Dain. It had been less than two months since the murder, and the memories still seared her soul.

Hannah took her place in line at the Records window. As the line shuffled forward, she thought about going back to the car. Hadn't last summer taught her it was better to leave the past alone? But Hannah kept her place. Her birth father's absence was like an amputee's phantom limb, causing pain without being there. If she didn't discover his identity, she would never begin to understand her own.

Something pulled at the back of her sweater, startling her out of her thoughts. Hannah turned around in time to see a paw retreating into the back-pack of the person in line behind her. She peered into the opening in the canvas bag and discovered a familiar whiskered face.

"Farley!" Although she wasn't a cat person, a few weeks of cat-sitting had converted Hannah to a fondness for this particular feline. The wearer of the backpack turned around.

"Hey, Hannah," Joe McGuiness said. "What are you doing here?"

What had begun as a casual acquaintance during a day-long continuing legal education course had become a friendship after Farley's stay with Hannah. In his mid-twenties, Joe was a lawyer with a small firm downtown.

Hannah's mind raced. "Er, picking up vaccination records," she stammered. "For a trip."

"Sweet. Where are you going?"

Scenes from Hannah's last surfing session through the Discovery/ Travel/National Geographic end of the channel spectrum popped into her head.

"Borneo," she blurted.

"Way cool! When—"

"So how's Farley?" Hannah asked with forced exuberance. She reached into the backpack to stroke the cat's proffered chin and felt the vibration of rumbled approval.

"Shh." Joe glanced around. "This is a cat-free zone. But I didn't want to leave him in the car, even with the engine running."

The man standing next to Joe leaned forward and spoke in a conspiratorial whisper. "Last time he changed all the radio stations."

Hannah laughed and withdrew her hand, earning a mewl of protest. "I believe it."

Joe's companion had broad cheekbones,

elliptical eyes, and smooth bronzed skin. A tur-
quoise earring hung from one ear, and his dark hair
was tied back in a ponytail. He was dressed casually
in jeans and a t-shirt emblazoned with the Tohono
O'odham circular maze.

The signature emblem of the tribe, the design
was routinely woven into baskets and chiseled into
rocks, always with a little stick figure at the top,
ready to find his way to the center. No shortcuts,
lots of wrong turns, and the entire path had to be
followed to complete the journey.

It struck Hannah that she had never seen a
drawing of the little man having made it to his
destination. *I know just how you feel, buddy.*

"Hannah Dain, meet Mike Chiago. Mike's my
team roping partner. And a PI."

"A private investigator? Are you here on a case?"

"Missing person," Chiago replied.

"Really," Hannah said. *Me, too.*

"Next," called the receptionist.

"You guys go ahead. That way you can get out
of here before Farley acts up."

"Thanks," Joe said.

"Have a good trip," Chiago added. Hannah
almost asked *Where?* before she caught herself.

After making sure Joe and Chiago were deep in

conversation with the woman behind the counter, Hannah slipped down the nearest corridor and found refuge in a recessed doorway, feeling her courage ebb. *Maybe this isn't such a good idea.*

Her cell phone went off in her purse, and from the ringtone, she knew it was Cooper. She let the call go to voicemail. Hannah knew if she talked to him, she would either lose her nerve or—worse—ask for his help.

"Excuse me." An older woman wearing glasses with fake diamonds at the temples pointed at the door behind Hannah.

"Sorry." Hannah moved out of the woman's way.

The woman inserted a key into the lock and opened the door, revealing a narrow room lined with metal shelves, each one overstuffed with manila file folders. The air that leaked into the corridor was stale and hot.

Hannah stared. "Is this the records room?"

"Sure is, hon. Can I help you?"

Hannah thought quickly. "I'm supposed to pick up my mother's hospital records. They told me to come here," she said, hoping the woman wouldn't ask who *they* were.

"They sent you instead of a runner? Well, come on in." The woman fanned a hand in front of her face. "Sorry about the temperature. AC's on the fritz again."

The woman flipped a switch and fluorescent lights lit up the space. At the far end of the room a computer monitor sat on a desk next to a copy machine. Sunlight filtered in through a single tall window.

"Give me a hand, will ya?" The woman walked over to the window and braced her palms against the frame. "It's easy once you get it started. Watch you don't cut yourself on the latch—it's broken."

Hannah stood next to the woman and gripped the strip of wood, her fingers touching a small butterfly decal stuck to a corner of the glass.

"One…two…three!" the woman said.

Hannah pushed, and pain pinched her still-tender shoulder. For a moment the window resisted, but after a second slid open smoothly.

The woman dusted off her hands. "Thanks. I thought records clerk would be a step up from nursing. That was before I saw the office that went with the job. What's your momma's name, hon?"

"Elizabeth Shelby Dain," Hannah said. She recited her mother's Social Security number.

"Current file?"

"No," Hannah said, hating the catch in her

voice. "She died when I was born."

"Is this by release, or do you have a court order?"

There it was—the question she had to get by. "Neither."

The woman's face became serious. "I'm sorry, hon. Without some sort of authorization, I can't give you the file."

"It's really important. I'm—"

"Hon, I can't—"

"—pregnant, and I'm worried my baby will have the same disease."

First Borneo and now babies. Well, if I'm going to lie, I might as well make them whoppers.

"The same disease?" the woman repeated.

"I just found out that when I was born, the doctors thought there was a chance I'd have some serious disease. The good news is, I didn't. The bad news is that my parents died when I was little, and I can't find any records of what disease they were worried about."

Hannah paused for breath and patted her tummy. "And now I really need to know."

The woman looked doubtful. Hannah didn't blame her. The story sounded ludicrous to her, too. She patted her tummy again and tried to look worried. Not hard to do, as it had just occurred to her obtaining another's medical records by fraudulent means was undoubtedly a crime. She thought of her scorn for Hepworth and his scheme. *So much for the moral high ground.*

"Well…I suppose it wouldn't really be breaking the rules to tell you what disease you *didn't* have." The woman tapped at the computer's keyboard, then jotted something on a notepad.

"Your momma's file isn't on microfilm—I'll have to look for it in the stacks. Might take me a while." She tore off the top sheet from the pad.

"I'm not in a hurry. Thanks for the help," Hannah said.

The woman disappeared down an aisle created by two rows of shelves. When she was out of sight, Hannah looked at the computer screen. It had gone dark. When Hannah moved the mouse a small box appeared, asking for user name and password.

Darn.

Hannah picked up the notepad the woman had used. She could see the faint marks left by the pressure of the woman's pen. Taking a pencil from the cup on the desk and using the side of the lead, she rubbed it back and forth over the indentations. A *D* was revealed, followed by a series of numbers: 70205639.

Hannah tore the sheet from the notepad and stuffed it in her pocket, proud but also a bit disappointed in herself. Today's string of falsehoods was becoming uncomfortably long.

And she wasn't sure the lies would get her what she wanted. Just because the woman had agreed to pull the file didn't mean she would let Hannah see it, or that it would have any information on her father.

The room was starting to feel close, and Hannah walked to the window, hoping to catch a puff of fresh air. The view wasn't much, just the back side of the hospital, overlooking the maintenance area. As she idly flipped the broken window latch back and forth with a finger, her cell phone again emitted the distinctive ringtone. Once more, she let Cooper's call go to voicemail.

Hannah knew she was letting her emotions whip through their relationship like flags snapping in the wind. But right now she couldn't help it. All she needed were a few answers. Then she would be ready to move on with her—*their*—life.

A framed photograph on the desk caught her eye. Hannah gave the latch a last flick and picked it up. The picture showed a chubby baby cuddled by a woman obviously his mother. The resemblance was unmistakable—same sharp chin, same angled eyebrows. Hannah had seen echoes of both in the face of the woman with the spangled glasses.

Was that why she was here? So that some day she could look into a face that bore traces of her own? Or did her search go beyond skin deep? The click of high heels on linoleum brought Hannah out of her musings, and she set down the photo.

The woman reappeared holding a manila folder with red tags along the side. *Elizabeth Shelby Dain* was printed in felt pen across the front. Hannah felt a jolt at seeing the name.

Flipping the folder open, the woman ran a finger down the top sheet, her lips moving as she read. She frowned, read some more, then closed the file, a funny look on her face.

"Is there a problem?" Hannah asked.

"Your mother's records—they've been sealed."

"Sealed?"

The woman looked apologetic. "Court order, signed by a judge. And stuff on some of the pages has been blacked out, too. I'm sorry, hon."

Richard. Hannah's mind whirled. Just how far had he gone to protect his reputation?

"Can you tell me who applied for the order? Or the name of the disease?"

The woman shook her head. "Sorry," she said, then brightened. "I can ease your mind on one thing. From what I can tell, only your dad had— um, what they were worried about. Not the disease, just the gene. That gave you a fifty-fifty chance of inheriting the gene, too. But you didn't—inherit the gene, I mean. So there's no way your baby can have it, at least not through you."

Hannah had gotten lost halfway through the woman's explanation, but she did manage to understand that the disease involved some sort of genetic testing. Now she was more certain than ever her birth father's name was in the file.

"Ma'am, I need to see that file for just one moment. It's really, *really* important." Hannah's voice was husky with want.

Reflexively, the woman hugged the documents to her chest. "I can't do it without official say-so. I've already bent the rules telling you this much. If anyone found out you actually saw the file, I would lose my job for sure."

For a moment, Hannah was tempted to grab the documents and run. But she knew it was futile. At three stories up, she would be lucky to get off the floor, let alone out of the building, before Security nabbed her. *Arrest, prosecution, disbarment...*

Hannah put her hand into her pocket and touched the piece of notepaper there. She wasn't giving up. At the moment, though, she couldn't take it any further.

"I understand. Thanks."

The woman smiled. "Glad it's good news."

Hannah suddenly found the room unbearably stuffy. Her head reeled, and her skin felt clammy. "Would you excuse me? I don't feel very well."

"Of course," the woman said sympathetically. "Isn't morning sickness just the most awful thing?"

Chapter Ten

Hannah pulled into the driveway of her condo, not altogether glad to see the red pickup at the curb. Sometimes Cooper could be more perceptive than Shelby, and Hannah wanted to keep the main events of her day—Richard, Tony, the hospital—secret for now. She hoped he wouldn't ask too many questions.

Carrying the hated heels in one hand, Hannah followed the smell of garlic and the sound of running water up the stairs to the kitchen, where Cooper stirred a pot on the stove with one hand while he rinsed fruit under the tap with the other. As usual, he had bought an overwhelming amount of food, arrayed his purchases across both counters, and was working in what appeared to be total chaos.

Hannah found a spot beside a stack of mail to set down her purse and keys. Until Cooper started staying over, she had been nearly compulsive about her housekeeping. Now it didn't seem as important.

Some mornings, she even left her bed unmade.

"Hey," she said.

Cooper glanced up from the pot. With a wide smile, he suspended his culinary endeavors and came around the counter to enfold her in his arms.

He really was nice to come home to. Hannah hugged him back—hard.

"Hey, Ms. Heimlich, I missed you, too." Cooper returned to the stove. "Your refrigerator was empty again, so I went shopping. After I saw all the food I had bought, I decided I better cook some of it. How did you not starve to death before I came along?"

"The freezer's full of frozen dinners!" Hannah protested.

"Like I said…"

"I know—Lean Cuisine isn't real food. So what are we having?"

"Pumpkin soup and veggie burgers, with sweet potato fries on the side. And dessert involves chocolate."

Cooper had brought his MP3 player, and the Dixie Chicks warbled at low volume through the portable speakers. Two candles sat in glass holders on the countertop, ready to be lit. Hannah shrugged off her jacket, feeling the stress of the day dissolve. After so many years of living alone, she had started to find a rhythm in sharing her space with someone else.

Gliding up behind Cooper, she wrapped her arms around his waist and pulled his hips close. "Sweet potato fries are my favorite," she murmured. She kissed his neck, tasting a hard day's work in the sun.

Cooper twisted around so he could face her. He ran a hand up her back, then twined his fingers through her hair. Sensations of pleasure moved down Hannah's spine, lodging below her belly.

"Thanks for making dinner," she said.

He brushed his lips against her ear. "I couldn't find the colander, or the long serving spoons."

"Packed up. But I've got some plastic forks from the deli. Would those do?"

"You're incorrigible." Cooper slid a hand under her shirt.

Hannah's condo was barely a couch and bed away from being unfurnished. Most of her things were in the mover's storage area, delivered there when she was still planning to take the Boston job. As a result, her place looked as though it had been burglarized, with the good stuff missing and everything the thieves didn't want left behind.

Hannah knew she needed to get her possessions back to Arizona. But that raised the question of where they should go. Cooper's overnights had gone from weekends to at least four nights a week. Lately, he had started dropping hints about getting a bigger place—together.

A timer dinged, and Cooper reluctantly released her. While he went back to whirlpooling the contents of the pot, Hannah kicked off her shoes.

"Take a last look—these puppies are going into the trash." She opened the cupboard under the sink and tipped forward the bin. "Farewell, vile instruments of torture."

"Never could figure out why women liked those things."

"This is coming from a man who wears cowboy boots?"

Cooper winked at her. "Can't have the cattle thinking I'm short."

Hannah rolled her eyes. "I thought men wanted women to wear heels. Something about making our tushes look good."

"Your tush already looks pretty good to me." Cooper dipped a spoon into the pot and took a tentative sip. "This needs more chiles, I think."

Hannah walked over to the pantry and scanned the shelves. "All these good smells are making me hungry. Mind if I spoil my appetite a little?"

"Go ahead."

Hannah found a foil bag of crackers. Salt, not sweet, was her weakness. She boosted herself up onto the counter and, legs dangling, munched on a surprisingly fresh cheddar-flavored bunny. Cooper was good about keeping an eye on expiration dates.

Hannah ate another cracker, content to watch him move around the kitchen. As far as she was concerned, *cook* was a noun not a verb, and a salad with more than five ingredients was haute cuisine.

"When did you learn to cook?" she asked.

Cooper grinned at her. "As soon as I found out you could play with all the things you were told not to mess with when you were a kid. Knives, food, and fire—doesn't get much more fun than that."

He dumped washed strawberries into a bowl and set them on the counter. Hannah popped one into her mouth.

"Thief." Cooper paused to brush cracker crumbs from her cheek, then kissed the tip of her nose before turning away to look for something in the pantry.

"By the way, I found a grocery that sells plantains," he said over his shoulder. "You busy on December twenty-first?"

Hannah felt an intensity push outward through

her upper body, filling her heart, forcing the air from her lungs.

She and Cooper had first met in Arizona, when Hannah was home during college spring break and he was doing some computer work for the firm. They had reconnected again by chance in Boston the week before Christmas, during Hannah's first year of law school.

As neither had plans for the holidays, Cooper had suggested a "winter solstice dinner" at a Caribbean restaurant. The meal was unmemorable, except for the dessert—fried plantains topped with cinnamon with a side of vanilla ice cream. They had fed each other spoonfuls of the sweet concoction, and plantains had become the signature treat of subsequent celebrations. Hannah hadn't eaten any since she had broken up with Cooper at the end of her second year.

"Sounds great," she managed to say when she had gotten her breath back.

While Cooper continued his food preparations, Hannah thought about the piece of notepaper in her pocket, the one she had taken from the hospital records room. Cooper offered far more love and affection than anyone she was related—or supposedly related—to ever had. So why wasn't it enough for her? She was her own person, complete unto herself. It shouldn't matter who her father was.

But it did. Hannah couldn't shake the sense that an element of her self *was* missing—a sense of belonging to something larger, and an understanding of what that something was. She had to know what other lives echoed within her.

A month, maybe two at most. By December twenty-first she and Cooper would be eating plantains and talking about a bigger place to live and potential law jobs for Hannah.

"Soup's on!" Cooper ladled his creation into two bowls, handed one to Hannah, then lit the candles. Hoisting himself onto the counter next to her—the dining table and chairs were among the items in Boston—he raised his spoon in a salute. "*Bon appetit.*"

Hannah took a tentative taste. "Delicious." She swallowed the rest of the spoonful with a noisy slurp.

Cooper set down his bowl. "Food as apology is a long-standing tradition in my family. I'm sorry for what I said about the Tohono O'odham job. How did the interview go?"

"I got the job."

"Congratulations!"

Hannah was touched by the sincerity in his voice. "You were right about the low pay and ordinary work. Looks like the only hard part will be managing the media. A reporter from the *Express* hounded me and my boss at lunch. You'd think the Indians were the Evil Empire the way he acted."

"Did you catch his name?"

"Zel Kassif. Ton—Mr. Soto, my boss, told me to stay away from him."

"I'll check him out, see what sort of articles he's written." Cooper hopped off the counter and began assembling the burgers. "A new job calls for a toast. What water would Mademoiselle prefer this evening? Le fizzy or le tap?"

"Le tap will be fine."

For a moment Hannah wondered what it would be like if they could go back to their time together in Boston—before she had fled their relationship the first time around, before she had moved back to Arizona, before she had uncovered too many family secrets. Would she make the same mistakes?

Maybe. Probably.

It didn't matter, she reminded herself. The past couldn't be fixed, only the future.

Hannah bit into her veggie burger. *The future.* Deep down, she knew continuing to exclude

Cooper from the main concerns in her life could only undermine their still-fragile togetherness. If she wanted the relationship to work, she had to treat him as a partner. Hannah put down her food, not hungry anymore.

"Cooper?" she said in a thin voice.

He stopped eating and looked at her, his expression attentive and, Hannah thought, a touch wary.

"I've found out something about my family..."

She poured out the whole story, beginning with Richard's revelation and ending with her visit to the hospital records room. Cooper didn't interrupt once, instead fixing her with a look so intense, she almost expected it to char her eyelashes.

"Oh babe," Cooper said when she had finished speaking, and reached out to hug her. His shirt smelled of hay and sweat, and Hannah pressed her face into the fabric and inhaled. He gently rocked her back and forth, his hand cradling the back of her head.

Hannah leaned back and looked up at him. "I didn't really understand what that records clerk meant about the genetics stuff. Do you?"

"I think so." Cooper helped her down from the counter and led her to the couch.

"Remember that stuff about Mendel's peas in high school?" he asked when they were seated.

"Barely. I didn't like my biology teacher."

"Here's a quick review. Genes come in pairs—one from each parent. In the case of certain diseases, if you inherit two genes for the condition, you have the disease. But if you inherit only one disease gene and one normal gene, you're a carrier. That may mean you have a much milder condition than the full-on disease, or even no symptoms at all. You can, however, pass on the disease gene to your kids."

"The science is coming back to me. Color-blindness works that way, too, right?"

"You got it. Colorblindness requires that *both* parents have the gene, either by being a carrier or being colorblind. Each parent has to have a color-blindness gene to donate to the offspring."

"I'm positive my mo—Elizabeth—wasn't a carrier for anything. It's something at least Olivia would have heard about."

Hannah realized she was developing an aversion to the words *my mother*, though there was no doubt that she was Elizabeth's child. She thought of the scene with Tony at the rock park, and the muscles in her jaw tightened. *Parent by blood but not by character.*

"If the father has a genetic disease, *all* his sperm contains the disease gene, and any child would be a carrier—the result of a normal gene from mom and a disease gene from dad. If a mother has no disease gene and the father is a carrier, half of his sperm carries the disease gene and half carries a normal gene, giving any child a fifty-fifty chance of having the disease gene."

"That's what the hospital clerk was telling me—my father was a carrier for some genetic disease, but he didn't pass on the gene to me. So how do I figure out what the disease was?"

"I don't know what they could test for thirty years ago, but it should be easy enough to find out. Your father was probably tested because he either showed symptoms or the disease ran in his family. Have you thought about trying to unseal the records?"

Hannah shook her head. "That means going public."

"Too bad all this happened pre-computers. Want me to see what I can find in the court files?"

Cooper's hacking skills were extraordinary, and the subject of more than one disagreement between them. Even though he never used them for doing bad or personal gain, Hannah didn't like the idea of rummaging around other people's cyber-drawers.

"No," she said, more abruptly than she had intended. "I mean, this is something I want to do myself."

"Got it." Cooper pushed himself off the couch. "How about some ice cream? I'll grab my jacket."

As he headed for the bedroom, Hannah tipped back her head and let her eyes close. She felt exhausted. As much as she cared for Cooper, there were just too many things going on in her life right now to make room for love. Everyone from the Greeks to the women's magazines said it was supposed to take up most of the available space, especially at the beginning. How was she supposed to fit in career decisions, parentage questions, Tony—

Tony? Where did that come from?

Hannah's mind flashed back to Sunday afternoon, when she was snugged into Tony's lap against the cliff face. The hardness of his muscles, the smell of his sweat, the smoothness of his skin… Hannah felt something rise up from the pit of her stomach, frightening and delicious. She resisted the urge to fan herself.

Cooper came back into the room with his jacket on and a sweater of Hannah's over his arm.

"We better hurry. The Creamery closes at eight."

Eight. The number nudged Hannah's memory. Wasn't there something—*Oh no.* She looked toward the kitchen in panic. The readout on the microwave read 7:40. *She was supposed to meet Tony in twenty minutes.*

"I've got to go!" She scrambled off the couch.

Cooper watched her sprint to the bedroom. "Where?"

"Something for work," Hannah called, unzipping her skirt while she flipped through the clothes hanging in the back of the closet, stopping when she came to a gold cocktail dress. The outfit had been purchased for last year's client party at the firm. Hannah yanked it off the hanger and pulled it over her head.

In the bathroom she dabbed gloss on her lips, gave her hair a few swipes with the brush, then inspected herself in the mirror. *Was the neckline always this low?* Hannah tugged at the fabric, then angled the mirrored medicine cabinet door so she could check the back. A small bottle sat on the top shelf and impulsively Hannah picked it up. A spritz at her throat and behind her ears, and the scent of wildflowers filled the air.

She returned to the closet to look for her one pair of evening shoes. After searching through the jumble of athletic footwear, she recalled her black slingbacks were at the repair shop getting new heels, a casualty of an encounter with a sidewalk grate en route to a bar association dinner four months ago.

Hannah threw down a skimmer in disgust. Even she knew wearing flats would look frumpy. She glanced at her crumpled skirt on the floor and got an idea. Not one she liked, but she didn't have a choice. She dashed into the kitchen and fished her red pumps out of the trash bin.

Cooper surveyed her ensemble. "This is a business meeting?"

"Casino inspection." Hannah hopped on one foot while she shoved the other into a shoe. "Ton— Mr. Soto wanted me to see it at night. Don't worry about waiting up. I'll probably be late."

She searched around the grocery bags on the kitchen counter. "Do you see my keys? I set them right here—"

Cooper put a hand on her shoulder. She looked into his eyes, a darker green than usual, and felt her mania ebb.

"You look nice. Smell nice, too." He picked up her keys from next to the stack of mail and handed them to her, then kissed her on the forehead.

"Don't want to mess up the lip gloss," he said

with a wry smile. "Have a good time."

Hannah thought about Tony and the park. *No, I won't. I promise.*

She picked up her purse, then hesitated as a peculiar feeling came over her—the sense that she had a choice to make, an action to take that would be irrevocable.

Kiss him on the mouth. Ask him to come with you. Tell him you'll call about your furniture tomorrow and move into a bigger place with him. The words ran through her head, and Hannah felt something tighten in her chest.

"Thanks," she said, and turned toward the stairs.

Chapter Eleven

His hand tucked under Hannah's arm, Tony strode confidently past the people seated at the slots, exuding a palpable *joie de vivre*. His smile gleamed, and his dark suit fit him like the hide of a racehorse.

He was, without doubt, the most social person Hannah had ever seen. Hopping from group to group like a magpie attracted to sparkly things—admiring this woman's earrings, that man's cufflinks—Tony flirted with men, women, kids, even animals. Hannah watched as an older woman in an aqua pantsuit received a peck on the cheek, two men playing poker were chatted up, a teenager received a gift of video game tokens, and a dog in a passing handbag got a pat on the head. Tony greeted each by name—even the dog.

She didn't know how he did it, particularly in the midst of such bedlam. A daytime person, Hannah wasn't comfortable in the after-dark world.

The fancy clothes, the cocktails with odd names, the din of chatter and music—all were foreign to her. She felt a bit overwhelmed. And her feet hurt.

The woman standing in front of her lit a cigarette, and Hannah waved a hand in an attempt to redirect the smoke. Catching Hannah's gesture, the woman glowered at her, and Hannah gave up the effort. She wondered why so many smokers acted like non-smokers complained just to annoy them. If she wanted to bug a smoker, she would do a lot more than create a breeze.

Tony bid good-bye to a couple and turned to her. "Hear that?"

Hannah cocked her head. The slots rang and chimed over the murmur of the crowd.

Tony grinned happily. "It's the sound of money falling into the tribe's pocket."

At the table next to them, a dealer turned up the final card in a poker game. One player threw down her hand with a curse, picked up her martini, and stalked away, slopping liquor onto her dress in the process. Another took a drag on a cigarette while a second butt smoldered in the ashtray beside him. The third snarled at the dealer to hurry up and start the next hand.

"Music to your ears," Hannah said. *Accompanied by hacking coughs from secondhand smoke, curses of addicts losing their rent money, and loud drunks. Maybe that reporter has a point.*

Tony nodded at a large slot machine. "Meet one of our star attractions, after the poker tables."

Chief Redfeather—Million Dollar Payoff read the neon letters across the top of the machine. *Only One Dollar.* A line of people waited, dollar tokens in hand, to pull its outsized handle.

Hannah raised an eyebrow. "Chief Redfeather?"

Tony held up his hands in a *don't-blame-me* gesture. "Ask the Marketing Department. They're also the ones who told us to put the Chief and our other popular games away from the entrance. Same reason grocers stock milk and eggs in the rear of the store—you have to walk by everything else to get to them."

Hannah nodded in understanding. "Makes people see more of your inventory. So where's the impulse buy?"

"You mean the candy bars next to the cash register? Those would be the high dollar slots near the doors, so low rollers can take a flyer on their way out."

"I guess I shouldn't be surprised that the art of getting people to lose money is really a science."

"You got it. And even better, we keep them from noticing. Free valet service, nominal gifts to big losers—we want customers to leave happy. Two-for-one show vouchers are the best. Patrons come back, and bring someone else with them, too."

Tony and Hannah watched a middle-aged woman, her hair pulled back by a purple scrunchie, feed dollar tokens into the oversized slot machine. The attendant cheered along with the woman as the tumblers fell into line, then commiserated briefly when no jackpot materialized before moving on to assist the next patron.

"So has the Chief paid out a million dollars yet?"

"Three times since the first of the year."

"Is the money paid over time?" Hannah knew Arizona's lottery jackpots were spread over twenty years.

"Nope—lump sum. Cashier's check within twenty-four hours."

"Wow." *Some serious money off the bottom line.* "How can the casino afford to pay out that much?"

Tony lowered his voice. "Are we covered by attorney-client privilege?"

"Since this morning."

"The casino takes in that amount every day,

more on weekends. The Chief is one of our biggest slot draws. That machine has paid for itself a hundred times over."

Hannah's jaw went slack. *A million dollars a day?* She glanced around at the hundreds—thousands?—of hands dropping quarters into slot machines, laying down five-spots on poker bets, using Benjamins to cover bar bills, and realized it must be true. *Definitely serious money.* Hannah could see why the casino—and the wealth it generated—had so many people up in arms.

Tony took three tokens from a pocket and handed them to Hannah. "Here—give it a try."

"I'm not really much of a gambler…"

He looked skeptical. "So why do you rock climb?"

"That's different. On the granite I'm in control of the chances I take."

"Oh really? So that wasn't you stuck on the cliff last night?"

"It's not the same. *I* was in charge of the events that got me there."

"Really? What about the weather, the condition of the rock, the muscle that fails—you can't control those. The possibility of falling, no matter how well you prepare—that's what gives climbing its buzz.

Risk is seductive, whether it's on a mountain or in a casino. Would you enjoy gambling if you knew you'd always win?"

"I suppose there's no thrill in the sure thing." Out of the blue, an image of Cooper came to mind, and Hannah felt the tightening again, like something elastic was being pulled inside her.

"Exactly! Gambling is a diversion, like going to the movies or a ball game. Part of the entertainment value is not knowing the outcome."

Casinos sold anticipation, Hannah realized. Numbers spinning, dice bouncing, a card in the air—all provided the thrill of uncertainty, and people were willing to pay for it.

Lights flashed and bells clanged on a slot machine several rows away. A young woman and her friend, faces flushed and smiling, squealed and hugged each other as coins rained into the machine's catch tray and overflowed onto the carpet. Tony watched with approval.

"There—that's what I'm talking about. Winning gives you the feeling you're special. It's a rush."

"A rush that only lasts until the handle is pulled again," Hannah said dryly.

"Does it matter if it's only for a moment? How many times do you think it happens otherwise in a day? Go on, try it." Tony signaled the attendant standing next to the large slot machine.

The woman, a young Tohono O'odham dressed in rustic clothing styled in hokey Indian mode—gaily painted and fringed, she reminded Hannah of Cher at her most flamboyant—held up a restraining hand to the woman in a lime green t-shirt who was next in line.

"Just a moment, please," she said.

The woman started to fume. "Hey! I've been waiting—"

"This won't be but a moment, ma'am," Tony said. "Here's a coupon for a cocktail on the house. And may I say, green is definitely your color." He flashed the smile he had been using all night. Hannah thought the smile had less to do with how he felt than how he wanted others to feel—entertained, intrigued, even beguiled. It seemed to be working.

Hannah quickly stepped up to the machine, dropped a token into the coin slot, and pulled the handle. The first tumbler clicked into place, and the word JACKPOT appeared in the pay-off line. For a moment, Hannah let herself think what she would do with a million dollars. *Travel, a small house...* Her daydream evaporated as a lemon and an orange appeared in the adjoining windows. She fed the machine another token, with a similar result. Pocketing the last chip, she rejoined Tony.

"I guess I'm not very lucky."

He winked at her. "The night's still early."

Hannah shot him a look. *What was that supposed to mean?* But Tony was occupied with flagging down a waiter. Seconds later a glass of champagne appeared in Hannah's hand. She took a sip, savoring the tartness.

"So do you gamble?" Hannah asked, and took another swallow. She didn't remember the last time she had drunk the bubbly beverage. Or that it tasted so good.

Tony barked out a quick laugh. "Not here. I don't mind taking risks, but only when the stakes are big and the odds are in my favor." He surveyed the room and looked pleased. "I come to the casino to enjoy the payback."

Hannah drank more champagne. "Payback?"

"For years the only thing the Anglo gave the Indian was disease, whiskey, and broken promises." Tony gestured at the crowd, which was nearly all white. "Now they line up by the tens of thousands to hand over their money."

For a moment his eyes went hard, and Hannah

considered whether the desire to help his people was the only thing that drove him. She raised her glass to her lips, belatedly realizing it was empty. At Tony's nod, a waiter relieved her of the empty flute, replacing it with one filled almost to the brim.

"I really shouldn't—"

"To your new job."

Hannah held up her glass. "To my new job."

Champagne sloshed onto her hand, and Hannah noticed Tony looked slightly out of focus. She stifled a giggle.

"Would you like to see the show?" Tony's voice seemed loud, amplified along with the rest of the casino noise.

Hannah had heard the entertainment featured impersonators of famous singers, like Madonna and Elvis. The concept creeped her out, but then she had been the only Brownie in her troop who had run screaming from the wax museum.

"Not really." She guzzled more champagne. Music pumped from one of the adjoining rooms, and Hannah swayed in time to the bass beat. "How about if we go dancing?"

Tony took her hand. "My pleasure."

Hannah quickly finished her drink and set down the glass, then let Tony guide her toward the room where the music was loudest. She kept a firm grip on his arm, her legs all of a sudden wobbly.

The bouncer admitted Tony and Hannah through the VIP entrance, and they found a place in the middle of the floor surrounded by dozens of writhing people. Seemingly oblivious to the dance track thumping through the speakers, Tony drew Hannah close, nestling his hand against the small of her back. Inches apart, they slowly circled, creating an island of near-stillness among the gyrating bodies. The music was loud and insistent, its beat pounding through Hannah at the cellular level. If the volume went up another notch, she thought she might vaporize.

Tony's cheek brushed hers. His hair smelled clean, with an underlying scent that reminded her of the desert after the rain. His fingers pressed into her skin, and a shudder rippled through her.

The song ended and Tony stepped away from her, his shirt front marked with perspiration. Hannah's dress clung to her shoulders.

"Man, it's hot in here. Let's get some air," he said.

Hannah realized she was staring at the outline of Tony's muscles under the damp fabric of his shirt. "Sure," she managed to say, letting Tony take her hand again.

Perhaps it wasn't Tony who was running hot and cold—maybe it was her. They made their way through the clanging slot machines toward the front entrance. *With the emphasis on hot.*

Once they were in the parking lot, Hannah took deep gulps of the fresh night air, trying to dispel the last of the champagne fog and cigarette smoke. It felt good to breathe air that was invisible again. Tony slid an arm around her waist, and their hips bumped lightly together as they walked toward her car.

Hannah fumbled in her purse for her keys, her fingers feeling thick. She pushed the button on the remote and Tony opened the driver's door.

"Thank you for coming this evening." His voiced had deepened and slowed, and desire gushed upward through Hannah like flowing water. She knew she should feel guilty, but she didn't. She felt great. *Was this how it had happened between Elizabeth and her father?*

Tony took a step closer. His eyes drilled into hers and he brought his face close. She leaned into him, mouth soft…

"Are you sure you're okay to drive?" he asked.

Hannah jerked backward, banging her elbow against her side-view mirror.

"I'm fine," she said, rubbing the spot she knew would be bruised tomorrow. It was true. Like a catalyst, embarrassment had burned off the last of the alcohol.

"Just wanted to be sure. I'll see you in the AM, then."

Tony started back toward the brightly lit entrance of the casino. After a few paces, he stopped and turned around. "Don't forget to wear jeans!"

Hannah got into her car, inserted the key into the ignition, and turned it partway. She hit the button for the sunroof and reclined her seat as far as it could go.

"Stupid, stupid, stupid," she said under her breath as she looked up at the sky sprinkled with stars. She felt as though she should slap herself. Almost cheating—*again*—on her boyfriend, and looking like an idiot—*again*—to her new boss. Instead of making a pass, all Tony had wanted was to tell her to—

Bafflement cut short her self-recriminations. *Wear jeans?*

Chapter Twelve

Tuesday, September 15

Hannah looked at the clock and groaned, not believing it was already seven in the morning. *I must have slept through the alarm*, she thought, then remembered she hadn't set it.

Champagne didn't make for sweet sleep. Hannah's mind had flitted from dream to dream, each set of images more disturbing than the ones before. In the last one, she had been sitting at a poker table in the casino. She didn't know the rules, and the pile of chips in front of her was rapidly dwindling. A woman passed by the table, and Hannah recognized Elizabeth.

Certain she would know how to play the game, Hannah got up from the table and followed her through the crowd, ears ringing from the cacophony of the slot machines. Elizabeth slipped through an unmarked door, with Hannah close behind.

They were in a narrow passageway, her mother's footsteps echoing ahead of her on the concrete floor. But no matter how fast she ran, Hannah couldn't catch up. After many twists and turns, the passageway ended at another door, and Hannah flung it open. She was standing by herself in the casino parking lot, empty except for one car.

The engine was running, and there was someone sitting in the driver's seat. *Elizabeth?* Hannah began to run again. But just as she was close enough to see it was a man behind the wheel, Hannah tripped and started to fall.

The moment she was about to hit the pavement, Hannah had awakened, the sheets damp and twisted around her. She had lain still in the darkness, waiting for her racing pulse to decelerate, while Cooper slumbered peacefully next to her. Many minutes passed before she had been able to go back to sleep.

Now Hannah pushed herself up in bed, squinting against the light. Her head felt overlarge and off-balanced, as though it belonged to someone else and she was just trying it on. She needed some hot tea.

"Cooper?"

There was no answer, and she vaguely recalled the rustle of denim and something whispered about an early morning at the ranch.

Padding into the bathroom, Hannah glanced into the mirror and immediately regretted it. Blotched skin, bloodshot eyes, and enough mascara smeared on her cheeks that she looked like a lineman in the fourth quarter. Apparently, a champagne hangover was just as unbearable as the after-buzz from wine or beer. Hannah thought it should feel classier.

After dry-swallowing three aspirin, she stepped into the shower, shampooing twice to get the smell of smoke out of her hair. At the end, she turned the dial all the way to *Cold* and stood under the icy pellets of water until she couldn't take it anymore.

With a towel wrapped around her, Hannah walked into the kitchen. No cowboy boots by the back door confirmed that she was alone. Opening one of the upper cupboards, she took out a box of her secret vice. *Great Source of 7 Vitamins and Minerals!* read the label.

Yeah, right. Using her teeth to tear open the foil packet, she dropped the Chocolate Chip Pop-Tart into the toaster, then opened the tea canister. It was empty, and Hannah closed the tin container hard enough to buckle the metal. Cooper wasn't a tea-drinker, so it was up to her to keep the supply stocked.

The carafe in the coffeemaker was half-full, left over from Cooper's breakfast. Hannah poured a few inches of the brown liquid into a mug. She hated the stuff, but was desperate for some caffeine.

Holding her breath, she took a sip. The bitterness tripped her gag reflex, and she spat the rest of the mouthful into the sink, then quickly opened the refrigerator to look for something to kill the aftertaste. Two blue-and-silver cans were behind a jar of peanut butter. Red Bull—Cooper's caffeine fix when he had a late-night computer programming project. With a taste only marginally better than coffee, it would have to do.

Hannah mainlined the first can, taking in as much air as liquid. While waiting for the resulting burps to pass, she pressed the second can against her forehead, hoping its coolness would smooth the pounding in her head. It didn't.

At least this will jump-start the aspirin. She opened the second can and drained it. Her Pop-Tart still heating up, she turned on the countertop flat screen that Cooper used to watch the commodity futures news in the morning. Hannah tuned to the local station, hoping to catch the weather forecast.

A news anchor looked earnestly into the camera. *Alleged Bribe in Deportation Case* read the electronic footer. A photo popped up in the corner of the screen and Hannah blinked in surprise. It was the immigration lawyer who'd interrupted her lunch with Tony. She turned up the volume.

"According to the District Attorney, Hepworth approached an INS official with an offer of twenty-five thousand dollars in return for destroying documents crucial to the deportation case against a Mexican national arrested in a narcotics sweep last month. Hepworth's attorney declined comment, except to say that he expects his client to be fully exonerated."

The toaster dinged. Hannah plucked the Pop-Tart from the slot, flipping it from hand to hand as it cooled. She recalled what Tony had said about the efficiency of Hepworth's practice. *Well, bribery was one way to cut through red tape*, she thought, now doubly glad she had rejected the lawyer's offer.

The TV picture switched to a split-screen shot of the news anchor and a man standing in front of the Tohono O'odham casino. Hannah gaped at the screen. It was Kassif, the reporter from the boycott protest who'd pestered Tony at lunch yesterday.

"—increase in bankruptcies, road repair and

other maintenance expenses, and a need for more police," Kassif intoned into his microphone. "Ignoring repeated requests from the City Council, the Tohono O'odham tribe refuses to contribute to the increase in infrastructure costs resulting from the casino."

"What about the money-laundering allegations raised at this week's City Council meeting?" asked the news anchor.

"There's no evidence of this yet, Jeanine, but no proof otherwise either. The tribe's books are closed to the public, and from all appearances, are going to stay that way."

"Thank you, Zel. Now in local sports—"

Hannah hit the *Power* button. Even after the picture dissolved, she continued staring at the darkened glass, feeling her intuition kick in. *Was this job is a bad idea?*

Hannah squashed the thought. If she quit now, she would be faced with choices she wasn't ready to make yet. Hannah's mind went to the file in the records room at the hospital. The past still beckoned, and she needed time to go there.

Hannah swallowed the last bite of Pop-Tart. The Tohono O'odham project would be finished in six, maybe seven weeks. She would be out of the loop and long gone before trouble, if any, hit. The warning bells she had heard in her head were probably ringing because of Tony. Well, she wasn't going to make that mistake again.

Tossing the empty Red Bull cans into the recycling bin, Hannah headed for the bedroom to find a clean pair of jeans.

The OTA building was surrounded by low, sparse brush—some mesquite, some palo verde, but mostly chaparral. Hannah had heard a lot of the little trees were over a hundred years old, and she believed it. The plants looks ragged, and had trouble standing up straight.

Just like me. Hannah walked across the parking lot, wishing her sunglasses were darker. Thank goodness she wasn't wearing heels. Although her headache no longer clamored for attention, her cotton mouth persisted, despite the full bottle of water she had downed during the drive from the condo.

The sun beat down on her head and shoulders, its force only slightly tempered from that of July and August. In the desert, seasonal rhythms of Nature were easily overlooked. There were few flashy natural occurrences—no return of a specific bird flock to a specific site, no large young animals frolicking in meadows, no changing colors on hand-sized leaves. Certain events did mark the passage of summer, though. When the really hot weather came, the out-of-staters left. When the temperatures cooled, they returned. Tourists marked the changing of the seasons in Arizona.

As Hannah neared the casino entrance, the doors opened to discharge the latest wreckage from the poker tables and slot machines. Two blue-collar workers, eyes downcast. A woman in an evening gown with its hem ripped out. A trio of tired-looking tourists burned red from the sun, fooled by the fact it was nearly October.

A million dollars a day ought to produce a lot of happiness. But this group didn't appear to have gotten its money's worth.

Both the OTA receptionists were on the phone. One of them covered the mouthpiece with her hand.

"Do you remember where your office is? Tony said to go ahead and get settled. He'll come by after his meeting is over."

Hannah found her office without any trouble. The room had been made further cramped since yesterday by an incongruous addition—a life-sized, carved wooden Indian. *Ironic art? Or was the figure too un-PC to display but too old to throw out?*

One desk was under the window, the other in the far corner, out of sight of the door. Both were made of plastic painted to look like wood. *Guess casino money hasn't trickled down here yet.* Hannah chose the desk in the corner, not liking the idea of someone being able to watch her while she was unaware.

After putting her briefcase into an empty drawer, Hannah sat in the desk chair. The sagging seat marked it as a hand-me-down from someone with a heavier and broader bottom than she. The wheels squeaked when she moved.

The space offered far less than her office at Dain & Dain—no state-of-the-art electronics, no marble finishes, no antique carpets. At the same time, it also offered far more. For the first time in a law office, Hannah was solely in the present. Her past had been erased, leaving just the future all around.

Maybe that was why Arizona didn't charm her the way Boston or other places did. Even with a different job or different house, it didn't matter—she could never truly start new. Living in Pinnacle Peak imposed a sense of backward motion, of being pulled through the door to the same old family dynamics.

But didn't every place eventually became ordinary, entangled in reality? And at some point, shouldn't the urge to construct a new set of needs and desires be supplanted by the enjoyment and comfort of the familiar? Hannah wished there were a calendar she could consult, one that laid out the milestones of her life.

March 4—fall in love. September 19—fall out of love. December 11—become an adult. July 23—no longer worry about what hair looks like on trips to the grocery store. It would make things so much easier.

"Right, Chief?" she said to the wooden Indian.

The tall figure wore buckskin trousers and a feathered headdress painted in garish colors. Bow and arrow in one hand, he stared stonily into the distance.

"Did you say something?" asked a female voice.

A young blond woman stood in the doorway. She wore a whisper of a skirt with a blouse cut to enhance her cleavage and too much perfume. Hannah could smell it from where she sat.

"Uh, hi." Hannah got to her feet, embarrassed at being caught talking to a piece of wood.

"Are you Hannah?"

"Yes. Are you—"

"Just a sec. I wanna set this stuff down."

The woman's arms were filled with an assortment of items—white leather jacket, striped tote bag, cup of coffee from the local java joint, and a set of hot rollers. The woman dumped her possessions on the secretary's desk where the note had been yesterday, then beamed at Hannah.

"Hi, I'm Wendi. This is going to be *so* great. I am *so* glad to be out of the typing pool." She wrinkled her nose. "All that typing—*so* boring."

Her secretary didn't like to type? Hannah had a feeling this was going to be *so* bad.

Wendi held up her hands, each finger tipped with an unsubtle coral. "That reminds me. Would it be okay if I stay off the computer on Fridays? Thursday nights I get my mani-pedi, and I don't want to chip my polish before the weekend."

Hannah tried and failed to come up with a suitable response. Wendi didn't appear to notice.

"I don't mind filing, but it can get old." Extracting a sheaf of fashion magazines from the tote bag, Wendi arrayed them along the desktop, then unpacked several plastic containers filled with chopped vegetables and what looked like pale fish. "And I've got food issues."

"Food issues?" Finally finding her voice, Hannah tried to make it as pleasant as possible.

"I'm on a really strict diet, so I can't get your coffee or order lunch. It'll mess with my hunger triggers."

Wendi's perfume had become overwhelming. Hannah rubbed her temples, feeling her headache start to return.

"What time are you supposed to be here?"

"Eight thirty, but don't look for me before nine." Wendi patted a framed photo next to her phone. It showed a dark-haired man glowering at the camera. "Personal reasons."

"Does your diet mean you skip lunch?"

"The eating part. But my Pilates class starts at noon, so I have to leave right at 11:45." Wendi plugged the curlers into a wall outlet next to the desk. "I hope it's okay if I cut out a little early tonight."

"Let me guess," Hannah said. "Personal reasons."

Wendi smiled happily as she draped her jacket over the chair. "You know, you're not as bad as Jenna thought you'd be. I'm telling her that stuff she said about woman bosses just isn't true!" She sat down and looked up expectantly. Her hair shimmered gold, white, chestnut, each strand a different hue.

Probably none the color she had been born with, Hannah thought as she leaned over the partition in front of Wendi's desk. The too-sweet scent of flowers was almost nauseating. "I need to tell you something."

"Yes?"

"I'm not paying you for today. Personal reasons."

Wendi stared at her, mouth slightly agape.

"Or tomorrow. Or the day after that." Hannah straightened up and went back to her office, closing the door behind her. She picked up the phone, already punching in Clementine's number before she sat down.

An answering machine came on.

"I'm busy. If you leave a message, I might call you back." Her former secretary's voice couldn't quite hide its New Jersey origins.

"Clementine, I don't care what soap opera you're watching, pick up," Hannah said after the beep. She heard the sound of the receiver on the other end being lifted.

"Now I won't know if Skylar really is Brett's brother," Clementine complained.

Hannah's secretary had quit Dain & Dain last month, telling Hannah she needed a break. "Crime, violence—I came West to get away from all that!" she had declared. Since then, Hannah knew she had done a smattering of temp work, and Clementine had mentioned something about taking night classes the last time they had talked.

But hours at home during the day had introduced Clementine to soap operas, and she quickly became an addict. Hannah had tried to encourage her to look for a full-time job, but Clementine wasn't to be persuaded.

"I'm getting career advice from a woman who doesn't even know what side of the country she wants to live on? Don't worry, Hannah. I'm on—what do you call it?—sabbatical."

"And the difference between that and unemployment is—?"

"If you're on sabbatical, you don't care that you're not working. Gotta go. My show's about to start."

That had been ten days ago, the last time they'd spoken.

"Can you live without Skylar for six weeks?" Hannah asked. "I'm doing a project for the Tohono O'odham, putting together a private offering. I could really use your help."

"You temping for the Indians?"

"That's one way to put it."

"Doesn't the job come with a secretary? You know I don't play well with others."

Hannah thought about Clementine's behavior at Dain & Dain. *No kidding.*

"Actually, I just fired her."

Clementine laughed, a deep rumble that matched her plus-sized figure. "So you're desperate, huh?"

"Pretty much."

"Job pay well?"

"No."

"Nice offices?"

Hannah glanced around the room, her eyes coming to a stop on the wooden Indian. "Interesting décor."

"Cute single guys?"

"N-None so far." *Why was she stuttering?*

"Will you buy me a TiVo so I can record *Passion Beach*?"

"*No.*"

"Shoot, Boss, you always were a hard woman. I'll be there in half an hour."

Hannah gave her the address for the OTA and hung up, feeling the ebb of her Pop-Tart and Red Bull high. She hoped Tony wasn't going to be irritated about Wendi. But putting together a private placement, especially one so high profile, was serious business.

As attorney for the deal, Hannah was responsible for collecting and verifying the relevant data, then incorporating that information into a private placement memorandum, the document used to solicit capital from investors. This past summer Hannah had learned firsthand the disastrous consequences of doing less than thorough due diligence. She didn't need the extra hassle of a diva secretary.

Not that Clementine was easy. She was obstinate and opinionated, voluble and volatile. But few had her secretarial skills, and even fewer could read Hannah as well.

Which was not always a good thing. Hannah resolved not to tell Clementine about the search for her birth father. At least Tony was out of the picture. Last night's embarrassing moment in the parking lot had effectively extinguished any remaining attraction as far as Hannah was concerned.

Wanting to get to work on the offering, she searched her file cabinets for paperwork on the first phase, but the drawers were empty. Walking into the hallway, she glanced over her secretary's desk. The hot curlers, fashion magazines, and Wendi were gone. There weren't any documents, either.

Tony would know. She walked to the lobby. According to the receptionist, he was almost finished with his meeting. Deciding to wait in the reception area, Hannah sat down in one of the leather chairs and picked up the latest issue of the tribe's magazine. The table of contents listed articles on luxury cars, collectible watches, and education trusts. She had just started skimming *Where to Buy Your Second Home* when the lobby door opened.

Hannah looked up, hoping it was Clementine. Instead, the reporter from yesterday walked in. He looked pleased to see her.

"Ms. Dain—Zel Kassif. You're just the person I want to talk to."

Light gleamed off his freshly shaved head and again he was beltless. This time he wore a gold-and-orange striped shirt that looked straight out of the eighties. Hannah was willing to bet he was the original owner.

Kassif sat down next to her without waiting for an invitation and freed a notebook and pen from his cargo pants. It was the first time Hannah had seen someone use the thigh pockets to carry stuff.

"How about a comment from the attorney for the tribe's real estate project? What's the projected rate of return? Isn't this just an attempt to smooth over the tension between the tribe and the citizens of Pinnacle Peak?"

Even though Zel's glasses were smudged with fingerprints, the eyes behind them were bright and lively. Hannah recalled Tony's warning.

"No comment, Mr. Kassif." She felt foolish saying the words— and felt the stirring of her intuition again. Did she belong in a job that required stonewalling the press?

With a rueful smile, the reporter flipped the notebook closed.

"You can't blame a guy for trying. And please, call me Zel."

The lobby door opened again, and in breezed Clementine. Just over five feet tall and almost half again as wide, she was resplendent in a cerise sweater set dotted with rhinestones. Plastic flowers adorned the toes of her shoes, and the red of her lipstick matched the hue of her full skirt.

"The secretary is in the house," Clementine announced, then opened her arms wide. "Hiya, Boss!"

Hannah was engulfed in a hug that drove the breath out of her. "Thanks for coming," she wheezed when Clementine finally turned her loose.

"Only for you would I give up mornings with Skylar and Brett to return to slavery."

"So do you think they're brother and sister?"

Zel got to his feet. "Zel Kassif, *Passion Beach* fan."

"Clementine Peters." Hannah's secretary held out her hand.

Zel raised it to his lips with the élan of a diplomat. *"Enchanté,"* he said.

The color heightened in Clementine's already rouged cheeks.

Hannah was astounded. The Clementine she knew would have slapped anyone who tried that stunt. "Be careful. He's with the *Express,*" she said.

Clementine wrenched her hand from Zel's grasp and Hannah hid a grin. She had never worried about her secretary disclosing something she shouldn't. Clementine had been well-schooled at Dain & Dain in the rules of confidentiality. And, as Hannah had recently learned, she came from a long line of people good at keeping secrets.

"Well, Zel, Zilch—whatever your name is— we're done here," Clementine said in a tone that could frost glass.

"I couldn't agree more." Clad in jeans and cowboy boots, Tony was standing next to the reception counter holding a cardboard banker's box. "Kassif, you know the OTA is private property. Out!"

"I was just leaving." Zel winked at Clementine. "Nice sweater. Call me if you want a *Beach* update."

"Humph," Clementine said. But Hannah saw her secretary's eyes follow the reporter to the door. *Uh oh*. Apparently she wasn't the only one capable of idiocy when it came to the opposite sex.

"These are the documents on the first phase," Tony said to Hannah. "I'll put them in your office, and then I want to take you downtown and introduce you to my bosses." He looked at Clementine. "I'm sorry—have we met?"

Clementine struck a pose. "If you have to ask, then we haven't. Because I am utterly memorable."

Tony looked questioningly at Hannah.

"Can I speak with you for a moment?" She fixed him with a bright smile.

Clementine flicked her wrist in a dismissive wave, setting a dozen bracelets jangling. "Don't mind me, I'll just look around." She strolled across the lobby to the basket display.

In a low voice, Hannah quickly explained the secretary changeover.

"That's fine," Tony said when she had finished. "All I care about is getting the deal done."

Prying Clementine away from her conversation with one of the receptionists, Hannah made the introductions.

"Nice to meet ya," Clementine said.

"Glad to have you on the project." Tony turned to Hannah. "Let me drop off this box, and then we should get going."

"I'll take care of the box," Clementine said.

Tony set the carton on the counter. "Thanks."

Behind his back, Clementine winked at Hannah and held up her fingers in the *OK* sign. Hannah shook her head and mouthed the word *no* before following Tony outside to the parking lot. *Maybe calling Clementine hadn't been such a good idea after all.*

Hannah expected Tony to drive something from the Axis—German, Japanese, maybe Italian. So she was surprised to see him stop next to a convertible Mustang from the mid-sixties, completely restored and painted a creamy yellow.

"Nice car."

"These days, O'odham think nothing of driving a Navajo, Cherokee—even a car named after our worst enemy, the Apache." Tony patted the running horse logo. "Me, I'm a traditionalist. Mind if we drive with the top down?" He was already fiddling with the latch.

"Fine with me," Hannah lied. Convertibles made her nervous. A few falls from her road bike had convinced her that travel above twenty miles an hour should involve as much protective metal as possible.

As they pulled out of the parking lot, Hannah glanced toward the OTA building in time to see a bald man in a striped shirt slip through the lobby door.

Kassif? Hannah started to look for her cell phone to warn Clementine before remembering it was in her briefcase—which was in the bottom drawer of her new desk.

She considered saying something to Tony. But what if she were wrong, and it wasn't the reporter? In any event, did she want to imply Clementine wouldn't be discreet?

Hannah decided to keep quiet. Tony already had seen enough foolish behavior from her, and Clementine had handled the press well enough on prior occasions.

Things will be fine, she told herself, trying to relax.

The car dropped into a dip in the road, taking her stomach with it.

Chapter Thirteen

Tony aimed the Mustang west toward town, passing columnar cacti and ocotillos bristling with green soft leaves, the only color in a landscape otherwise as relentlessly brown as an old sepia-tinged photograph. In the distance, clouds curled over mountain peaks like giant crashing waves.

Once on the main road, the car picked up speed, and Hannah's hair began to whip Medusa-like around her head. Sixty-five miles an hour with the top down felt like sitting in a convection oven. She could feel her skin baking in the dry desert air.

Tony draped one hand over the top of the steering wheel. "I love driving here. In LA, there's always too much traffic to really let a car run." He punched the gas pedal and the Mustang responded with a surge of power. The back of Hannah's skull hit the headrest.

Tony tapped the brakes. "Sorry about that. Cars bring out the Mexican in me. You can never go too fast or have too many horses under the hood."

Eyes on the speedometer, Hannah rubbed her sore neck. *Guess that rules out Latina as one of my possible nationalities.*

"What does your family think of your move back to Pinnacle Peak?" Hannah asked. She was sure Richard and Shelby would have been happier if she had passed on trying to fulfill her perceived legacy expectations.

"Both sides think I'm nuts. Why else would I give up a condo on the beach and partnership track with the bank?" Tony shrugged. "They don't understand."

"You probably could build up a good investment business managing the tribe's casino money."

"That's not my goal. When my mom and I lived on the rez, one of my chores was standing in line for surplus government food. Cheese mostly. No bread, no meat, no vegetables—just cheese. I still hate the stuff." Tony ran a hand through his hair. "Too many O'odham remember those days, too. They're afraid to seize the power that the casino money gives them. I want to help change that."

Hannah studied his set jaw and narrowed eyes.

Gone was the ready smile and deferential manner he had displayed at the office and in the casino. Tony was a chameleon of the highest order, not just changing his skin to survive, but also to get his way. She wondered if he had generated friction within the tribe's hierarchy, especially from those who might not be as altruistic.

"At a million dollars a day, isn't every Tohono O'odham rich by now? Where are the mansions and airplanes?" she asked.

"Some tribes pay out casino income directly to members. The O'odham decided that would just be trading one form of welfare for another. Look what instant wealth does to kids who become NBA players. While a stipend is paid to individual tribe members—don't get me wrong, it's generous—most of the money goes to funding projects and creating jobs."

They hit the edge of town, and Tony slowed the Mustang to the speed limit. Just past Scottsdale Road he turned left into the area known as *El Mercado*. This part of Pinnacle Peak always made Hannah feel as though she were in Mexico. The air smelled of cinnamon and cooking grease, and there were more people on the streets, most of them brown-skinned. The signs in store windows read *Abierto* and nothing at all in English. To Hannah's ears, even the bells over the doors tinkled in Spanish.

They continued south, each block shabbier than the one before, entering a section of town that white people usually visited only if they were curious about trouble or wearing a badge. The Mustang rolled by houses with oil stains on the concrete driveways and lawns that were more dirt than grass. *For Sale* signs dotted chain-linked front yards, some so old Hannah couldn't read the Realtor phone number. The walls of the commercial buildings were marked with Spanish graffiti.

"Welcome to the *barrio*," Tony said. "You know, that used to be a nice word—it means *neighborhood*. Now the media have made it synonymous with a bad place."

He parked in front of a two-story building. Cracks ran up the walls and the structure's roof sagged, signs of wear that could only be remedied by a bulldozer.

"Here we are."

A group of young boys, dressed in baggy pants and athletic jerseys, stood on the opposite corner eyeing the yellow Mustang. Hannah wondered if the car would still be there when they returned.

Tony got out and waved at the boys. "Hey, *ese,*

watch my ride?" His accent had become thicker, more guttural.

A short, dark-haired boy stepped forward from the pack. He wore what Hannah imagined were the latest sneakers and a blue bandana tied to a belt loop.

"*No problema, Antoñio.*"

"*Gracias.*"

As Tony escorted Hannah into the building, a lone wolf whistle sounded from across the street. Hannah glanced back to see the boys collapse into guffaws and a medley of hand slapping and fist bumping.

"They're not as bad as you might think—not yet, anyway," Tony said. "Most of them are wannabes, trying to look like they're down with the genuine *cholos*. But give them a few more years of hanging out, and they'll be in the life for real." He nodded toward a set of stairs rising out of the lobby. "Sorry, but the elevator's out."

Hannah followed Tony up the once-carpeted steps. The fabric was worn through to the wood underneath in most places. "Looked like they were just being kids to me."

"That's the problem. Hanging out, killing time—fine to do if you're a kid. But too many people in this neighborhood never get past it. If you want to move up in the world as an adult, you have to get out of the *barrio* and step up to the white man's tempo. Your timeline needs to be next month, next year, the next five years. If you stay here, it's because you like the pace or don't want to think past the short term. One day blends into the next, and you're a winner for just making it through another Saturday night with pride and life intact. *Suerte o muerte.*"

Luck or death. Hannah thought Tony's view overly harsh. Not everyone remained in the *barrio* out of choice. Economics, family responsibilities, and lack of education or employment weren't always surmountable barriers. And she wasn't sure leaving was required to make something of life.

The stairs led to a corridor lined with doors. Many bore the marks of removed nameplates or traces of scraped-off gold lettering.

"Aren't there any other tenants?" Hannah asked.

"P&M is the only one. The partners bought the building last year—got a bargain price, and a tax break for investing in the neighborhood. They have plans drawn for a major remodel, and are going to use their investment fee from the tribe's real estate offering to pay for it."

At the end of the hall, *Peña & Moreno—Private Equity* was lettered on a small brass plaque mounted next to a door. Tony tapped the square of metal.

"You should have heard the argument over this. Peña wanted to use the Spanish *Y* instead of an ampersand. Moreno was having none of it. They finally ended up flipping a coin. I was surprised they didn't quarrel over whether it should be a peso or a quarter." Tony opened the door and they walked inside.

The reception area looked like most others she had seen—visitor chairs, low side tables, a half-height counter. Behind the counter was an empty secretary's desk, backed by rows of filing cabinets. Conditioned air wheezed out of an overhead vent.

"Hello?" called a voice from a hallway to the left.

"Hey, Alex, it's me. Ms. Dain is here, too. Do you and Roberto have a moment?"

"Of course!" A short, portly man appeared from the hallway and hurried toward them carrying a glass of frothy pink liquid. He had thick black hair touched with gray and a moon-shaped face.

"Alexander Moreno." He shook Hannah's hand enthusiastically. "Welcome."

Moreno pronounced his name without inflection, his accent more Southampton than south-of-the-border. He had skin paler than Hannah's (she could see the laser marks from the lightening procedure along his jaw line), and wore a navy suit and a red tie with little boats on it.

"Robert, we have company!" Moreno said in an amplified voice.

Hannah noticed his use of the English version of his partner's name. Was Moreno trying to lose his beginnings as much as she was trying to find hers?

"How's the diet going?" Tony asked.

Moreno grimaced at the pink liquid in the glass. "This is a truly foul-tasting beverage, Anthony. But the doctor was adamant I must trim my waistline if I didn't want another *incident*." He patted his chest in the region of his heart.

Tony shook his head. "I agree with Hunter Thompson. It's better to arrive at the Pearly Gates totally thrashed, shouting, *'Ay Carumba!* What a ride!'"

"You'll understand when you're older, Anthony. And I wish you wouldn't use that street expression. Now if you'll excuse me, I'll see what's keeping my partner." Moreno disappeared back down the hallway.

"Street expression?" Hannah whispered.

"*Ay Carumba*," Tony whispered back. "Bet you didn't know Bart Simpson was a *cholo*." He shook his head. "Poor Alex. He still hasn't forgiven his parents for being Hispanic. It probably kills him that his last name means *brown* in Spanish. I'm surprised he hasn't changed it."

Moreno reappeared with a man Hannah presumed was Peña. Almost six feet tall, he had dark brown skin and longish hair that lapped over his collar. His suit pulled tight across his hunched shoulders, the sleeves showing too much shirt cuff.

"Roberto, this is Hannah Dain," Tony said.

"*Mucho gusto.*" Peña's coal-black eyes were large and dark-rimmed, reminding Hannah of the big-eyed children in the paintings on velvet peddled by *El Mercado* street vendors.

"Dain & Dain has an excellent reputation. We're so pleased you're going to be the attorney on the offering," Moreno said.

Dain & Dain? "Mr. Moreno, I'm not—"

Moreno put a hand on her arm. "By chance, does your firm practice immigration law?"

Peña frowned. "Alejandro, Ms. Dain is here to discuss the tribe's private placement."

Moreno waved him off and continued. "We do some immigration consulting for our clients, and the attorney we were using is—"

"Alejandro!" Peña said.

"It's okay, Roberto," Tony said. "Hannah met Hepworth yesterday. Anyway, there's no reason to keep what happened secret. His indictment led the morning news."

"What a disaster!" Moreno's cheeks were pink with agitation. "Our clients will—"

"—have to be patient until we find a suitable replacement," Peña interjected. "Mr. Hepworth's services were valuable but not unique. An inconvenience, Alejandro, that's all this is."

"You gotta take the Latin view of things, Alex. It'll keep your blood pressure down," Tony said.

"Latin view?" Hannah asked.

"My Mexican grandmother used to say white people had a lot to learn about happiness. She thought the Anglo mentality—you know, that everyone deserves to be happy, that everything ought to be the best—only set you up for disappointment. As a Latino, you expect unhappiness, then are pleasantly surprised when the occasion comes along that brings you joy."

"Sounds like a blueprint for depression to me," Hannah said.

"Is that worse than the misery of constantly falling short?"

Hannah recalled how much it had hurt never to measure up to Richard Dain's expectations. Maybe Tony's grandmother had a point.

Thinking of Richard reminded Hannah that she needed to clarify her employment status. "Mr. Moreno, you should know I'm not with Dain & Dain anymore."

"Oh?" Confusion flitted across his features. "But Anthony said—"

"—that the tribe was very fortunate to have the top transactions lawyer from Dain & Dain working on its private placement," Tony said.

Hannah gave him a sideways glance. *Why hadn't he told his partners that she had left the firm?*

"The Tohono O'odham project is our first Native American deal," Moreno said to Hannah. "Usually we invest in Hispanic-owned businesses. The companies are privately owned, rather than publicly traded, so we act as the conduit for equity capital. Our firm has about two hundred million dollars under management, primarily from large companies or pension funds."

"Feel-good money," Peña added sourly. At Hannah's questioning look, he added, "Investors who care more about the PR value of putting money into a Hispanic-owned enterprise than potential return. They look at it as charity, and are shocked when their investment makes money."

"Nothing wrong with that. Helps us build a track record," Moreno said.

"What *is* wrong is Hispanic businessmen bowing and scraping like peasants, as though they don't deserve Anglo money," Peña retorted.

"Robert, it's a fact that mainstream equity capital has been slow to flow to Hispanic investment opportunities. Things are changing, but it takes time."

"The Anglos better wake up soon. We're the largest minority in the country—forty million plus. They need to be paying attention to us instead of a handful of Indians."

Was this Dump On White Men Week? First Tony was upset at Anglo oppression of Indians. Now Peña was mad that whites weren't supporting the Hispanic business community. Did they expect her to play the woman's card, and carry on about equal pay for equal work? Not that Hannah didn't endorse the concept. But she preferred to keep her politics private.

"Is the two hundred million fully committed?" she asked, hoping to steer the conversation onto a more neutral topic. P&M sounded like a pretty vanilla investment operation, with perhaps less capital than most. That could change in a hurry if the partnership were tapped to manage even part of the casino revenues. The partners' pro-Hispanic bias notwithstanding, Hannah was sure they would be thrilled to get the Indian business. No wonder Moreno wanted a top lawyer from a top firm putting together the deal.

"About ninety percent," Moreno said. "We've got several investments under consideration and are expecting a new influx of capital by the end of the month, thanks to Anthony here." He clapped a hand on Tony's shoulder.

"This place is a two-way street, professionally as well as financially," Tony said to Hannah. "P&M allows me to earn on my own business. That means I get to eat a big chunk of what I kill. This real estate deal is only the beginning." Tony glanced at his watch. "Hannah and I need to get going. We have one more appointment."

After another vigorous handshake from Moreno and a restrained nod by Peña, Tony and Hannah were on their way. When they hit the street, there was no sign of the boys, but the yellow convertible looked intact.

"Your bosses seem nice. And *very* different from each other," Hannah said as Tony started the car.

"They're an unlikely pair, that's for sure. Roberto has smiled maybe twice since I've met him, and is a card-carrying member of La Raza. Alex is a classic coconut who runs on pure enthusiasm. If you met them separately, you'd never guess they were partners."

"What's a coconut?"

"Brown on the outside, white on the inside." Tony merged onto Scottsdale Road, the town's main artery heading north. "But I don't mind their differences. Both have been very good to me. Alex told me last week if things keep going well, I'll be a partner in two years."

The Mustang zipped through traffic, finally pausing when confronted by a light several seconds into the red wavelength. Hannah felt the car vibrate beneath her.

"So why did you want me to wear jeans?"

"You'll see."

The light changed. Tony hit the gas, and the car leaped forward with a throaty roar.

Chapter Fourteen

Half an hour later as the Mustang flew, Hannah and Tony were somewhere northeast of Pinnacle Peak. Traffic thinned as buildings became sparser, the area between them bigger. Soon just desert rolled out on either side of the road in great, spreading swells. Sunlight reflected off metal fence posts while hawks stood sentinel on top of tall saguaros.

After the hemmed-in, forested East, it had taken Hannah a while to adjust to Arizona's emptiness and scale. Sometimes driving down the long ribbons of asphalt made her feel curiously light-headed, even slightly out-of-body. With Tony at the wheel, though, all she felt was nervous.

As they neared what Hannah recognized as the northern boundary of the rez, yellow-and-black-edged signs began to appear along the roadside. Each one bore the admonition *Control Growth!*

"What do those signs mean?" she asked.

"It's the name of one of the anti-Indian groups. A bunch of white businessmen are opposed to the tribe buying land to expand the rez. They can't legitimately block the sales, so they try to bully owners into not selling to us."

Hannah recalled an *Express* article that had quoted one ranch owner who had sold out to the Indians. *They offered me double the market value. What was I supposed to do?* She thought about what Tony had told Hepworth yesterday at lunch. *From northern Mexico to southern Arizona... I wouldn't mind having it all back.* No wonder some whites were worried.

The Mustang sped along the two-lane road, catching up to a slow-moving motor home traveling in their direction. Tony tailgated for a moment, then passed with a bad-mannered flash of headlights, clearing the other vehicle's front bumper by mere inches when he steered back to the right. The blare of the motor home's horn faded as they pulled away.

Hannah glanced over at Tony, noting his firm hold on the wheel, the relaxed set of his shoulders. *I don't mind taking risks, but only when the stakes are big and the odds are in my favor.* Hannah wished she had asked how big of an advantage he needed on the road. In the future, she was going to insist on driving.

Barely braking, Tony turned right at an unmarked exit. The pavement gave way to gravel, and the car began to climb. They passed a chain link fence decorated with a collage of *No* signs—*No Shooting, No Hunting, No Trespassing, No Public Access.* The road S-ed up the mountain, finally dead-ending in front of a small barn and attached corral. Two horses were tied to the fence rail.

Tony put the car into neutral and turned off the engine. Hannah uncurled her hand from its grip on the door handle, her fingers leaving dents in the leather.

"Welcome to the rez taxi stand." Tony picked up a cowboy hat off the floor of the backseat and jammed it onto his head.

Hannah looked at the two horses with dismay. The rez stretched out over a hundred thousand acres, with only the casino and limited commercial areas along the borders open to the public. Although looking forward to going where few non-Indians were allowed, she wished they were using another means of transportation. A bad experience at summer camp had led to a lifetime avoidance of all things equine.

With Hannah's help, Tony raised the convertible's top and latched it into place. For the first time since they'd met, neither his handsome face nor the bulge of muscle beneath his shirt registered on her sexual chemistry scale. *Zero catalytic reaction*, Hannah thought with satisfaction and something akin to relief.

One of the horses was brown, the other a medium gold with white legs. Both were fitted out in bridles and Western saddles. The brown horse watched their approach with its ears pricked, greeting them with a whinny. The gold one appeared to take no notice. It continued to doze with its head down, barely opening its eyes even when Tony rubbed its ears.

"Meet Buttermilk," he said.

Hannah gave the gold horse a tentative pat on the neck.

"Have you done much riding?" Tony asked.

"Do merry-go-rounds count?"

He laughed. "Don't worry, she's a real babysitter. After a few pointers, you'll be good to go."

Hannah concentrated on Tony's quick rundown of riding fundamentals—*neckrein to steer, heel bump to move forward, hold on to the horn if you want, say Whoa! to stop*—even though she knew she wouldn't remember most of it. Too soon the talking part was over.

Tony grasped a stirrup. "Put your foot in this." He boosted her into the saddle, then untied the reins from the fence and handed them to her. "Wait here while I get my horse ready."

As though I would go galloping off into the desert. Hannah could feel the warmth of the saddle leather through her jeans as she wriggled from side to side, trying to get comfortable. Buttermilk let out a small sigh.

"Believe me, I'm as thrilled about this as you are," Hannah said under her breath. The mare flicked an ear in her direction.

A small ground squirrel appeared on a nearby rock and balanced upright on its hind feet, eyes hopeful. When it was clear Hannah had no food to share, it chirred its disappointment and darted back into hiding.

Tony mounted up. "Let's go, Buttermilk," he called, and clucked his tongue against the roof of his mouth.

With Hannah clutching the saddlehorn, Buttermilk jogged toward Tony's horse, slowing to a walk once the two animals were side by side. Just beyond a shiny metal sign that read *Tohono*

O'odham Tribal Lands—Members Only, Tony turned his horse onto a narrow dirt path. Buttermilk fell into line behind.

"Mind if I ask where we're going?" Hannah asked, thankful not to be bouncing anymore.

"My grandmother's. Last night you saw where the money comes from. Now you'll see how it's changed things. I want you to understand what life was like on the rez before the casino."

"Wouldn't driving be easier?" Already the insides of her thighs were sore.

"We're on the main road."

Hannah eyed the jagged rocks, deep sand, and needle-studded cacti. Anything less than a military-issue SUV wouldn't have a chance of getting through.

Tony flicked the ends of his reins at a fly. "I visit every Tuesday afternoon. One of my cousins leaves a horse for me at the trailhead. Last night I called and asked him to tack up Buttermilk, too."

The trail started to gradually climb, wending through splintered rocks and clumps of chaparral. Hannah was quiet, lulled by the rhythms of her walking horse. Here and there she caught the shine of aluminum off singlewide trailers presumably abandoned for housing built with casino revenues.

A muslin curtain flapped in the breeze from a glass-less window of a cinderblock house.

No electricity, cardboard siding, water only when it was carried in—this was poverty Hannah associated with countries far poorer than her own. In her view, the tribe's gambling windfall was well deserved and long overdue. She was impressed how far Tony had come from such beginnings.

"Your family must be very proud of you," she said as they rode past a shack pieced together from sheets of corrugated tin and plywood.

Tony nodded. "And a little intimidated, too. They don't really understand my world." He shifted sideways in the saddle and hooked a leg over the saddle horn.

"My dad graduated from high school and got married on the same day—wedding at four, commencement at eight. My father's family didn't come to either. They weren't too thrilled about *the mixing of the races*, as they called it, even though Tohono O'odham traditionally speak Spanish and intermarry with Mexicans. His bride—my mother—was sixteen. She had quit school after eighth grade. Both their fathers were dirt-poor. Neither could read English, and my mother's family didn't even own a car. They could have bought one, but because her father drank too much, her mother thought it was a better idea not to. So my grandmother never got used to cars. She still doesn't like them much."

"How come your grandmother doesn't live in the housing development near the casino?"

"Both my mother and I have tried to get her to move. It wasn't until last year that she let me replace her trailer with a real house. A few months ago I put in a generator so she can have electricity. She still won't use the dishwasher or washing machine. Doesn't think they get stuff clean enough."

"Is it modern things she doesn't like?"

"Not exactly. She doesn't want to leave where she grew up. Says she likes living where she knows everybody and the roads are straight. *Makes it easier to see where you've been and where you're going*, is how she puts it. Funny thing is, now I'm thinking about building a place near hers and living there part-time."

"So this is a *Roots* kind of thing?" Hannah knew something about sacrificing self for family expectations. She hoped Tony would do a better job than she had in figuring out how far to go.

Tony grinned. "Maybe. There's also something appealing about the utter impossibility of the place."

Hannah imagined him washing his pricey dress shirts in a bucket. "Are you sure you can handle it?"

"When I lived on the rez as a kid, it was like a Third World village. The streets weren't paved and most of the dogs didn't wear collars. All we had was a church and a convenience store that stocked canned food and potato chips. No pay phone, no television. Seventy houses that were little more than miner's shacks—damn cold in the winter and broiling in the summer. My grandmother's had a tin roof." Tony's tone softened. "It made the best sound when it rained—*p-tat, p-tat*. I loved falling asleep to that sound."

He shrugged, and his expression became as hard as the surrounding rock. "Poverty always is better to talk about in retrospect than to live through. But to answer your question, I can handle living here."

The trail leveled off, taking them past upthrusts of granite with the presence of statues. The shadows had lost their noon-day edges and now pushed out from under bushes, reclaiming territory. Albeit technically autumn, the temperature was still ten degrees above comfortable. The heat lay heavily on the desert floor like a thick wool blanket, muffling both sound and movement.

Even with his hard upbringing, Hannah envied Tony his sense of family. *Where you've been and where you're going.* She would settle for knowing the answer to either question.

"You don't miss LA?"

"No. I never really fit in as a Latino. My dad's second wife is from Mexico and I have a bunch of half brothers, but we aren't close."

I know how that is. "Are you married?" The question popped out before Hannah could stop it.

Tony laughed. "No, I'm still living a la carte. That's one of the reasons I came back to the rez—better chance of finding an Indian bride."

Hannah couldn't tell if he was kidding, and decided it wouldn't be polite to ask.

"You know, it's funny. In LA, when people look at me, they see a short, chunky, dark-skinned man. But on the rez I'm tall, thin, and nearly white. Labels aside, this is where I feel at home. I guess Indian skin fits me best."

The heat pressed against the top of her head, making Hannah wish she had worn a hat. She looked wistfully at the horizon, where horsetails of clouds trailed across the mountain peaks. *What kind of skin would she feel right in?*

"Don't get me wrong—the rez isn't a perfect

place to live," Tony said, guiding his horse around a cactus. "Especially when it's ten o'clock at night and you want to buy toner for your printer or rent a foreign film. And the traditional way of doing things can be slow and *very* frustrating." He spread his arms wide. "But there's something about the place that will always pull me back."

Hannah understood the allure of pomegranate-tinted rock, sculptural cacti, ethereal light. But she also saw a landscape that couldn't quite hide its menace—the obvious lack of human presence, the brush that harbored desert things. She thought something out of the ordinary persisted among the rocks and sand and tough-looking plants. Something unstill, never sleeping, just possibly past reason. A dormant maliciousness, waiting for the weak.

"I'm more of a city girl. The desert is too… too…" She searched for the right word. "Alien. Hostile, even."

"True, but you can't take it personally. That's the key to surviving."

Life in general or just on the rez?

Tony suddenly reined his horse to a halt. "Hold up. We've got company." He unhooked his leg from around the saddle horn so he was sitting astride his horse again.

"Whoa," Hannah said, even though Buttermilk had already stopped.

Tony maneuvered his horse sideways until his knee was snugged up next to Hannah's. "Look," he said in a hushed voice, his eyes on something trailside.

Hannah peered through the green candelabra of cacti. "Where?"

Tony draped an arm over her shoulder and, pressing his torso against hers, pointed into a thicket of chaparral. "There. Under the palo verde."

At first Hannah didn't see anything. Then she spotted the tic, the one-nerve flicker, and what had appeared to be a shadow took form. *A coyote.* With gold-clear eyes, it stared at her for a long moment. Then, almost casually, the animal got to its feet and broke into a trot, heading down the trail ahead of them. Not hurrying but purposeful, glancing back now and then across one shoulder. The next moment it was gone, pepper-gray fur melting into the barren landscape.

Hannah wasn't really superstitious. Except when she was. A chill went through her, and she moved closer to Tony.

His arm still resting across her shoulders, Tony looked down at her. A glimmer came into his eyes, darkening their coffee hue, and Hannah felt a warmth that didn't have anything to do with the outside temperature.

He stroked a finger along her cheek, and a hum started up deep in Hannah's throat.

Snake, apple… I'm going to leave Paradise again.

Tony must have taken off his hat. Hannah wasn't sure, because in less than a second they were holding each other tightly, the saddlehorn digging into her thigh, lips crushed together. A rumble that sounded like approaching hoofbeats pounded in her ears, but Hannah ignored it. She gave herself over to the kiss, knowing there was no way she could stop, no way at all.

It wasn't until Buttermilk spooked, nearly unseating her, that Hannah realized they were no longer alone.

Chapter Fifteen

Three riders were arrayed across the trail a hundred feet away. They wore light blue denim shirts and jeans, with blue bandanas tied over their faces outlaw-style, like in an old Western.

The guns they held, though, looked straight out of the latest action movie. The metal barrels gleamed malevolently in the sharp light.

For a second, Hannah thought she was imagining things. She was ready for someone to appear and yell *You've been punked!* But no one said anything.

Save for the high whine of insects, the desert was startlingly quiet. One of the riders' horses tossed its head, the jingle of its curb chain harsh against the stillness. The air smelled of sage and dust and sweaty animals.

Hannah's knees began to tremble. *This can't be happening again.* Just last month someone else had pointed a gun at her, wanting her dead. The trembling worsened.

"Where's the damn cavalry when you need 'em?" The humor in Tony's comment was belied by his voice, tense and low. He stared at the men.

Even though she couldn't see their faces, Hannah had the impression the riders were in their twenties. They were beefier than the average teenager, but lacked the bulk usual in older men.

The rider in the middle gestured at Tony with his weapon.

"Get off your horse," he ordered, his voice muffled by the bandana. Hannah thought he might have an accent.

Tony didn't move.

The man raised his rifle and leveled it at them. Hannah's heart started to beat in her throat. Almost nonchalantly, he slid back the bolt and, without warning, pulled the trigger.

Hannah screamed and ducked as the bullet barely cleared their heads. Buttermilk shied sideways, and Hannah clutched at the mane to keep from falling off. Tony reached over and grabbed the frightened horse's bridle.

"Easy, girl, easy," he said, stroking the palomino's neck.

Hannah re-centered herself in the saddle, feeling as though Tony were talking to her as well as the mare. After a few more snorts and head tosses, Buttermilk settled down.

"Looks like I better go see what he wants." Tony dismounted in one easy motion and, after handing the reins to Hannah, walked toward the riders.

Hannah stared at the three men, committing to memory as many details as she could. *Dark eyes, brown skin, thick black hair.* Each was clad in continuous blue—bandanas, shirts, pants. Even their gun barrels were a dull, metallic indigo.

Tony halted about eight feet in front of the riders. Feet planted in the sand, he crossed his arms and waited. While the man in the middle kept his rifle at the ready, the rider on the left spurred his horse forward until it was beside Tony. Then he kicked his foot free of the stirrup and extended an arm.

"Step up," directed the man who had fired the rifle.

Hannah felt a rush of terror. *They want him to get on the horse?*

"Step up," the man repeated.

Tony didn't move. The man slid back the bolt on his rifle again and aimed the weapon at Tony.

Get on the damn horse! Hannah felt the unsaid words vibrate against the back of her clenched teeth.

His face tight with anger, Tony grabbed the offered hand, stepped into the stirrup, and swung up behind the saddle.

The man in the middle sheathed the rifle in the scabbard hanging from his saddle, then locked his eyes onto Hannah. She stiffened under his scrutiny, the sweat trickling down her ribcage. Briefly, she considered making a run for it, but the memories of being shot at last month held her back. A target had to be lucky every time, but a shooter needed to be lucky only once.

Slowly the man raised his hand and pointed an index finger at Hannah, thumb cocked, the rest of his fingers folded back like a gun. He sighted along the "weapon" and dropped the hammer, his hand jerking from an imaginary recoil.

Hannah flinched, feeling an upwelling of terror as flashbacks from last month's trauma overwhelmed her senses. The needle-like sting of rain, the crack of the rifle, the smell of fear on her skin—it was as though she were living through the nightmare all over again. Her stomach heaved, and Hannah thought she might be sick.

She was still fighting to regain her equilibrium when the three masked riders wheeled their horses and galloped away, taking Tony with them.

Chapter Sixteen

Tony's horse whinnied and pawed at the sand, frantic to follow the three riders, who were now out of sight. Hannah wrapped the reins around her saddlehorn and pulled.

"Stop that! Whoa!"

The panicked animal jerked its head up and down, then crashed into Buttermilk, who laid back her ears and nipped at her stablemate. The brown horse squealed and kicked out, and Buttermilk bit again, harder this time. With a last rib-shaking whinny and toss of its head, Tony's horse stopped fighting the reins. Pushing up against Buttermilk as though seeking forgiveness, it lipped at Hannah's saddle.

Hannah stared at the hoof prints in the sand where the riders had been only moments before. Tony's cowboy hat lay upturned next to the trail.

What was going on? This was Arizona, not South America—kidnapping was supposed to happen only on television. Various scenarios ran through Hannah's imagination, all of them bad. Tony held for ransom…injured…*killed.*

Chasing the kidnappers was out of the question. Even if Hannah had the riding skills and were able to follow their tracks, what could she do against three armed men? Her only choice was to go for help. But first that meant getting back to the car.

"Okay, Buttermilk. Home, girl. Home!"

The mare didn't move.

Maybe I sound too nervous. Hannah concentrated on steadying her voice. "Dinnertime! Back to the barn!"

Buttermilk let out a sigh and lowered her head.

Hannah thought about dismounting and walking back, but she doubted she would make it to the corral before dusk. Navigating an unfamiliar trail through the desert at night wasn't something she wanted to do. Nor was leading the horses—staying off the ground and away from eight hooves seemed much safer.

Another thought crossed her mind, adding to her fear. Why hadn't the kidnappers taken her, too? Were they coming back? She squinted against the glare in the direction where the riders had disappeared. No one was there—at least no one she could see.

"C'mon, Buttermilk!"

Nudging with her right heel and tugging on the left rein, Hannah managed to get the mare turned around and facing back down the trail. She squeezed with both legs, and Buttermilk started walking. Tony's horse, his reins still tied to Hannah's saddlehorn, followed.

"Let's go, girl." Hannah tried to imitate Tony's clucking noise. Buttermilk broke into a slow jog, Hannah holding on to the mane to avoid bouncing off.

It was an interminable ride back to the corral, even after Buttermilk, apparently deducing they were on the way home, accelerated her pace into a springy trot. Hannah's legs were quickly rubbed raw against the stirrup leathers. With every jarring step, the top of her spine felt as though it were being hit with a mallet.

Perspective became misleading, and landmarks that looked attainable kept their distance, like mirages on the horizon. The foreboding that had struck Hannah earlier returned, stronger than before. She fought the urge to keep looking back over her shoulder. When the barn and corral finally came into view, Hannah thought she would faint with relief.

Instead, she slid off the saddle onto unsteady legs, tying both horses to the fence rail as best she could before staggering to Tony's car. Once in the driver's seat, she locked the doors and sat there for a moment, breathing deep into her chest. It wasn't until her pulse was approaching normal again that she realized she didn't have the car keys.

Hannah pounded on the steering wheel in frustration. *I will never go anywhere without my cell phone again.* She opened the car door to start on the two-mile run back to the main road, and her foot nudged a lump under the car mat. A lump that jingled.

She flipped back the piece of rubber, uncovering a pair of keys attached to a keychain stamped with the Tohono O'odham man-in-the-maze emblem. She scooped them up and with shaking fingers inserted the correct one into the ignition.

Her Subaru was a stick shift, but Hannah had never driven a car with three on the tree. After a few miscues, she worked the car into second and started down the dirt road. Once on the pavement, she got into third gear and beelined for town at twenty miles over the limit.

Half an hour later, she sped down the street that led to Pinnacle Peak's only police station. Leaving the car next to a sign that read *Patrol Car Parking Only—All Others Towed*, she ran up the stairs to the main entrance.

Hannah rattled off her name to the deputy behind the counter. "I need to speak with Detective Dresden *now*. It's an emergency!" The events of last summer had introduced Hannah to Karl Dresden, Pinnacle Peak's sole homicide detective. He was the only law enforcement officer she knew.

The deputy disappeared down a corridor while Hannah paced, too wired to sit. Two minutes passed, then another two. She was about to ring for the deputy again when Dresden opened the door that led from the reception area to the back of the station.

"Ms. Dain?" he said in the remembered baritone.

Hannah launched into her story. "Out in the desert, we were just—"

He held up a hand. "Let's go to my office."

From her prior experience with the detective, Hannah knew arguing would only delay things more. Instead, she impatiently followed Dresden through the doorway and down the corridor.

Dresden led her into his office and closed the door. From flattop haircut to highly polished shoes, he looked the same as when she last had seen him. Hannah perched on the edge of a visitor's chair, drumming her fingers on the chair arm, while he seated himself behind his desk and took out a small digital recorder and a waiver-of-rights form from a drawer.

"*Now* can I start?" she asked.

"After I turn this on." Dresden pushed a button on the recorder. He identified himself and Hannah, stated the date, time, and location, then read the Miranda rights listed on the waiver form and asked Hannah to sign it.

She scrawled her name. "This is ridiculous. I'm trying to report a crime and you're—" The look on Dresden's face stopped her in mid-sentence.

He thinks I'm here to confess. Hannah rubbed the scars on the palm of her hand with her index finger, momentarily at a loss for words.

Last month, she had refused to own up to doing something monstrous—directly denied it to Dresden, in fact. Even though she had been legally blameless, her mind wouldn't—couldn't—acknowledge that she was capable of such an act. The detective had let her falsehood go at the time, while leaving no doubt that he knew the truth.

Dresden's eyes were of such faded blue they looked almost colorless. "Do you want to call a lawyer?"

"No! This isn't about…I mean…something happened *today.* My new boss—his name's Tony Soto—he and I were riding on the rez this afternoon and…"

The story of the kidnapping tumbled out, broken up by Hannah's backfills of information. Dresden took out a notepad and pen, writing while she talked.

"…and then I drove his car here." Hannah sat back in the chair, drained.

Dresden paged through his notes. "The three men—were they Tohono O'odham or Hispanic?"

His question brought Hannah up short. All she could remember was brown skin, black hair, and eyes that were hard and bright, like some predatory bird's. *Indian? Mexican?*

"I—I don't know," she stammered.

"Were they wearing gang colors?"

"What do you mean?"

"Were they dressed in mostly one color? Or wearing the same item in the same color, especially red or blue?"

"Well, they had on jeans and light blue denim shirts. The bandanas over their faces were blue, too, I think. But I'm not sure if they were *colors*, like you're talking about."

"What about the horses, their gear? Any brands or distinctive marks?"

The horses had just looked like horses to Hannah. She wasn't even sure what color they were. "Not that I remember."

"Tell me again what you and Mr. Soto were doing right before you saw them."

Making out like a couple of teenagers. "He was showing me a coyote in the brush," Hannah said, hoping the quaver in her voice wouldn't trip the detective's internal lie detector.

Dresden switched off the recorder and looked thoughtful. "Gang activity has been on the rise lately. Two Fantasmas Azules were arrested last week driving a truckload of illegal aliens. What they'd want with one of the O'odham, though, is beyond me. Usually the *cholos* leave the rez to the Indian crews."

"What are Fantasmas Azules?"

"Means The Blue Ghosts in Spanish. They're a local Hispanic gang that moves people and drugs from the border northward, usually to Salt Lake

City. The rez is becoming their highway of choice because law enforcement can't patrol there. As you may have guessed from their name, members wear blue. Trouble is, so do most of the Indians on the rez, and half the town, for that matter."

He reached up to massage the back of his neck. It was the only concession to tiredness or frustration that Hannah had ever seen him make.

"The kidnapping…from what you said, it sounded pretty emotional, as though things could have spiraled out of control pretty quickly."

Hannah nodded.

"That isn't how gangs operate. Their violence is dispassionate, part of the business. They'll kill someone they've got a beef against, or give them a beat down to send a warning. Unless they're looking to collect a big ransom from the tribe, kidnapping doesn't make sense as a gang crime."

"So now what happens?" Hannah wanted Dresden to start *doing* things—making phone calls, assembling a posse.

"Technically, a kidnapping on the rez belongs to the FBI. But the local office is backed up with that string of bank robberies in Phoenix. We've worked together before. They won't mind if I do some preliminary work."

Dresden turned to a clean page in his notepad. "First, we need to contact Mr. Soto's family in case there's a ransom demand. Do you have a home number?"

"I'm pretty sure his mother and grandmother live on the rez. He works for a private equity firm called Peña & Moreno. They should know how to get in touch with his family."

Dresden jotted some more notes on his pad, then stood. Hannah did, too.

"I'll be in touch. For now, it would be best if you kept quiet about this. I don't want to put Mr. Soto at any greater risk than he already is."

Hannah nodded, unconsciously rubbing the scars on her palm again. The detective's eyes flicked downward, and she balled her hands into fists and pressed them against her sides.

Dresden relaxed his military bearing just a fraction. "I don't think you need to be concerned, Hannah. If those guys wanted to, they would have taken you, too. The bandanas mean they won't be worried that you can identify them. Sounds as though you were in the wrong place at the wrong time."

Hannah's answering grin was stiff. "Story of my life, Detective."

For a moment, Dresden looked as though he

were going to say something else. Instead, he reached over and opened the door. "I'll walk you out."

Hannah and Dresden reached the lobby just as a deputy was escorting a large bearded man, his hands cuffed behind his back, through the front door. The man's t-shirt read *Harley-Davidson* instead of *White Power*, but Hannah had no trouble recognizing him. Wishing she were wearing sunglasses, she ducked behind Dresden.

"This is the guy we were looking for on that assault in the casino parking lot, sir," the deputy said. "Indian vic decided to press charges."

"Good work, Frampton," Dresden said. Hannah sidled toward the exit, her face averted.

"He was carrying when we picked him up. Jim's vouchering the gun now."

"I got a permit for that, you red-ass-kissing—" The bearded man lunged at the deputy, trying to land a head butt.

Terrific—White Power *man has a gun.* Taking advantage of the fracas, Hannah slipped out the door, glancing back only once she was safely on the other side of the glass. Her eyes met the furious glare of *White Power* man, now pinned against the wall by Dresden and the deputy.

She turned hastily away and ran for Tony's

car, relieved to see that it hadn't been towed. With only a slight amount of gear-grinding and one stall, Hannah maneuvered the Mustang back onto the street. Moving almost robotically, she drove to her condo, parked the car in a visitor's space, and turned off the engine.

White Power *man. Kidnappers.* It was too much, too soon after the events of last summer. Hannah sat in Tony's car and clasped her hands together. Despite the heat, she was shivering.

Chapter Seventeen

Wednesday, September 16

"Mr. Moreno, I promise to call the moment I hear *anything*."

Hannah hung up the phone. Beside himself with worry, Tony's boss had peppered her with questions for almost twenty minutes. When Hannah had asked who might want to kidnap his employee, Moreno's response was immediate and certain.

"Nobody! Like I told the police, there've been no threats, no problems with clients—nothing! Everyone *loves* Tony!"

Maybe not everyone, Hannah thought. *Like Control Growth...protesters at the park...* White Power *man...*

Cooper had stayed at the ranch last night. *Work to do* was all the note on the kitchen counter said. Hannah hadn't told him about the kidnapping because she knew what his reaction would be. Worried about her safety, he would want her to quit the OTA job. Not an irrational response—the events of last month were undoubtedly just as fresh in his mind, too—but one she wanted to avoid just the same.

Hannah's eyes felt gritty and her head ached. After a night of insomnia, she had finally fallen asleep at five. Disrupted by chaotic dreams, the short slumber hadn't done much good—as her secretary had confirmed.

"Girl, you look terrible!" Clementine had exclaimed when Hannah arrived a half hour late for work that morning.

"Bad dreams," Hannah had mumbled. A mug in one hand and a briefcase in the other, she was trying to tear open the foil wrapper around a teabag with her teeth.

"You, too? In mine, I found a whole rack of sequin tops on sale at Tacky Duds, but I had to leave the store without buying any. What was yours like?"

At that instant Hannah had tugged too hard, shredding the tea bag and spilling green powder onto the counter.

"Dammit! Clementine, could you—" Her secretary had shooed her away from the mess, and Hannah had escaped to her office.

A new computer had appeared on her desk overnight, and after her phone call with Moreno, Hannah immersed herself in work on the private placement. Part of her hoped that if she acted normally, things would return to normal—including the reappearance of Tony. It was absurd, but she couldn't help it.

An hour later she was in the midst of drafting the due diligence questionnaire when her cell phone rang. The read-out on the screen read *Private*. She answered it anyway.

"Hello?"

"Hey, it's me."

"*Shelby?*" Hannah couldn't believe it—her sister never called. *Something must be wrong.* "Are you okay?" she asked, her voice taut with concern.

"Relax, I'm fine. That is, as fine as someone can be locked up with a bunch of drunks."

"That bad, huh?"

"I hate this place. Group therapy is the worst. As though I care about all these other people's problems! If I hear there's no *i* in *team* one more time, I'm going to scream."

Hannah was glad to hear Shelby complain. It meant her sister was getting back to her old self. "You can always point out there's a *me* if you jumble things around a bit," she said.

"And get assigned an extra counseling session? No thanks."

Shelby fell silent and Hannah waited, wondering at the reason for the call. *Money? Contraband request?*

"The jelly beans…they're pretty good," Shelby finally said. "Next time, you can drop them by my room if you want."

Was Shelby asking her to visit? "Um, okay."

"If you come early Thursday morning, I can get out of Group. But no more dumb-looking hats!" The line went dead.

Leopards and spots… Had she been wrong about her sister? Hannah went back to work, the stacks of paperwork not seeming so tall anymore.

Nearly two hours passed, until close to noon the smell of fast food drifted into her office. Ready for a break, Hannah went to the door to investigate.

A man leaned against the partition in front of Clementine's desk eating French fries out of a red cardboard box with a yellow *M* on it. He wore an ill-fitting sport coat, jeans, and sneakers. Hannah's secretary talked to him as she typed.

"Say what you want about Tang, it prevents scurvy," Clementine said over the click of the computer keys. "And just so you know, I *never* eat things grown in the ground."

"But that means no French fries!" the man said.

Clementine stopped hitting the keyboard long enough to snag a fry from the red box and pop it into her mouth.

"Don't be silly," she said, still chewing. "Everyone knows these are really sticks of grease that McDonald's has brainwashed us into thinking come from potatoes."

Hannah recognized Zel Kassif. His sense of fashion hadn't improved, but he had shaved off the goatee attempt. *Did he know about the kidnapping?* A newspaper story could put Tony in greater jeopardy.

"Mr. Kassif! What are you doing here?" she asked.

"Good to see you again, Ms. Dain. I was in the neighborhood and thought I'd stop by."

Hannah glanced from the reporter to her secretary. *Yeah, right.* Clementine was a gossip, a true inside-dope dealer. *Had she heard about the kidnapping and passed on the news to Kassif?*

"You know what Mr. Soto said about the OTA being private property. I'm going to have to ask you to leave. *Now.*"

"No problem." Kassif handed the box of fries to Clementine. "Here. Next time I'll take you to a real lunch."

"Whatever," Clementine said. Hannah noticed her pleased expression. *The reporter and Clementine at lunch?* Her anxiety went up a notch.

Kassif headed for the lobby, then stopped and turned toward her. "Interesting choice in office décor, Ms. Dain. Tell Tony I'm sorry to have missed him." He continued down the hallway, a funny little bounce in his step.

He had been in her office? And what did the remark about Tony mean? Was he baiting her or did he know something?

"What was that all about?" she said to Clementine when Kassif was out of sight.

"Nothing! He just came by, that's all." Clementine toyed with the bangles on her wrist. "I think he's kinda nice."

"Clementine, he's a reporter. It's his *job* to be nice to people he wants information from."

Her secretary's dark eyes snapped. "You don't have anything to worry about."

"Good." Hannah exhaled the word, and with it, her anger. Realizing she had been foolish, she attempted to salvage her pride. "And please get that

Indian out of my office. It's undignified."

Hannah went back to her desk, now awkwardly aware of the wooden figure in the corner. She imagined she could feel the statue's eyes on her, reproach in its gaze. After a few minutes of trying to work, she looked up.

"Look, Chief, it's nothing personal. You're a great guy—low maintenance, quiet, don't drink. The wardrobe could use some help—what guy's couldn't? But I'm seeing someone else."

The Chief stared impassively into the distance.

"That's settled, then. I'm glad we had a chance to talk."

Hannah could hear Clementine loudly opening and shutting drawers, a sure sign her secretary was still mad. Wanting to end the feud, Hannah grabbed up the apple and sandwich she had brought from home and went to the doorway.

"I'm going to lunch. Want to come?"

Clementine shook her head. "I've already eaten." She tossed the empty French-fry container into the trash.

Even though the calendar said it was nearly fall, the courtyard west of the OTA building was still uncomfortably warm. But the walled patio was the only place Hannah could find to be alone. Sitting on a bench shaded by a sculpture of an Indian woman, she bit into her apple.

First White Power *man, and now Clementine and the Chief.* The week was barely two days old, and already she was running out of people to tick off. At this rate, she wouldn't have to buy Christmas cards.

Not that she ever did. Hannah hated holiday gestures lacking real or original sentiment. Cards bearing only a preprinted greeting went straight into the trash, and she ignored the "holidays" concocted by Hallmark altogether. As she had asked Clementine once, wasn't it supposed to be Boss' Day all the time?

"No," Clementine had replied. "You're thinking of Secretary's Day."

A black-haired woman with bronzed skin entered the courtyard. Her smart jacket was decorated with rows of buttons and matched her dark pants. She strode briskly toward Hannah.

"Are you Hannah Dain?" Her voice had a musical lilt.

"Yeth," Hannah said through a mouthful of apple.

"Hi. I'm Delores Alvarez, Mr. Baptisto's assistant."

Hannah swallowed the last bit of fruit. The name Baptisto rang a bell, but she couldn't place it.

"The tribe's chairman," Delores added, as though sensing Hannah's confusion.

And, Hannah now recalled, the owner of the development company created with the proceeds from phase one of the real estate project. "Of course! He's president of Gee—" She stopped, unable to pronounce the development company's name.

"Ge Oidag Development," Delores finished for her. "It means *big fields* in Tohono O'odham."

"How can I help you?"

"Mr. Baptisto needs the notebook."

"Notebook?"

"The one Tony put together on the private placement."

Hannah hesitated, unsure whether Dresden had told the tribe's upper echelon about the kidnapping yet. If he hadn't, she didn't want to be the messenger.

Delores sat next to Hannah on the bench. "We know what happened to Tony," she said in a low voice.

Hannah tensed. "Is there any news? Have they asked for a ransom?"

Delores shook her head. "The police came by

this morning. They don't have any leads on the three men, or any idea why they took Tony. The tribe is doing everything it can to cooperate—Tony's safe return is obviously top priority. But, in the meantime, Mr. Baptisto wants to keep the private placement on track. Tony's the only one who knows the whole picture—projections, costs, that kind of stuff. He kept everything in a spiral notebook, a thick burgundy one with *ASU* embossed on the cover. Without Tony, or at least the information in the notebook, we won't be able to pull together the final figures for the offering in time."

And Ge Oidag Development will be in trouble, Hannah thought. According to the documents that Tony had given her, if the second phase weren't sold out by the deadline, the three million raised by the first private placement would have to be refunded to investors—which might be tough to do if the money had already been spent on bulldozers and building supplies. Small wonder Baptisto wanted the private placement to go forward. *With or without Tony.*

"I haven't seen any notebook," Hannah said. "But Tony gave me a box of documents yesterday. Maybe it's in there."

"It's not." Seeing Hannah's raised eyebrows,

she added, "I took the liberty of checking. When it wasn't in his office, I thought he might have given it to you." Delores' shoulders drooped. "I don't know where else to look."

The sorrow in her voice roused Hannah's compassion, blunting her annoyance at having her office rifled without permission. "I'm sure it will turn up. And that Tony will, too."

"I hope so." A tear rolled down her cheek, and she hastily scrubbed it away, her mouth puckered with sadness.

She likes him, Hannah realized, wondering if the affection were returned and then immediately annoyed at herself for caring.

"I better get back," Delores said. "Mr. Baptisto is out of the office today, but he would like to talk to you about the private placement. Can you meet him for dinner this evening? La Ristra at seven o'clock?"

"I'll be there." Hannah said, a little surprised at the choice of Pinnacle Peak's nicest restaurant. Baptisto wasn't sparing any expense on the casino expansion.

Back in her office, Hannah tried to concentrate on

sorting through the material from the cardboard carton—Delores had dumped everything on the floor searching for the notebook—but her eyes kept drifting to the phone. At last unable to bear it any longer, she put aside the documents and punched in the number she knew by heart.

"Cooper Smith."

Hannah loved the Texas in his voice. She imagined him sitting in his red pickup, surrounded by cowboy paraphernalia.

"Hey," she said. "It's me."

All Hannah had planned to tell him was that she wouldn't be home for dinner. But images of yesterday's terror began to spool through her mind, intermingled with memories of last month's awful events. Before she knew it, the story of Tony's kidnapping had poured out.

Cooper's response was as she had expected, his expressions of sympathy quickly giving way to concern.

"You can't keep working there!"

"Dresden said the kidnapping had nothing to do with me."

"If those men think you can identify them—"

"They won't because of the bandanas." Hannah interrupted. *Was that a whine in her voice?*

"What I don't understand," Cooper said, measuring his words, "is how a job that you've had for only two days becomes so important that you're willing to put yourself in personal danger."

Because I need time to find my father, because I don't know where to go from here, because Tony—

"I don't know," Hannah said. "But I can't quit. Not yet."

"Well, I know once you get a goal in your head, there's no stopping you." Someone who didn't know him would have said Cooper's tone sounded matter-of-fact. But Hannah had heard something else underneath—exasperation, maybe even resignation. She felt the denial rise in her throat, but made herself keep quiet.

"Single-mindedness can be a good thing—unless it's a cover for something else." There was a snag in his voice. "Whatever it is that you're doing, be careful, okay?"

"Cooper—" Hannah said, but he had already hung up.

She set down the phone. Seeing the empty cardboard carton on the floor, she kicked it. The carton ricocheted off her desk, and Hannah kicked it again.

Why couldn't he understand? The OTA job

was just a placeholder for her career and her mind while she delved into the questions surrounding her mother and father. What Cooper saw as obsession was simply focus and determination. She wasn't pushing him aside, not really. Even if she were, it was only temporary.

Hannah debated whether to call him back. Deciding it was a discussion better had in person, she forced her attention back to the mess Delores had created.

Kneeling on the floor, she started sorting through the last of the documents that had been in the carton. From an oversized envelope, she pulled out what looked like accounting ledgers. Skimming through the columns of numbers, Hannah felt something click in her brain.

She reviewed the figures again, slower this time, then sat back on her heels. *The raw numbers for the second phase.* Hannah was fairly certain the ledgers contained everything needed to recreate the information Delores had said was in Tony's missing notebook. She felt the beginnings of excitement.

Although legal work had taught Hannah a lot about balance sheets, her computer skills were limited. Cooper was far more qualified than she to interpret and program the data.

She picked up the phone, punched in his number, but hung up before the call could go through. Guilt—pride—she wasn't sure of the reason, but it didn't feel right to ask for his assistance. Instead, she collected the spreadsheets and took her seat in front of the computer.

Hannah logged on, feeling like the little man in the Tohono O'odham maze—she knew where she wanted to end up, but wasn't sure how to get there. And like the little man, she would be navigating the trip alone.

Chapter Eighteen

The interior of La Ristra was so dark, Hannah felt nearly invisible in her navy trouser suit as she followed the hostess through the maze of tables. The restaurant's namesake—pods of chilies harvested after they had turned red and hung to dry in strings—were tacked to the walls and dangled from the ceiling beams. Hannah hoped there were non-pepper dishes on the menu. Her tongue's spice capabilities usually maxed out at the Taco Bell Mild level.

The table, set for three, was in an alcove off the bar. Hannah was surprised to see Delores seated in one of the chairs. Dressed in a copper-colored top and gold jewelry, she glowed with warmth in the candlelight. But the nod she gave Hannah was more recognition than friendly.

"Hi," Delores said, sipping a martini. If the discarded olive skewers were any indication, it wasn't her first.

Hannah sat down, tucking a stray piece of hair behind her ear. She had tried to create what the magazine she had bought to give Shelby called *Sophisticated Up-Do*. The end result looked neither sophisticated nor like the photo accompanying the article. Now the *up* part was failing, too. Another strand came loose as the waiter appeared with menus, and Hannah decided to ignore her hair for the rest of the evening.

"Let's order appetizers. I'm starving," Delores said as the waiter hovered.

"Shouldn't we wait for Mr. Baptisto?"

"He's always late. Calamari Hidalgo for me." Delores tapped the rim of her martini glass. "And another one of these."

The waiter smiled and nodded politely in that stilted way of personal service providers dependent on tip income. He looked at Hannah. "And for you?"

Hannah could barely read the menu's tiny print in the low light. She pointed at an entry in the salad section—"no fish or dairy, please"—and declined wine in favor of mineral water.

"Party pooper," Delores said. She put her elbows on the table and propped her chin in her hands.

"So what's the Hannah Dain story?"

"A pretty short one. College and law school

back East, three years with a local firm doing business law." *And a family situation you wouldn't believe.* "How about you?"

Delores' answer was interrupted by the ring of her cell phone. She picked it up from the table and held it to her ear.

"Hello?" She listened for a few seconds. "Okay. Thanks." She snapped the phone shut. "Mr. Baptisto has to cancel," she said, eating the olive from her drink.

Hannah saw the waiter approaching. "Should we skip dinner?"

"No way! He's got an account here that I can sign on."

They chose entrées, and Delores ordered a bottle of wine. After the waiter had left again, Hannah sipped at her water, feeling awkward. She wasn't very good at small talk. *Or the bigger kind, either*, she thought, recalling her last conversation with Cooper.

Delores gulped down more martini. "Do you think I'm Indian or Latina?" she asked.

Hannah fumbled for an answer that wouldn't offend. "Part Indian?" she said, figuring Delores wouldn't be Baptisto's assistant otherwise.

"You're right, although I would have denied it

a few years ago." Delores raised her glass, the glisten of her drink reflected in her eyes. Hannah realized Delores had entered the contemplative phase of drunkenness. *Morose will be next.*

"My *papa* is Hispanic and my *madre* is Tohono O'odham. We didn't have much money—the best jobs my parents ever had were with Wal-Mart. In their world, Mexicans were looked down on, but Indians were treated worse. So my mother and I pretended to be Latina. It wasn't until college that I told anybody I was part Tohono O'odham."

The waiter arrived with their dinners. He arranged the plates and performed the requisite fussing with the pepper mill and cheese grater. Hannah had always wondered why restaurants trusted patrons with steak knives but not condiment dispensers.

When they were alone again, Delores resumed her monologue. "Ten percent of the students at ASU are Hispanic, so I thought I would fit in. Even majored in Chicano Studies. Then I met a boy who was half-Pima. He was great—taught me about sex and how to be an Indian. Before I met him, I had never even been to the reservation!"

Delores had raised her voice again, and Hannah saw several heads turn in their direction. "Mmm," she said through a mouthful of food. *If she starts in on their love life, I'm faking an urgent call on my cell phone.*

"So I changed my major to Native American Studies. It was fun hanging out with the radical types. After a while, though, their approach seemed pointless. I mean, seceding from the US just isn't going to happen. And it didn't matter why your skin was brown if you were dying of diabetes or getting pregnant at fifteen. So after the Pima guy dumped me, I transferred to Social Work."

Delores had changed over from martinis to wine. She paused to freshen her glass, clanging the bottle against the rim of the goblet.

"After a semester's internship at the Governor's Office, I realized there was a better way to help people than through the system. Money—that's what it's all about. So I became a Business major."

Hannah tried to accelerate the story. "When did you start working for the OTA?"

"A month after graduation, three years ago. My main job is running the tribe's visa program."

"I didn't know the tribe had a credit card."

"Not that kind of visa!"

Delores dissolved into a fit of giggles and Hannah suppressed a sigh. She had forgotten about the hilarity stage of inebriation.

"I do the paperwork for the border crossings," Delores added after catching her breath.

From reading up on the tribe before her job interview, Hannah knew what Delores was talking about. Tohono O'odham had been living on both sides of the Rio Grande since before there was a US-Mexico border. Even after 9/11, the two countries made it easy for tribe members to travel back and forth.

"And you're also Mr. Baptisto's assistant?" Hannah said while glancing around for their waiter in the hopes she could signal for the check.

"Just on this deal. Officially, I'm the liaison with the outside professionals, like you and Peña & Moreno. That's how I met Tony."

Hannah drank some water, still searching for their waiter. Her eyes slid over a familiar-looking face at the bar and she nearly gagged.

What is White Power *man doing here?* Hannah hunched down, hoping he hadn't seen her.

"Why were you out in the desert with Tony?" Delores said loudly enough to earn a dirty look from the woman at the next table.

"We were going to see his grandmother," Hannah said, debating whether to call Dresden. *Why wasn't* White Power *man in jail?*

Delores unleashed a barrage of Spanish at such volume and inflection that Hannah could practically see the upside-down and right-side-up exclamation points bracketing every sentence.

"Shhh! Keep it down!" she whispered to Delores. Putting her hand up to her forehead to shield her face, Hannah snuck a look toward the bar. But *White Power* man had disappeared.

"He's never taken *me* to meet his family," Delores whimpered, switching from Jekyll to Hyde. "It's because I'm half-Latina."

"What does that have to do with it? Tony is, too." Hannah covertly scanned the restaurant. She didn't see *White Power* man anywhere.

"Tell that to Mr. I-Want-An-Indian-Wife!" Delores noisily drained her wineglass. "Tony can be Indian or Hispanic. Just because he's made a choice, why can't his kids have the same option?"

Thinking about it, Hannah could understand Tony's desire that his children escape the ambiguousness of belonging to two races, instead enjoying the certitude of near full-blood. She wished for the same sense of security in her own life. *This is who you are, one hundred percent.*

They declined dessert and the waiter brought the check. Slumping dejectedly in her chair, Delores scrawled a signature at the bottom. The restaurant was beginning to empty out, and Hannah looked around one more time. Still no sign of *White Power* man.

"Tony, Tony, Tony," Delores murmured with the sweet mournfulness of a woman who was never going to get the happy ending she had once thought attainable. A moment later, she sat up and pointed an accusatory finger at Hannah.

"I know you like him!" Her mood shifted again, and she began weeping silently.

Definitely the morose stage. Hannah offered a tissue from her purse. "Delores, Tony and I aren't dating. I have a boyfriend."

Delores cried harder. "I know he's never coming back!"

"Of course he will. As soon as they pay the ransom."

Delores raised her head to stare at Hannah. Mascara tracked down her cheeks.

"Ransom?" she repeated incredulously.

"The police said the call should come anytime. And thanks to the casino, the tribe will have no problem paying it."

"Don't you know about Tony's brothers?" Delores' speech had lost all trace of alcohol.

Hannah was confused. "The ones in LA?"

"They're *cholos*. One of them is in prison for killing another gang member."

Hannah remembered the scar on Tony's wrist. *A gang tattoo? Had Tony attempted to erase a past connection? When it came to gangs, was that even possible?*

"If those people kidnap someone for payback, they don't hold him for ransom," Delores said.

One look at the bleakness in the other woman's eyes, and Hannah knew what she was going to say next. Her insides clenched, and she forgot all about *White Power* man.

"They kill them."

Chapter Nineteen

Thursday, September 17

Cooper had bunked at the ranch again. He sometimes stayed there during the work week, and Hannah usually didn't mind a night with the covers to herself. So she didn't know why she hadn't slept better. *Stress from recent events, no doubt.*

By the time she arrived at the rehab center, the sun was already high in the sky, suspended above mountain peaks so uneven and jagged they looked like a readout for an irregular heartbeat. Hannah hurried through the front door—glad not to be lugging a potted plant—and asked for Shelby. A nurse led her down the corridor to the room at the end.

This time her sister was wearing lavender sweats, the sleeves pushed up to reveal wrists as delicate as swan's necks. The jacket's pale hue highlighted her even paler skin.

Hannah deposited a sack of jelly beans on the

bureau with a thump. "Licorice and cinnamon, as requested. Would you like to throw them on the floor or do you want me to?"

"Very funny." Shelby was sitting in the chair by the window again. "Stay for a while. If you do, I won't have to go back to Group."

"Okay." Hannah chose a spot on the bed, careful to avoid the stuffed dog nestled among the pillows.

"So what's new in the outside world?" Shelby asked.

Let's see… I'm on the run from a biker whose motorcycle I totaled. I made several passes at my boss, the last one right before he was kidnapped. At least I don't have some yet-to-be-identified genetic disease.

"My new job is more interesting than I thought it would be," Hannah said.

"You're kidding. What's your boss like?"

"Well, he's smart, really committed to the tribe, and amazingly generous, not too-bad looking, and—"

"You're hot for him!"

Hannah felt her neck become warm. "What are you talking about?"

"As though I can't tell. Did he make a pass at you?"

Hannah shifted on the bed. "Not exactly."

"Oh my God—you went after him? Tell me you're not sleep—"

"Of course not! It was just harmless flirting."

"You have one of the world's greatest guys for a boyfriend and you're fooling around with someone else? You're an idiot! Are you sure you went to Harvard?"

Irritated, Hannah grabbed the stuffed dog and held it up.

"You're one to talk about fooling around. What about whoever gave you this? I thought it was against the rules to hook up with fellow patients."

"Leave Sparky alone. And the person who gave him to me has nothing to do with this place."

"Then how did you meet? Are you going over the wall at night?"

"Of course not. He was doing a safety inspection of the building, and we ran into each other in the hallway." Her usually self-assured sister looked almost bashful. "He's a firefighter."

Hannah took another look at the toy dog, now recognizing the Dalmatian spots. *A firefighter?* Obviously a relationship of convenience, one that would end as soon as her sister got out of rehab. In real life, Shelby would never be interested in a "regular" guy, especially of the blue-collar variety.

Hannah was about to make a joke about fire hydrants and Sparky when she saw the happiness in Shelby's face. Cooper's words floated into her mind.

You never know—she might have changed.

Hannah dismissed the thought. *Leopards and spots.* She glanced at her watch.

"I better get to work." Hannah opened her tote bag and pulled out the current issue of *Vogue* magazine. "Here—I thought you'd want to know green is going to be big this fall."

Shelby feigned astonishment, but Hannah could tell she was pleased. "Was this mis-shelved with the sports magazines?"

"You still don't believe I can say *chic* without sounding like I'm going to the henhouse. Next time I'm bringing you *Fireman's Quarterly*."

"And you better start reading *Modern Rancher*." She shot Hannah a look. "Unless you prefer the I'm-cheating-on-my-boyfriend articles in *Cosmo*."

"I told you, there's nothing going on."

"Good, because Cooper's a great guy. Don't blow it." Shelby started flipping through the glossy pages of the magazine. "Now go away."

So much for sisterly bonding. Hannah was almost out the door when she heard the muttered "Thanks."

As the Subaru sped toward the OTA office, Hannah cranked up the CD player, her fingers drumming out the beat on the steering wheel. She couldn't remember the last time she'd had a purely social, let alone personal, conversation with her sister. Even more amazing was that between the two of them, Shelby was the one on track—working through her addiction, sure about her job, committed to a single romantic interest. It was Hannah who was flirting with one guy while holding her boyfriend at bay, uncertain about her family and career.

Leopards and spots.

Chapter Twenty

The wind blew on Hannah's neck, its breath hot and dry, as she walked across the casino parking lot. Flurries of seeds from the cottonwood trees scudded across the ground before settling into drifts of false snow, and the palo verde branches made a rattling sound.

Hannah didn't like the wind. Too often when she was out cycling it had enveloped her in sandstorms that left her tasting the desert for days no matter how much water she drank. And when she was clinging to a remote cliff face, its roaring silence could be too loud to bear.

The OTA lobby was empty except for two receptionists, a different pair than had been behind the counter yesterday. At least Hannah thought they were different. Given her recent lack of brilliance at cross-racial identification, she wouldn't bet on it.

"Morning," Hannah said, wondering whether to introduce herself before deciding it was better to appear rude than stupid. "Any messages?"

What she really wanted to ask was *Any word on Tony?* But she wasn't sure if news of the kidnapping had filtered down to the staff.

One of the women glanced up from her computer terminal. "No, Ms. Dain. Just your appointment."

"Appointment?"

Hannah thought back to last night. Delores hadn't said anything about meeting with someone this morning. Maybe all that alcohol had made her forget. Hannah hurried down the hallway to her office.

Clementine's chair was empty, but Hannah could hear her chatting with a deep-voiced male in the coffee room. Her secretary was an old hand at entertaining visitors when Hannah was running late.

"When it comes to ab workouts, I'm a fan of crunches," the male voice said. "Basic and side, sometimes reverse."

"The only crunches I like are from Nestlés," Clementine responded. "And the only reason I would go to a gym is if it had a bigger TV and better cable than I did at home."

Hannah was about to walk into her office when she caught sight of a spiral notebook balanced on top of the partition that surrounded Clementine's desk. Long and narrow, it had *Property of Pinnacle*

Peak Express printed across the bottom in black marker pen, followed by *Z. Kassif* in smaller letters.

That reporter was here again! Hannah was ready to storm into the coffee room and confront Kassif when her eyes went to the notebook again.

Did he know about the kidnapping? Almost unconsciously, she reached for the notebook, then hesitated.

It's not illegal.

It's not right, either.

Before she could talk herself out of it, she picked up the notebook, flipped back the cover, and started reading.

There weren't any notes on the kidnapping or casino finances, no interviews with Control Growth or tribe members. Instead, Hannah found nothing but information on Clementine. Page after page—address and phone numbers, what looked like Clementine's MP3 playlist, notes on the outfits she wore, a page titled *C's Pesto Sauce.*

Hannah was momentarily miffed. For two years she had asked Clementine for her pesto recipe without success. She skimmed the ingredient list, somewhat assuaged by the discovery that the secret ingredient was truffle oil.

"I wondered where I had left that."

Kassif's voice made Hannah jump. She closed the notebook with a guilty snap. Then indignation got the better of her.

"Why are you collecting information on Clementine?" Hannah asked, sure she already knew the answer.

Kassif held up his hands. "Hey, take it easy. I like her, okay? I just came by to ask her to lunch."

The ingenuous look on his face made Hannah believe him— almost.

Clementine may have divulged a family recipe, but Hannah knew there was one secret her secretary would never let slip. It was the one that she had shared with Hannah in the course of last summer's events, a secret that would make headlines locally, if not statewide—and go far in reestablishing a disgraced reporter's reputation. Kassif must somehow have discovered it. A feeling of protectiveness coursed through Hannah.

"Nice try. Anyway, you know what Tony said. Are you going to leave or do I need to call Security?"

Kassif started to respond, then apparently thought better of it. Instead, he picked up his notebook and slipped it into the pocket of his jacket, a charcoal plaid model that clashed with the gray in his trousers.

"I'll be on my way. By the way, where *is* Tony these days?"

"Haven't seen him," Hannah said, keeping her expression bland.

The phone rang on Clementine's desk and she picked it up, glad for the interruption. Covering the receiver with one hand, she looked pointedly at Kassif. "*Good-bye.*"

He winked. "See you later."

Was that a threat or a promise? Hannah waited until the reporter was out of sight, then raised the receiver to her ear.

"This is Hannah Dain."

"Ms. Dain, I'm calling for Chairman Baptisto. He would like to see you now, if it's convenient."

"That's fine." After his no-show last night, Hannah had wondered if the chairman would call. She got directions—the executive council offices were in a nearby building—then stopped by her desk to pick up the notes she had made after reviewing the ledgers. *Never hurts to impress the boss,* she thought while noticing the Chief was still in residence.

Clementine was back at her desk when Hannah emerged from her office.

"Have you talked to anybody yet about that Indian statue?" Hannah asked.

"It's handled." Clementine's tone was as wooden as the Chief.

"Look, I'm sorry about what I said to that reporter, but—"

"*Nice try,*" Clementine snapped, and went back to her typing.

Hannah blew out a mouthful of air. Clementine could be tenacious when it came to holding on to a grudge. Sometimes Hannah thought her secretary would give a kidney to a stranger before offering a friend a second chance. Deciding a cooling-off period was in order, she set off for Baptisto's office.

She found the walkway that connected the OTA with the rest of the complex, the path meandering between long-stemmed ocotillos and brittlebrush, the latter's velvety coat of white hairs creating its own shade from the sun. The wind had turned and was at her back now, blowing her toward her destination. Hannah was tempted to turn and resist the push of air, but she kept walking.

A secretary showed her into Baptisto's office. "He'll be right in," she said, and left. Hannah walked to the window and looked out. When viewed from behind glass, the desert had a spare, bleached-clean kind of beauty that even she could appreciate. Still, Hannah preferred leaves and grass to spines and sand.

The door to the office opened. "It's good to finally meet you, Ms. Dain. I'm Gordon Baptisto."

The tribe's chairman was a big-sized, big-voiced man. As he walked across the room, Hannah noted the expensive cut of his suit, the highly polished shoes, the hint of bling. He looked more like a drug dealer than a businessman.

Baptisto sat down behind his desk and took out a pack of cigarettes from a drawer.

"One of the advantages of being exempt from federal law—I can smoke in my office."

He offered her the pack. Hannah declined.

"You don't mind, do you?" Baptisto was already shaking a cigarette free.

If you want to kill yourself on the installment plan? "Go ahead," she said.

The tribe's chairman lit the cigarette with an engraved silver lighter, then leaned back in his chair, shot his linked cuffs, and took a deep drag.

"So tell me how the private placement is coming."

Hannah was a bit taken aback. She had been expecting a comment or question about Tony's kidnapping, or maybe an apology for missing last night's dinner. "Fine."

Baptisto waved a hand toward the window.

"This development will be the first of its kind in this area—ecologically sensitive, environmentally sound. My people have been stewards of this land for thousands of years, and I aim to carry on that responsibility."

His comments rang false in Hannah's ears, sound bites for media consumption. According to the plans she had reviewed, the proposed project would be like the thousands of others being built in the Southwest—wood and sheetrock, stucco and tile. Unless she was missing something, its only environmental advantage over buildings constructed forty years earlier was the absence of lead paint and asbestos.

Baptisto leaned forward as though he were about to impart a secret. "All while making a good profit for the investors, of course."

Hannah's smile congealed. *Of course.* So Baptisto was kin to most other developers after all. His love for the desert was like that of the coyote for the sheep—real estate was something to be devoured, not preserved. Hannah thought about Delores' thorough search for the missing notebook. Had Baptisto put a similar effort into helping find Tony?

"Is there any news on the kidnapping?" she asked.

Baptisto's expression became grave. "I'm afraid

not. But I'm sure Tony will turn up. If he's any-where on the rez, someone will report it." Baptisto took another drag on the cigarette, then blew out a stream of smoke. "Indians help one another."

Hannah didn't think that was so, any more than it was true that black people helped one another, or people with green hair helped other people with green hair. She thought it was one of those things people told themselves to make their world seem better.

Baptisto knocked ashes from his cigarette into a shallow dish on his desk. "Did you enjoy dinner last night?"

"It was very nice, thank you. I'm sorry you couldn't make it."

"I think it's good for staff to socialize without the boss around."

So why invite me to dinner with you? Hannah's irritation was curtailed by a sudden thought. *Unless he hadn't.*

Had Delores faked the cell phone call? Why would she want to dupe Hannah into going to dinner? Sizing her up as a potential competitor for Tony? To cry on the shoulder of someone in the loop on the kidnapping? Or was there another reason?

"Have you found Tony's notebook?" Baptisto asked.

"No." His focus on the deal was beginning to grate. "But I found what looks like the underlying financial data. I'm using them to reconstruct the projections and cost analyses."

Baptisto broke into a delighted grin, his teeth as white as his shirt.

"Splendid! I'll have Dolores pick up what you've got."

"I can bring everything over when I'm fin—"

"*No.*" As though hearing the edge in his voice, Baptisto forced another grin.

"I'd like to see what you have so far."

White smoke enveloped the chairman's head, slightly obscuring dark eyes that suddenly made Hannah uncomfortable. She felt a queasy shifting in her perception of reality, a sense of something happening that she wasn't seeing.

Don't be ridiculous. Baptisto's company goes under if this deal doesn't close. Of course he's concerned.

Hannah was about to hand him the notes she had brought when again something held her back. *Make a copy first.*

She abruptly stood. "Everything's in my office. I'll go get it," she said, making it out the door before he could respond.

Outside the wind had built to a howl, blowing

its autumn rhapsody through the chaparral and over the tile roofs. Hannah leaned into it, eyes narrowed against flying specks of sand. She was still shaking grit out of her hair in the OTA lobby when one of the receptionists rushed up to her.

"They said they were from the FBI!" she blurted.

Hannah froze. "FBI?"

"They said they had a warrant. While I was calling the council's offices to find out what to do, they disappeared." The woman twisted one hand in another. "I didn't see where they went."

News on Tony? Hannah hurried toward her office, slowing when she saw Clementine standing outside the door.

"What's going on?"

Her secretary tossed her curls over an ample shoulder. "Seems like I should be asking *you* that question. Two guys showed up, said you sent 'em to pick up some papers for your meeting. I told them to knock themselves out. A few minutes later, they walked out with a couple of boxes."

Hannah looked into her office. The desktop and floor had been stripped of paperwork—all the documents pertaining to the real estate deal were gone. Unaccountably, she felt relieved to see the

Chief still in his corner.

"After the two guys left, *she* got here, and that's when all hell broke loose." Clementine jerked a thumb toward her desk.

Delores was sitting in Clementine's chair, arms wrapped tightly around herself. She looked abandoned, like a child separated from her mother in a crowded department store just before the enormity of her plight hits. At the sight of Hannah, she jumped to her feet with a little cry.

"They took everything, Hannah! The spreadsheets, the paperwork on the first phase, the due diligence files—it's all gone. First Tony's notebook and now this. The offering will never be finished in time!" She collapsed back into the chair, her body wilting like an inflatable doll's with its plug pulled.

Hannah turned back to Clementine.

"The receptionist said these guys told her they were from the FBI. Did you see any identification?"

Her secretary shook her head. "They didn't say anything about being feds. I thought they worked here. For sure, though, they weren't no real police." Clementine tapped the side of her nose for emphasis. "In my family, you learn to smell cops."

Given where Clementine's father was spending his retirement years, Hannah didn't put much stock in Clementine's olfactory abilities. But the two men certainly hadn't acted like law enforcement agents. Hannah's nerves began to thrum. She had a bad feeling about this.

"What did they look like?"

Heedless of the damage to her carefully applied lipstick, Clementine gnawed at her lower lip.

"They had black hair and were Indian…no, Mexican…no…" Clementine shrugged. "I'm not sure. It was hard to see their faces because of their hats." She brightened. "The hats! They were blue, like their jackets and pants. Dark blue."

The words skittered around Hannah's mind. Briefly she was back in the desert with Tony, facing three kidnappers. Three kidnappers all dressed in dark blue.

Hannah's bad feeling became worse.

Chapter Twenty-one

Hannah called Dresden, realizing as she punched in the number that while she had to look up the listing for the beauty salon that cut her hair, she had the Pinnacle Peak detective's direct line memorized.

"Detective Dresden."

Hannah identified herself.

"What can I do for you?" His tone was guarded.

He still doesn't trust me. Shelving her feelings, Hannah told the detective what had happened.

"Those guys weren't FBI," Dresden said. "The local office doesn't know about kidnapping yet. The chairman asked me to hold off telling the federals for a few days. I agreed to treat it like a missing person situation to give the tribe a chance to resolve things by itself."

Hannah couldn't believe it. "What if To—Mr. Soto's hurt?" *Or about to be killed?*

"There wasn't much choice. I'd be facing the red wall of silence unless I gave the tribe a little leeway. They are a sovereign nation, don't forget. I'll send out a deputy to take statements and collect evidence on the burglary, so don't touch anything or let anyone else in your office."

"Do you have any idea yet who the kidnappers are?"

"We're narrowing it down. For one thing, it doesn't appear Soto has any gang affiliations."

"Have you talked to—" Hannah caught herself. She had started to ask about Tony's half-brothers, the LA gangbangers Delores had mentioned. *A very drunk Delores*, Hannah reminded herself. She didn't want to repeat possibly false rumors—her credibility with Dresden was thin enough already. And hadn't Delores said one of Tony's brothers was in prison? If that were true, Dresden surely would have found out about it by now.

"What about a ransom?" she said.

"Neither the tribe nor the firm that Soto works for has been contacted. At this point, it's getting a little late to expect a demand. If this isn't gang-related"—Hannah thought of Delores' comments on initiation killings and a chill rippled through her—"Soto may just be a random victim."

Hannah heard voices in the background on Dresden's end. "Excuse me for a moment," the detective said.

While listening to the white noise created by his hand cupped over the receiver, Hannah considered, then dismissed, Dresden's conclusion. If Tony were simply a chance target, why hadn't the three men taken her, too? And what about the theft of the deal papers from her office? Hannah thought as little of coincidence as she did of karma. Tony had to have been the intended victim. *But why?*

Dresden came back on the line.

"A deputy is on his way to the OTA. In the meantime, you should be care—"

Hannah knew what he was going to say and cut him off. "I will." The last time Dresden had warned her to be careful, events had turned out more horribly than she could have imagined.

"Things have changed, Hannah. This time they came to *your* office. They might—"

"As you said before, this has nothing to do with me. Good-bye, Detective."

Hannah hung up the phone. Almost immediately, it rang again and she snatched it up, irrationally hoping it was Dresden with more news.

"Ms. Dain? This is Alexander Moreno."

Hannah forced the disappointment from her voice. "Yes?"

"Would you join Robert and me for a breakfast meeting tomorrow? While Tony's safe return remains our chief concern, we thought it prudent to discuss the status of the private placement with you. Responsibilities to the shareholders and our client, et cetera."

First Baptisto, now Peña & Moreno. Was Tony the only one interested in this deal as something other than a way to make money?

"Fine," Hannah said, biting off the word. Stress was making her peevish.

She considered telling Moreno about the burglary, then decided to wait until tomorrow. *He better bring his heart medicine.*

"Shall we say the Trading Post at eight?" Moreno asked.

"I'll be there." Hannah broke the connection and looked at her watch. Already it felt like a long day, and it wasn't even ten thirty yet.

Without any documents, she couldn't move forward with the drafting or due diligence. Hannah knew she should wait and talk to the deputy, but decided she couldn't bear staying in the denuded office another minute. She turned off her computer and collected her purse.

Clementine was seated at her desk, talking to a man in a tan uniform. She glanced toward Hannah, then pointedly looked away. Careful not to attract the man's attention, Hannah walked toward the lobby, making a mental note to call her secretary later.

A strong breeze propelled her across the parking lot. Hannah had to clutch the front of her jacket together to keep it from flapping. She got into the Subaru and pointed it toward home, the wind growing stronger as she drove. Sand blew across the pavement like a silk scarf trailing across a bureau, while the chaparral was flattened and fluffed by errant gusts.

For a change, Hannah turned into her condo's main entrance. Passing Tony's yellow Mustang in the visitor's space, she did a double-take—she had forgotten about the car. After parking the Subaru, she looked again at the Mustang. A piece of paper was pinned under one of the car's windshield wipers, and Hannah felt hope blaze through her. *A ransom note?*

She darted across the asphalt and yanked the paper out from under the wiper.

NOTICE: PARKING IN THIS SPACE IS LIMITED TO THIRTY MINUTES OR LESS. VIOLATORS WILL BE TOWED. FOR IMPOUNDED VEHICLES, CALL (480) 555-7563. P.P. ORD. NO. 103-22(A).

Hannah crumpled the piece of paper in frustration, then checked the car over just in case, but didn't find any other notes.

May as well move it now before the tow truck does. She rummaged in her purse for Tony's keys. Her fingers closed around the key fob bearing the man-in-the-maze symbol.

"I'm as lost as you are, buddy," she said to the piece of metal.

Hannah unlocked the Mustang's door and slid behind the wheel. When she set her purse on the passenger seat, it flopped over, spilling its contents into the passenger footwell. Hannah sighed, then leaned over to collect the scattered items. Groping under the seat for her cell phone, her hand encountered what felt like a stack of papers. She grabbed a corner and tugged.

A moment later she was gazing at a burgundy notebook, *ASU* embossed on the cover.

Chapter Twenty-two

Hannah's initial exhilaration at finding Tony's notebook was replaced by dismay once she began studying the pages. There was an outline of a business plan, but its projections didn't match the ones in the documents that had been stolen from her office. And the cost figures differed from what she remembered Tony telling her.

She skimmed through to the end, hoping for an explanation. The numbers only became more confusing. It was like reading a menu in a Chinese restaurant—when the restaurant was in Beijing.

Hannah had never been great at accounting. On the other hand, Cooper was fluent in the language of numbers, a native speaker. Asking for assistance, though, required telling him that the other documents were gone. Once he had heard about the theft, she knew what he would say.

But with Tony still missing, and no one apparently able to do much about it, she needed Cooper's help. What if something in the notebook could help the police identify the kidnappers? Steeling herself, Hannah called his cell phone.

She hadn't underestimated his concern—or his reaction.

"That's it, Hannah. You have to get out of there. *Now.*"

"Not until I figure out what's going on with this deal. I'll be fine. They wanted the documents, not me."

"Why are you putting yourself at risk like this?"

Because if I quit I have to make a real choice about my career. Because focusing on Tony and this deal gives me a reason to delay confronting Richard about my father. Because if you and I work together on this, maybe we'll know why you haven't stayed at the condo the past two nights and why I wasn't that upset you didn't.

"Will you take a look at the notebook? Please?"

Cooper didn't respond. Hannah waited, the stillness feeling like a weight between them.

"I've got a work crew in for a full day of mending fences," he finally said. "Have the notebook couriered out, and I'll look at it during a break. We can talk at the end of the day. Water station on the west side around six?"

Gratitude flooded through Hannah. "Thank you." But her words were met with the buzz of a dial tone.

The road to the ranch was not much more than a strip of rain-runneled dirt. Hannah held tightly to the steering wheel as the Subaru shuddered over a cattle guard, the parallel metal bars shiny in the late afternoon sun.

The sky was just starting to bruise when the car bumped to a stop next to the oversized water trough. On the far side of the field Hannah could see a cluster of pickup trucks. Beside them a group of men worked on stringing barbed wire between fence posts.

She lowered her window. Everything was still—no insect drone, no machinery hum, not even the slightest breeze to give the comfort of sound. In the sodden earth surrounding the metal trough she could see the imprints from countless cloven hooves. The water caught in the cattle tracks was a muddy golden color.

Hannah beeped her horn, then watched as one of the men detached himself from the work crew and walked over to a red truck. A moment later the truck headed across the field, dust trailing from its tires.

The truck pulled up next to the Subaru, and Cooper climbed out. He wore cowboy boots, workday jeans, and an ironed plaid shirt. The shirt was misbuttoned, one half hanging lower than the other below his waist. His shirt sometimes ended up that way when he got dressed in the dark, like on the mornings he left the light off so she could keep sleeping.

Something clenched in Hannah's chest, and she thought back to when they had met for the first time in Boston. She recalled the feeling of fragile intimacy, the sense their relationship required nurturing. *Cooper isn't the only one who has fence-mending to do today.*

"Hey." He reached out to hug her, and Hannah's breath caught in her throat. Stepping into his arms, she laid her cheek against his chest, the fabric of his shirt smooth against her skin. She felt him lace his fingers together, then snug them against the small of her back, right above the top of her jeans. They stood there for almost a minute, until Cooper released his hold.

"As nice as this feels, I have to get back to the crew." He retrieved Tony's notebook from the truck cab.

"I went through everything twice, enough to

know what's going on. You want the long or the short version?"

"Just the verdict. Thumbs up or thumbs down?" When he didn't immediately answer, Hannah felt a twinge of nervousness.

"There are two sets of projections. One shows a decent rate of return for investors, the other predicts much lower profits. Not bad, just more in line with much less risky ventures."

"Which means no smart investor would ever touch it." Her unease was starting to feel like a premonition.

"Bottom line, under the lower projections, the deal doesn't cash flow." Cooper rubbed a thumb over the embossing on the burgundy cover. "A year, maybe eighteen months, and the project will be underwater."

Part of Hannah's job as offering attorney was to certify the financial projections. If the deal cratered, her name would be on the list of those sued by investors. Proving she had been duped by her client would be expensive—and iffy. She could hear opposing counsel now.

Ms. Dain, were you romantically involved with Mr. Soto?

No. I mean, not really.

A crow swooped past them, then settled on the edge of the water trough and cackled derisively.

"I'm sorry," Cooper said.

Hannah felt her temper flare like autumn foliage. She hated pity. Anyway, how could he be so sure the offering was a fraud? The tribe wasn't hurting for money, and Tony wasn't stupid. Why would he put the reputation of the Tohono O'odham at risk?

"Nothing to be sorry for—or to worry about. The financials I was given support the deal."

"But the notebook—"

"Doesn't prove anything. This deal isn't a scam. Ton—Mr. Soto and the tribe want it to succeed."

"Yes, but—" Cooper paused and looked at her. "Hannah, what's really going on here?"

His words hung in the air. Hannah thought she could almost see them, like skywriting on a clear day. The band across her ribs squeezed so tightly she couldn't get her breath.

"Nothing," she choked out, feeling wetness on her cheek. Another tear fell, and it was as though a dam had broken.

Cooper held her while she cried. When her sobs had abated some, he gently kissed the hollow of her neck, and Hannah thought of the ocotillo outside her bedroom window and how its tongue-shaped blooms licked at the sky. The tightness in her chest dissolved, giving way to arousal, and she kissed him back on the mouth.

Cooper hooked a finger under one of her belt loops, pulling her closer. Hannah moved her hips against his groin and he made a little sound. Their first kiss was followed by another, and then another.

Hands cupped around her butt, Cooper lifted her up, and she wrapped her legs around his waist. He walked them awkwardly to the pickup, opened the door, and set her on the seat.

Hannah lay back. Heavy-lidded, she looked up through her eyelashes at him. "What about your crew?"

In response, Cooper touched her lips as though shushing her, then trailed his hand across her cheek and down to the angle of her jaw. Hannah sighed and arched her back as his fingers traced the length of her collarbone through the thin fabric of her sweater.

He paused, and Hannah knew what he was asking. In answer, she grabbed a handful of his shirt and pulled hard, knowing that she was starting something there was no way either of them could stop. Buttons were undone, jeans unzipped. The late afternoon sun streamed through the windshield, its heat magnified by the glass. Sweat slicked their bodies, muscles tightened and stretched, as they climbed up the cliff, then let themselves fall, together.

Afterward they lay across the truck's front seat, Cooper propped against the door on the passenger side and Hannah snugged against his chest. His hand curled around her hip.

"Meant to tell you that I found out about that reporter," he said drowsily.

It took Hannah a moment to recall the name. "Kassif?"

"That's the one. He was fired from one of the New York papers for missing deadlines. And that wasn't the first newspaper job he's lost. Apparently he has a substance abuse problem."

Hannah could feel his breath against her hair when he talked. "How did he end up at the *Express?*"

"Knew somebody who knew somebody. Claims he's climbing the twelve steps, with the aim of getting back on the staff of a big city paper."

An exposé of problems with the tribe's private placement would boost his prospects. And a story on Clementine's family wouldn't hurt either.

"I'll be sure to warn Clementine again."

"Mmmm." Cooper was starting to drift off. Hannah could feel his muscles slacken, his breathing become slow and regular.

She stayed awake. The sun rested on the edge of the horizon before her, the late light transforming the landscape into glowing golden hills and dark violet canyons—colors so brilliant that, even after seeing them countless times, Hannah still thought them unreal.

What was the matter with her? She was in the arms of a man who was, by modern standards, flawless. No ex-wife or children, no stressful, time-consuming job. No interest in drinking or drugs. Self-made, with more than adequate means. He, too, disliked all things peach-flavored, and shared her passion for doing rather than watching sports. Cooper made her laugh, reached for her hand in public, always had time to talk when she called. So why couldn't she put the past behind her and commit to their relationship?

The kidnapping, the stress of finding out about her birth father... Even as they came to mind, Hannah knew they were excuses without merit, just as she knew her attraction to Tony had been foolish and indulgent. She might not always know the reason behind her behavior, but she knew when it was wrong.

Hannah realized that she had arrived at one of

life's unanticipated junctures—the moral equivalent of standing at the bottom of a mountain, plotting the best route for an ascent. Her heartbeat slowed and her head cleared. She could see the obvious safe pick, recognized which holds risked a fall.

She leaned back and pressed her lips against the scratchiness under his jaw, letting herself feel the connection. Although thin, it was there.

"I'm sorry," she murmured.

Cooper stirred under her. Hannah twisted so she could see his face. Their eyes met, his a summer lake-green.

"You were right. I've been way too caught up in things," she said.

He smoothed a strand of hair off her forehead. "I just want you to be safe."

"Well, you don't have to worry anymore. Tomorrow I'll turn over the notebook and back off. I promise."

Chapter Twenty-three

Friday, September 18

Hannah poked carefully at her oatmeal. The cereal had arrived topped with nearly three dozen blueberries, and she knew a wrong move with her spoon would send fruit rolling onto the tablecloth. As she ate, Hannah considered her two dining companions.

Moreno ate British-style, precisely slicing his melon slices with the knife in his right hand, then ferrying the cubes of fruit into his mouth with the fork in his left. His dark suit, tailored to hide his bulk, was protected by a neatly folded napkin.

Peña didn't bother switching utensils from hand to hand either. He cut apart his bacon strips with the edge of his fork, speared a piece of the meat along with some scrambled egg, and, using a triangle of bread as a backstop, scooped the whole bite into his mouth.

Each was so different from the other, Hannah wondered how they had become partners in the first place. A case of playing off one another's strengths? Or was there a connection she wasn't seeing?

So far the conversation had been dominated by Moreno, who alternated between voicing worries for Tony and his theories about the kidnapping. Peña had remained largely silent, but Hannah had the impression he was just as concerned.

His food gone, Moreno laid his knife and fork across his plate, then reached into his jacket pocket and took out a silver box. Opening it, he selected a pill from one of the sectioned compartments, put it in his mouth, then took a sip of water. He snapped the pill container shut and looked longingly at what remained of his partner's meal.

"Richard, if you're not going to eat that last bit of bacon…"

"I am." Peña slathered butter onto a piece of toast.

Tearing his eyes away from the food on his partner's plate, Moreno put the pill container back into his pocket. "Hypertension tablets, aspirin, beta-blockers, nitroglycerin—the doctors have turned me into a walking drugstore."

Hannah trapped an escaping blueberry with

her spoon. "Mmm, this is good fruit," she said, hoping to head off a detailed discussion of Moreno's health. In her view, casual acquaintances should never answer the question *How are you?* with an answer beyond *Not bad* or *Fine.*

But Moreno wasn't to be deterred. "Angina worries me the most. A big meal, exercise, stress— anything that increases the oxygen required by the heart can trigger an episode. If it lasts longer than thirty minutes, that's a heart attack. Part of the muscle dies and can't pump—"

"Alejandro!" Peña interrupted. "Ms. Dain doesn't want to hear your medical history, especially over the breakfast table. If you eat like the fat white man, you get the fat white men's disease. You wouldn't have these problems if you went back to *maiz con frijoles, amigo.*"

Moreno sniffed. "You know I don't care for beans or corn."

"At least you still remember your Spanish."

A flush spread across Moreno's gourd-shaped jowls. "Robert, I was only—"

"—here to talk with Ms. Dain about the private placement." Peña turned his attention to Hannah. "What's the status?"

Last night Hannah had explained to Cooper

that while the notebook might raise suspicions, without more it didn't provide her with a legal basis to withdraw as attorney for the deal. As the deadline for putting together phase two of the project was fast approaching—assuming the offering was still on—Hannah risked a malpractice claim if she quit without client permission.

"If Baptisto says the tribe wants to go ahead with the deal, I have to complete the offering documents. But that's all I'll do," she had said.

Cooper had still been troubled. "What about the kidnapping and the second set of numbers in the notebook?"

"They're someone else's problem."

When Hannah had called Baptisto's office the following morning, the chairman was unavailable. Instead, Delores got on the line—a very agitated Delores, once she had heard Hannah's question.

"Of course the deal is still on! You can't back out now!"

"I don't intend to," Hannah had replied. "But because of the missing documents, I'll need some help with the due diligence. Is there a paralegal available?"

"I can help. Your office this afternoon?"

Hannah had reluctantly agreed. Still unsure of Delores' agenda, she would have preferred someone else, but at this late date, she didn't have much of a choice.

She intentionally hadn't told Delores about finding the notebook. Tony was an employee of Peña & Moreno and his work product belonged to the private equity firm, not the tribe. Also, Hannah was concerned about confidentiality—Tony's jottings could include information on other P&M deals. That was why she had decided to deliver the notebook to the two partners at their breakfast meeting.

Hannah swallowed some cold oatmeal and surreptitiously looked at her watch. If she didn't leave soon, the meal would qualify as lunch.

"I called Mr. Baptisto's office this morning to ask if the tribe still wants to go ahead with the deal—" she began.

Moreno's face turned pink. "If they cancel, they better be prepared to pay us the fee would we would have collected from our investors!"

"Alejandro…" Peña said.

Moreno ignored his partner. "The balloon payment is due in three weeks. If we don't get paid—"

"Alejandro!"

His mouth turned down in a pout, Moreno sat back in his chair and crossed his arms.

Balloon payment? Hannah wondered if the

lump sum were due on the office building. *None of my business*, she thought, remembering her pledge to Cooper.

"Mr. Baptisto's assistant confirmed the tribe wants to go forward. In fact, I'm supposed to be meeting her now to work on the due diligence. But before I go, I want to give you this." Hannah leaned down and took the burgundy notebook out of her briefcase. She handed it to Peña, then signaled the waiter for the check.

"That's Tony's notebook!" Moreno said. "He was always scribbling things in it. Where was it?"

"In his car."

"Don't you need it for the private placement?"

Not with that second set of numbers. "No. I thought you should have it in case it has information on other projects."

"The Indian deal is the only thing Tony had going," Moreno said. "*Has* going, I mean." Reaching across the table, he took the notebook from his partner. "I'll put this in Tony's office. For when he comes back."

Hannah signed her name on the credit slip, hoping Moreno's *when* turned out to be more than wishful thinking.

Hannah walked down the hallway to her office to find Kassif leaning against the partition in front of Clementine's desk. Her secretary wore what Hannah knew to be her favorite dress, a multi-flowered print trimmed with fabric flowers that she had sewn on herself.

"Your family's Italian? What does your dad do?" Kassif was asking as Hannah approached.

Clementine glanced coyly away. "Oh, the usual Italian stuff."

You're not kidding, Hannah couldn't help thinking. She hastened her pace, the heels of her shoes clicking crossly on the tile floor.

"Mr. Kassif, what are you doing here? You know you've been banned from the premises."

He held up his hands in a gesture of innocence. "Banned as a reporter. But I'm here to pick up my lunch date."

Clementine stuck out her chin defiantly. "Do you have a problem with that?"

"No," Hannah replied, unhappy at the prospect of what she was about to do. She wished she had remembered to call her secretary last night. Now it was too late. "But I do have a problem with someone taking advantage of you."

Clementine's face squinched into a mask of hurt. "I didn't think you believed *fat* also meant *stupid*, Hannah."

"I don't. But I also don't want Kassif or anyone else to use you to resurrect his career. You, me, the tribe— we're just potential stories. That's why he's here."

"I don't believe you!"

"It's all in his notebook," Hannah said quietly.

Moving with surprising agility for a woman of her bulk, Clementine stood and plucked Kassif's notebook from his shirt pocket. She opened it and began to read. After a few pages, she looked at the reporter, her eyes sparkling with tears.

"How did you find out all this stuff?"

Kassif looked stricken. "S-some things you said, Google… But it's not what you think, Clemmy! I really—"

Clementine flung the notebook at Kassif. It bounced off his chest and onto the floor.

"Get out," she said in a tight voice.

"If you just let me explain—"

"Get out!" Clementine fled into the coffee room, slamming the door shut behind her.

Kassif snatched up his notebook from the floor, then pointed it angrily at Hannah. "You have no idea what you just screwed up!"

Hannah reached for the phone on Clementine's desk. "That's it, I'm calling Security."

"Don't bother. I'm leaving." Kassif started down the hallway, then stopped.

"I'll phone you tonight, Clemmy!" he called in the direction of the coffee room, then pointed the notebook at Hannah again.

"You have no idea," he said darkly, and left.

Another name off my Christmas card list, Hannah thought, then looked toward the coffee room door. *Clemmy?*

Ten minutes later as she was still trying to coax Clementine out, her cell phone rang. It was Shelby.

"Good news," her sister said. "They're letting me out of here next Friday."

"That's great!"

"There's just one thing." Shelby paused. "A family member's supposed to pick you up. Daddy's got a meeting. Can you come?"

Richard wouldn't change his schedule for his real *daughter? Especially for something as important as this?*

"Of course I'll be there." Hannah bit her lip, knowing she should keep quiet. But she couldn't help herself. "I can't believe Richard won't—no, I can believe it. What a self-centered—"

"Hannah, would you cool it? Daddy doesn't have a choice. He's got the settlement conference in *DEB v. Cornwell.* Lawyers are flying in from all over the country. Why are you on his case so much lately?"

Because I'm mad he won't tell me what I want to know. Because I'm mad that there's something to tell. Because I'm just mad. In the middle of her mental tirade, Hannah glimpsed Delores at the other end of the hallway.

"Shelby, I have to go. What time Friday?"

"Five o'clock. Dress nice, and make sure there's no bike stuff in your car. I don't want to get grease on my clothes."

Hannah closed her phone with a smile. *Rehab notwithstanding, the leopard still had some of her spots.*

"I'm ready to go to work." Delores looked with mild curiosity at the still-closed coffee room door.

From past experience, Hannah knew Clementine wouldn't budge until she was ready. The best thing at times like this was to leave her alone. She picked up her briefcase. "Let's do it."

Delores was a quick study. With little direction, she compiled projections, did Internet searches, even found a set of financials for the first phase in Baptisto's files. Meanwhile, Hannah drafted the investor documents. They worked steadily and mostly without speaking. Whenever Delores left the room, Hannah would check her secretary's desk, but the chair at Clementine's desk remained empty.

She'll be fine, Hannah told herself. *Better that she found out about Kassif sooner rather than later.*

A little after five, she saved the draft on which she had been working and powered down her computer. "Ready to stop for today?"

Delores burst into tears. "It's my fault that he's dead!"

Hannah stared at her.

"If I hadn't talked Mr. Baptisto into doing the private placement, Tony would have never been involved. I should have known something bad would happen!"

Hannah pulled up a chair next to the distraught woman. "This has nothing to do with you—it just happened. All we can do now is wait and hope for the best."

Delores wiped the tears off her cheeks. "I thought he would like me if I came up with an idea to help the tribe." She sniffed. "It's the only thing he cares about."

Hannah awkwardly patted Delores' arm. "You can't be sure of that. Sometimes people get so wrapped up in their work, they don't pay enough attention to the people they care about."

"You don't say," Clementine said from Hannah's doorway.

"Clementine, I—" Hannah began.

"You got a phone message." Clementine slapped a piece of paper onto the desktop. "That detective called. He wants you to come down to the station."

Chapter Twenty-four

When Hannah called Dresden's direct line, there was no answer. She next tried to reach him via the main number, also without success.

"I'm sorry, but Detective Dresden isn't available," said the deputy who answered the phone.

Hannah hung up, not overly concerned. *Probably some follow-up questions on the document theft, or maybe he wants me to look at a mug book.*

Delores, though, was in hysterics.

"It's Tony! I know something's happened to Tony!"

Hannah tried to stifle the annoyance in her voice. "If the police had news, they would leave a message, not ask me to stop by."

"You were with him that day! They probably think you're his girlfriend, and want to tell you first!"

Out of patience and short on sympathy, Hannah picked up her jacket. Between Clementine and Delores, she'd had enough romantic drama for the day. After she found out what Dresden wanted, she was going straight home to bed.

Hannah stood at the counter in the police station lobby. "You wanted to see me?"

"Let's talk back here," Dresden said.

Hannah followed the detective down the familiar corridor. But instead of taking her to his office, he instead walked into a small interior room furnished with a metal table and four chairs built for durability more than comfort. Hannah noticed the rings welded to one side of the table and the small camera mounted high up in a corner.

The room made Hannah feel jumpy. She tried to joke away her tension. "Isn't this Interrogation? Do I need a lawyer?"

"That's your decision. You can call one if you'd like."

Hannah searched his expression for humor, but Dresden's face was a blank canvas. Just then, the door swung open and a deputy poked his head into the room.

"Oh—sorry, sir. Didn't know you'd already started."

Already started? Already started what? Hannah looked from one man to the other, her unease increasing.

"Can I help you, deputy?" Dresden asked.

"What should I do with him?"

The deputy jerked his head, and Hannah realized there was someone standing next to him. Leaning forward, she glimpsed an overhanging belly, thick beard, and eyes that were watchful and angry. She sucked in her breath. It was *White Power* man.

"If it were up to me, I'd charge him with one count of disturbing the peace and numerous counts of stupidity. But it's the DA's call. Put him back into holding and tell legal his alibi checked out."

"Yes, sir." The deputy disappeared.

Hannah relaxed just a bit. *This was about running over that motorcycle.* Her mind went back to that day in the rock-climbing park. *Wasn't an impending riot a defense to leaving the scene of an accident? And what* alibi *was Dresden talking about?*

Dresden looked thoughtfully at Hannah. "How has your day been?" he asked with studied casualness.

Not great, Hannah wanted to say, but didn't. Instead, she cut to the chase.

"Look, it was his fault. If he hadn't attacked—"

"Wait," Dresden said. "You're not denying what happened, but you're claiming self-defense?" His eyes were like two pale stones.

Hannah wrinkled her brow. "I think so…well, not exactly. Unless you're talking about my car. I mean, if they hadn't tried to—"

Dresden abruptly got to his feet.

"Wait here."

He left the room, closing the door behind him. Hannah heard the snick of a deadbolt.

Wait here? I'm locked in! Worry percolated in her gut. *Just what was that motorcycle worth?*

After several minutes Dresden came back into the room, accompanied by a deputy wearing sunglasses. Both men sat across the table from Hannah.

"Ms. Dain, this is Officer Frampton."

Hannah recognized the deputy *White Power* man had attacked when she was at the police station to report Tony's kidnapping.

"Ma'am." Frampton nodded, and took out a notepad and pen from a drawer in the table. Hannah could see a distorted reflection of herself in his mirrored lenses.

Dresden put a waiver-of-rights form on the table. "Before we begin—"

Hannah took a pen from her purse and signed. *I*

should just give them a Xeroxed stack of these things.

"I believe you were about to tell me about your day. Something about your car and an attack…?" Dresden's voice was like January wind, cool and impersonal.

"Did he tell you it happened *today*?" Hannah said, indignation supplanting her anxiety. "He's probably backdating an insurance claim. It was last weekend at the rock-climbing park. And it was an accident—I was trying to get away from the pro-testers. Anyway, nothing would have happened if he hadn't picked up my car!"

Frampton and Dresden exchanged a look. The deputy leaned over and whispered something in the detective's ear.

Dresden raised his eyebrows. "The ME's sure there weren't any marks on the body from a vehicle?"

At the word *body* Hannah's spine went rigid.

Frampton nodded. "Just two GSW, both through and through."

Hannah was utterly confused. And certain something was very wrong.

"Why exactly am I here?" Her voice was reedy.

"Ms. Dain, I think we should begin again. Where were you this afternoon?" Dresden said.

"I'm not saying anything else until you tell me

what this is about!" Hannah felt a small vein pulsing in her temple and hoped the twitch wasn't visible.

"Gordon Baptisto was found dead this afternoon."

"*What?*" Hannah felt as though she were caught in a riptide, the current becoming stronger by the minute, pulling her forward to unknown but certain disaster. Why would Dresden think she knew something about the murder? She didn't—

All of a sudden things became clear with an intensity that was blinding. *He was questioning her because of what she had done last month.* Hannah stared at the detective in horror.

"You don't think I…I mean…my God! I didn't have anything to do with whatever happened to Mr. Baptisto!" Hannah felt outraged and helpless—and scared.

"Why don't you just tell us about your day," Dresden said. The look in his eyes reminded Hannah of a coyote tracking prey.

She rattled off the chronology—breakfast with Moreno and Peña, working at the office with Clementine and Delores, even her confrontation with the *Express* reporter. Every time she mentioned another name, Frampton scribbled it on his notepad.

"…And then I got your phone message and

came here." She crossed her arms, then realizing what she was doing, uncrossed them. Her shirt felt clammy against her back.

Frampton stood. "I'll make the calls, sir." He left the room.

Dresden placed his hands, palms down, on the tabletop. His movements, like his speech, were precise and accurate.

"Now what's this about Stanley Kawarshki's motorcycle and your car?"

In spite of the circumstances, Hannah felt the urge to laugh. *A lawyer and a* Law & Order *addict—and still, I blab to the cops.*

"Last Sunday, when I went rock-climbing…"

When she was finished, Dresden allowed himself a wry grin.

"I don't think you have to worry about Stanley pressing charges. Those protesters did a lot of damage. He's already spent several hours telling us he wasn't anywhere near the rez over the weekend."

"Do you know where he was when Mr. Baptisto was killed?" Hannah recalled how *White Power* man had whipped the crowd into a frenzy. And what about his assault on the casino worker?

"Stanley's your average, ignorant bigot. Blames the Indians and everyone else for all that's wrong in his life. Anonymous violence is his style—he's too much of a coward to act by himself, and too dumb to plan anything. In any event, he's got an alibi for the murder. He was sitting in a bar the entire afternoon. Unless we can tie him to the shooters, he's in the clear."

There was a knock on the door, then Deputy Frampton stuck his head into the room. This time the sunglasses were missing.

"She checks out, sir—three confirms. I still have a call in to the reporter."

Hannah felt an upsurge of relief that was almost physical. "So my *alibi* holds up?" she asked. Sarcasm aside, she knew that, in truth, Dresden had shown restraint. After what she had done last month, he would have been justified sending a patrol car to pick her up for questioning. The phone summons had been a courtesy.

Dresden's expression relaxed around the edges. "You're in the clear. And I'm sorry you were upset. But under the circumstances, I didn't have much of a choice."

"I understand," Hannah said, her tone curt. She didn't want him to elaborate.

Dresden pushed back from the table. "You're free to go. Again, I would appreciate your discretion on this."

"You can count on it." Her status as a murder suspect wasn't something Hannah planned on broadcasting.

Getting to her feet, she realized neither Dresden nor Frampton had mentioned the elephant in the room—Tony's name hadn't come up once. Did that mean they thought the kidnapping and the murder were unrelated? She had to find out.

"What exactly happened to Mr. Baptisto?"

"He was shot twice, sometime this afternoon. His body was dumped in an irrigation ditch north of the rez." Dresden looked grim. "That makes him my problem instead of the feds'."

North of the rez—where Tony had been kidnapped.

"Nothing we've seen links the kidnapping to the murder," Dresden added, as though hearing her thought. "Right now, we're assuming it's just a coincidence that both victims were Tohono O'odham. Of course, that doesn't mean we won't keep looking for a connection between the two."

You mean like the fact both men are key players in a major real estate deal for the tribe—a deal that has two sets of financials? Hannah knew this was the type of information Dresden would want to know.

She also knew it was protected by attorney-client privilege.

Dresden held open the door. "Do you know of any connections we've overlooked?"

Poker-faced, she shrugged. "This is my first week at the OTA. I barely know the way to my office."

Hannah followed him to the lobby. *But I seem to have no problem finding trouble.*

Chapter Twenty-five

Hannah set the cartons of Chinese take-out on the kitchen counter and checked her voice mail. There were two phone messages, and she was tempted to hang up without listening to them. After her visit to the police station, she didn't feel like talking to anyone.

But what if Dresden had called with more questions? Or to say that Tony had been found? And that he's alive or—

She hit the *Playback* button.

"Boss, it's me. Why aren't you answering your cell? Did you forget it again? Anyway, about today… that reporter…he was…well, you know. And I have a copy of that pesto recipe if you still want it. Later."

The beep sounded. Hannah was mildly astonished—she couldn't remember Clementine ever getting that close to an apology before. She cued up the next message.

"Hey, Hannah."

She stopped unpacking her food and stood still to listen.

"The well pump went out, so I'm stuck at the ranch tonight. Call me when you can."

Hannah depressed the *Disconnect* button. She wasn't looking forward to telling Cooper about the day's events. *Might as well do it on a full stomach,* she thought, dumping the carton of tofu and broccoli onto a plate. No telling which would upset him more—Baptisto's murder or the police needing to verify her alibi.

Or would Cooper be most worried by the same feeling that had niggled at Hannah since Tony's kidnapping? The sense that she was getting too close to something—something big, possibly as large as what had happened last summer. *At least this time she was staying out of the way.*

Hannah filled the kettle with water for tea and set it on the stove, then put the empty cartons and chopsticks in the trash. The Chinese may have had a lot of good ideas, but eating with wooden sticks instead of forks wasn't one of them. The fortune cookie was put aside for later. She could never resist reading the message.

The aroma of warm food filled the room, and Hannah's stomach rumbled in response. She found a fork in the drawer and speared a piece of broccoli, pleased with its slightly rubbery feel. Hannah had loved the vegetable since she was a child. Olivia had once told her it was one of Elizabeth's favorite foods.

She bit into the floret. *What else did she and her mother have in common?* Did Elizabeth have days like this, when it seemed as though she were living a life that didn't quite fit? Was that why she went to New York, had an affair? Or was there a wildness—a badness, even—deep in her bones that marriage and career couldn't subdue?

Hannah ate a cube of tofu, then checked to see if the water was about to boil. She caught her reflection in the side of the kettle, wavy and distorted. If she opened her mouth and pressed her hands to her face, she would look like Munch's screamer.

And feel just as tormented, if the search for her birth father didn't start going better. With no one else to talk to, all she had left was Elizabeth's medical records, which she couldn't access without overturning a court order and exposing her secret to the world.

Hannah took a mug out of the cabinet and dropped a tea bag into it. The kettle whistled, and she lifted it off the burner, then filled the mug with hot water. Waiting for the tea to steep, Hannah leaned against the counter.

What if my birth father can't answer my questions about Elizabeth? What if he wants nothing to do with me?

She picked up the fortune cookie and cracked it open. The font on the white slip of paper was supposed to look like Chinese kanji.

You aspire to great heights—
don't be afraid to climb.
Lucky number is one.

So that's why I got stuck on the cliff last Sunday. She tossed the cookie fragments in the trash but left the slip of paper on the counter.

Noticing that her climbing shoes and orange crash pad were still by the front door where she had left them after the weekend, she moved to put them away. As she grabbed the shoes, Hannah thought about kissing Tony that night. She still couldn't explain why she had done it.

Was that how it had started between Elizabeth and her father? Had her mother given in to one-time desire, a capitulation that led to unforeseen consequences of unimagined magnitude? The thought troubled Hannah. She wanted the differences between her and Elizabeth to be more than merely outcome.

Hannah kicked the crash pad in frustration. If

she could just talk to her birth father! Maybe then she would understand her mother's behavior—as well as her own recent actions. Hannah booted the crash pad again.

As her foot connected with the foam, an idea popped into her head. An outrageous, ludicrous, dangerous idea.

You aspire to great heights.

Her common sense weighed in. *Disbarment... arrest...jail...*

Don't be afraid to climb.

Hannah headed for the bedroom, where she traded her work clothes for black climbing tights and long-sleeved top. Poking around in the closet until she found an old black ski hat and her climbing headlamp, she stuffed them into her navy daypack along with her chalk bag.

Don't be afraid to climb, Hannah silently repeated to herself as she slung the daypack over her shoulder. She grabbed her shoes from by the door, wishing the fortune in the cookie had said something about not falling, too.

Less than an hour later she was standing in the empty parking lot. She had left the Subaru behind, choosing instead to walk the five blocks from her condo. With the proliferation of surveillance systems and webcams, Hannah didn't want photos of her car for the police to find.

It was a cool starry night, with no clouds to dim the constellations overhead. A breeze rattled nearby palo verde branches, and Hannah shivered. She was still more accustomed to the canopy of darkness created by the blaze of urban lights. Stars made her uncomfortable—she imagined they made it easier for whatever was out there to see her. *Spy holes in the universe.* Hannah shivered again.

In front of her loomed the hospital. She was at the rear of the building, away from the glare of the emergency entrance. Windows of unoccupied offices looked out onto the deserted swath of asphalt, rimmed with landscaping that shielded the space from the main road. The building wasn't really a shape, but more a blackness where the stars weren't.

Hannah switched on her climbing headlamp and a faded circle of light appeared on the ground. She was peeved—the batteries were less than six months old. *That lying pink bunny.*

She aimed the headlamp at the second story

and found what she was looking for on the fifth window from the end. The metallic butterfly decal danced in the wavering beam, looking as though it were in flight.

Threading through clumps of teddy bear cholla—taking care to avoid the platinum blond needles—Hannah walked the length of the building's exterior. Save for a facade of locally quarried granite, the three-story oblong was without architectural aspirations, the stonework giving it a dour presence. While she had never seen one, Hannah thought it looked like an asylum.

A wafer moon appeared over the roofline, and Hannah took off the headlamp and put it into her backpack. Better to save the batteries for once she was inside. Using the window with the decal as her guide, she plotted her ascent.

Her first holds—a positive side pull on a stone bulge for the right, a window ledge corner for the left—were neatly outlined in shadow. The next ones were less obvious, but Hannah thought they would be apparent once she was up there. She placed the crash pad under her intended route, positioning it between two clusters of prickly pear. A fall that missed the square of foam would mean a bone-jarring landing on hard ground or cactus spines.

This is no different from Sunday's climb, she told herself. *Except for the illegal part.* Getting caught risked a fine and jail time for trespassing or even burglary. *First the rehab center, now the hospital. What was next—the local bank?*

Hannah took the chalk bag from her daypack and dusted her hands with the white powder. She put the daypack back on, then strapped the chalk bag around her waist. A glance around the parking lot revealed no late-night joggers, no dog walkers, no hospital employees sneaking a smoke. She was alone.

Deciding that putting on her climbing shoes was enough of a warm-up, Hannah reached for a protruding stone and pulled herself off the ground. Her feet found traction on the rock as she crimped the ledge of the window with her other hand. Inch by inch she climbed, feeling for finger-sized edges and not-too-slopey footholds among the chunks of granite. Residue from car exhaust and other air pollutants mixed with the chalk on her hands, leaving her fingers a dirty gray.

Five minutes later Hannah pulled level with the top of the first floor and paused to catch her breath. The breeze had picked up, its cool air chilling her damp skin. Hannah spat stone dust from her mouth and grabbed the next hold.

By the time her right hand touched the sill of the second-story window marked with the decal, she was ready for the climb to be over. Her injured shoulder throbbed with pain and her legs trembled with weakness. Blood dotted her fingertips.

Hannah braced the heel of one hand against the moveable part of the window frame and with a foot wedged into one of the deeper cracks for leverage, pushed upward. The window didn't budge. She pounded on the glass with her fist and tried again, but the wooden frame stayed put.

Somewhere close by a coyote cut loose with a long dolorous aria, punctuated with staccato barks and yips. Hannah leaned her forehead against the stone. She felt cold, tired, and in pain. According to her climbing instructor, any of the three was sufficient reason to discontinue an ascent. She didn't even consider it.

Instead she leaned back as much as she dared, squinting through the darkness at the next window over. In the moonlight a butterfly decal winked back at her from the corner, identical to the one pasted onto the glass next to her.

Two windows in the records room. Two butterfly decals. But only one broken latch.

Hannah knew she didn't have enough strength

left to descend to the ground and then climb back up again. But sideways was a different matter. Three lateral moves, and she would be at the other window.

Three moves that would take her away from the safety of the crash pad to the risk of a fall onto hard ground or spiky cactus. And this time there would be no Tony to rescue her.

Don't be afraid to climb.

Willing resolve into her spine, pushing it through to the rest of her bones, Hannah reached for the first hold, a short pull to the left. Two more moves and she was clinging to the stonework around the adjacent window.

This time when she pushed against the frame, it slid upward a few inches before balking. Hannah slipped her fingers through the newly created slit and gripped the edge of the inside sill.

She needed more than the strength that was left in her one arm to open the window all the way. If she got the timing right, her legs would act like springs, pushing her up with enough force to slide the window open, while at the same time propelling her into the room.

Lucky number is one.

Hannah hoped the fortune cookie was right, because one chance was all that she would have. If the window stayed stuck, she would peel off the wall and plummet two stories to the ground. Hannah briefly considered the risk of a fractured leg or vertebra, weighing it against the ache that had been inside her since she had found out about Elizabeth's deceptions.

Some pain hurts more than broken bones. Hannah got into position.

Her right hand was wrapped around the underside of the frame when a single headlight appeared at the far end of the parking lot. The buzz of an engine cut through the night's stillness.

Hospital security? Hannah couldn't believe it. She hugged the building wall, its rough exterior snagging her shirt like cactus thorns. The pale light of the moon, now fully overhead, etched her into a dark shadow against the bleached stone. Hannah's heart pounded as she watched the beam rove across the asphalt like an errant firefly. If the security guard looked up, he would see her. She had to get inside—now.

Tightening her grasp on the window frame, Hannah heaved upward at the same time she pushed off her stone perch. After a fraction of hesitation, the window slid upward with a groan of protest. She tumbled through the opening and onto the carpeted floor.

Hannah lay still and let her gaze rove the room. Overhead, fluorescent lights glowed at random, their illumination sufficient for her to see the desk next to the copy machine, the shelves of files. She was in the right place.

Outside, the engine noise droned closer and then abruptly stopped. Hannah began to perspire again.

Had the security guard seen her?

She slipped the daypack from her shoulders, then crept to the window and peeked over the sill. Below was parked a golf cart-like vehicle, headlight still on. As Hannah watched, a small yellow flame flared in the driver's compartment. A minute later the smell of cigarette smoke wafted through the open window.

Backing away, Hannah dug into the daypack for her headlamp. She put it on her head but didn't turn it on. She knew it would be smart to wait until the guard had finished his smoke. But she couldn't.

Afraid of being silhouetted by the overheads, Hannah stayed on all fours. She crawled toward the section of the room where the records clerk had retrieved Elizabeth's file. After a few feet she stopped, pain searing her lower leg. Hannah pulled up her pant leg and examined her shin in the dim light. Blood oozed from an angry gash just above her ankle.

Someday I'll find a sport that doesn't involve bleeding. Hannah reached into her daypack, found a stray tissue, and held it against the wound.

The white square quickly turned crimson. *Blood*—the reason she was there. The bits of information encoded in genetic material flowing through her veins from parents, grandparents, and the generations who preceded them, playing a siren song she couldn't ignore.

Hannah turned on the headlamp and shone it at the closest shelves. The end of each tier was labeled with a letter followed by a series of numbers, just like the one she had lifted from the notepad during her prior visit. Hannah checked the inside of her wrist, where she had written the sequence in pen on her skin before she left the condo. According to the code system, her mother's file should be somewhere in the next shelving unit.

She turned off the light and started to crawl again. In less than five minutes she was holding Elizabeth's medical records. The folder smelled old, and the paper felt powdery. Hannah handled it gingerly, trying not to dirty the pages with the gray soot on her fingers.

For a moment, she was tempted to put the file back onto the shelf. But burying the past wouldn't be the same as never knowing it at all. Having come this far, Hannah couldn't resist a chance to find the connection she had wanted for so long. She flipped open the chart and, using the headlamp's dim light, began to read.

On top was a copy of a court order stating that for "purposes found just and satisfactory to the Court, the identity of and references to individuals other than Elizabeth Dain and Richard Dain are to be expunged from the medical files of Elizabeth Dain maintained at Pinnacle Peak Hospital."

So the records clerk had been only partially right. Elizabeth's medical records weren't sealed, only the names of anyone other than Elizabeth and Richard. Hannah turned to the next page.

Patient: Elizabeth Dain. Husband: Richard Dain was typed across the top, followed by lab test results that appeared standard for a pregnant woman at the time. Hannah read the doctor's notes. Richard—a man who wanted his dentist to make office calls so he wouldn't have to leave the law firm—had

attended every one of Elizabeth's initial appoint-
ments.

A comment Olivia had once made came to
mind. *Sometimes people's best-kept secrets are in plain
sight. We see them without recognizing them for what
they are.* Hannah wondered if she would have found
out the truth about her mother if she had tried harder
to mend the fissure between her and Richard. Would
she have recognized his aloofness as heartbreak if they
had been close? She continued reading.

As Elizabeth's pregnancy advanced, Richard's
name disappeared from the chart. *Because the doctor
saw no reason to mention it, or because he had stopped
coming?* A month before her mother had been due
to deliver, additional tests had been ordered. The
typing was barely legible in the weakening light of her
headlamp. Hannah squinted at the faded letters.

Dain, Elizabeth. CBC w/ DIFF. Under *Notes*
was printed *Disease/Trait: Negative.* The rest of the
writing in the section had been lined through with
a black marking pen. *Per Court Order* was written
in the margin next to it.

From the physical exams required for bicycle
racing, Hannah knew *CBC w/ DIFF* meant Complete Blood Count with Differential. *Differential*
referred to the percentage of various types of white

blood cells. A description of the red blood cells was also part of the test.

So Elizabeth had been tested for a blood-borne disease. Hannah couldn't imagine what it could be. She surmised that *Disease/Trait: Negative* meant her mother neither had the disease nor carried the gene for it. She turned to the next page.

It was another set of blood test results. The name of the person tested had been blacked out, along with the information listed under Address, Telephone, Date of Birth, and Social Security Number.

Hannah's heart beat faster. When she read the *Notes* section, it really began to thump.

Disease/Trait: Positive for Trait. A few lines had been skipped, then the following was written in a different hand: *Patient is male parent of Baby Dain. (See DAIN, ELIZABETH) Family history of [blacked out]. Results: [blacked out].* The rest of the page had been torn off.

Male parent of Baby Dain. The unknown test subject was Hannah's birth father. And as the records clerk had said, he had the gene but not the disease.

The beam from her headlamp flickered, indicating its batteries were nearly drained. Hannah turned the page, to a copy of her birth records.

When she had first started looking for her father, she had obtained a set from the hospital. These, though, were more complete.

According to the doctor's notes, Richard had been in the waiting room during her birth, and he had taken Elizabeth and Hannah home the following morning. The chart also noted that Baby Dain's blood had been tested, and that *no [blacked out] have been detected.* No other name—redacted or otherwise—was mentioned.

There were only a few pages left in the file. Tears in her eyes, Hannah skimmed the stark medical details of her mother's death two days later. Again, no name other than Richard's had been noted.

Nowhere in the folder was the piece of paper that had been torn from the second set of test results. Hannah flipped through the file twice, but the missing scrap wasn't there.

As much as she wanted to, Hannah decided against taking the two test results with her. She didn't want to raise doubts about the integrity of the file that might have an adverse effect on an action to unseal the records.

She did unfasten the clips holding the file together and remove the court order. No doubt the records of the court proceedings had been sealed as well, but it was worth a shot. She looked at the signature line, not surprised to see Judge Rothberg's name. Aaron was an old family friend, and one of the principal backers of Richard's judgeship bid. The name of the applicant had been redacted, but Hannah was fairly certain *Richard Dain* lay under the pen strokes.

Her headlamp flickered again. Hannah hurriedly closed the file and put it back onto the shelf just as the light finally went out.

Fortunately, getting out of the hospital was a lot less complicated than getting in. Guided by the indirect lighting, Hannah crawled to the door and cracked it open. It was the wee hours of the morning, and the hospital's corridor was empty. She slipped out, easing the door shut behind her, and walked to the elevator, trying not to favor her sore shin.

Most people leave here bleeding less than when they arrived, she thought as she limped out the ER entrance. But she had to admit that she did feel better. It was as though something vital had been restored in her, a piece replaced that had been missing.

Except for the ache in her leg, the walk back home was uneventful. As she neared the condo, Hannah wondered—hoped, actually—if Cooper would be there. But the space where he usually parked his truck was empty.

Leaving her climbing gear in the foyer, Hannah hobbled up the stairs. She set her daypack on the kitchen counter and took out the court order.

Now that her initial excitement had cooled, Hannah felt a bit of a letdown. All she had really accomplished was confirm what the records clerk had told her. She still didn't know her birth father's name, and was no closer to finding him. *Not much to show for an evening of multiple felonies.*

Discouragement washed over her, along with a sudden tiredness. Resisting the urge to crawl under the covers as she was, Hannah peeled off her dirty clothes and stepped into the shower.

Fifteen minutes later, wearing Cooper's bathrobe, Hannah collapsed onto her living room sofa, feeling weary to the core. She wrapped her arms around one of the sofa pillows, stretched out, and closed her eyes. *I'll just rest for a few minutes…*

Hannah was deep into sleep that was more like a coma than a nap when her cell rang inside her purse on the kitchen counter. She moaned, but there was nothing to do but answer it—middle-of-the-night phone calls couldn't be ignored. Groggy, she staggered to her feet.

"Hello?"

A digitized recording began playing.

What telemarketer is stupid enough to call at two AM? Hannah was about to hang up when her brain registered what the mechanical voice had said.

Will you accept a collect call from…

"Of course! Yes!" Hannah said, pushing damp hair out of her face.

The recording clicked off.

"Hi, Hannah," Tony said. "Did I wake you?"

Chapter Twenty-six

Saturday, September 19

"There it is," Delores said, the first words she had spoken in ten minutes. After her flurry of questions were met with a string of *I-don't-knows* from Hannah, she had gone quiet, staring out the car window while Hannah drove through the empty streets.

The Subaru's headlights swept across the front of the convenience store, illuminating the empty parking lot. They were in a neighborhood a Realtor would call transitional, although Hannah didn't think going from *worst* to *really bad* was much of a change. Following Tony's instructions, she parked next to the dumpster, where the car couldn't be seen by the clerk behind the counter.

Delores started to open the door. Hannah put out a restraining arm.

"Wait. He told me to stay in the car, that he'll come when it's safe." *Safe from what*, Hannah hadn't asked, although she assumed Tony's departure from the kidnappers wasn't consensual.

Delores reluctantly shut the door. They sat for several minutes, peering into the darkness. Just as Hannah was wondering if they were in the right place, Tony stepped out of the shadows.

"Antoñio! Dios mio!" Delores scrambled out of the Subaru and flung herself into Tony's arms, almost sending them both to the pavement. Hannah stayed behind the wheel, hoping it hadn't been a mistake to bring Delores. She was beginning to worry her attraction to Tony was more akin to that of a stalker than a lover.

"Easy there," Tony said, extricating himself from Delores' grasp. "My ribs are pretty sore." He glanced up and down the street. "Let's get in the car. Hurry." He ushered Delores into the backseat and slid in after her.

Delores clutched his arm. "What happened? Where have you been?"

"It's a long story." Tony leaned forward. "Did you call…?"

Hannah looked over her shoulder at him. "No, not yet."

"Good." Tony let his eyes close momentarily. "Jeez, I'm tired."

Hannah started the engine. "Where do you want to go? Home? Hospital?"

"Neither. Did you bring the stuff I asked for?"

She nodded.

"There's a motel to the left around the corner. Let's go there."

Hannah studied Tony in the rearview mirror while she drove. There were smudges of blue under his eyes and lines in his face that hadn't been there before. He had on the same jeans and shirt he had worn while riding, only now the pants were filthy and one of the shirtsleeves was ripped. But his cocksure gleam was intact, undimmed by his bedraggled appearance. If being kidnapped had frayed him, Hannah couldn't see it.

After she had gotten over her initial shock at hearing Tony's voice on the phone, their conversation had been brief.

"I'm at the Circle K on Yucca, south of Palo Verde. Can you pick me up?"

"I'll call Dresden—"

"Don't! There's something I have to do first. I'll explain when you get here. Can you bring some food and money? A change of clothes and a razor would be nice, too."

Hannah had hung up without pushing the

police issue, even though she had the sense that she was agreeing to more than a postponed phone call. Truth be told, she wasn't that eager for Dresden to be involved yet, at least not until she had talked to Tony first. This might be her only opportunity to get straightforward answers on the kidnapping and the second set of numbers in the notebook, perhaps even Baptisto's murder.

She had hurriedly collected sweatpants, socks, and an old t-shirt of Cooper's, and put them into a paper grocery bag, along with shampoo, a disposable razor, all the fruit in the bowl on the kitchen counter, bottled water, and some energy bars.

When she was about to leave, Hannah had decided to call Delores. Given how she apparently felt about Tony, Hannah couldn't bring herself to exclude her.

Now, seeing them together for the first time, Hannah was struck by the lopsidedness of their connection. Delores couldn't stop staring at Tony, her hands gripping his as though she were afraid he would disappear again. She radiated a depth of emotion that Hannah expected to see only between a couple of long standing. But here the feeling ran only one way—Tony wasn't simply ignoring Delores' questions, but her presence, too.

"Turn right here," Tony said. Hannah steered the Subaru past the *Come On Inn* sign. She really disliked cute business names. Hair salons were the worst offenders.

"Ask for the end unit. And pay cash, okay?"

Pay cash? If Tony didn't want her to use her credit card, did that mean he thought someone was after her, too?

While Delores and Tony waited in the car, Hannah roused the night clerk and paid for one night. Pocketing the change back from her three twenties, Hannah wondered why Tony had chosen the place. It was the type of lodging where the television was bolted to the bureau and the bathroom amenities stopped at a bar of cheap soap and a paper strip across the toilet lid. If Hannah had just spent three days in the same clothes without a shower, she would want to be home or in the nicest hotel in town.

"Drive around to the back so the car can't be seen from the street," Tony said when Hannah got back to the car. At her questioning look, he added with a lopsided grin, "General paranoia."

Hannah didn't believe him, but did what he said. She parked in one of the rear slots, and the three of them got out of the car. Carrying the overstuffed grocery bag, Hannah unlocked the door to the room. Her expectations hadn't been far off—dingy bedspread, battered furniture, and curtains reeking of cigarette smoke. Everything was neutral-colored, as though not to offend.

Tony collapsed onto the bed and, folding his arms behind his head, shut his eyes. Hannah set the bag on the nightstand while Delores pulled the lone chair close to the bed and sat in it.

"Why didn't you call *me*? You know I would have come," she said.

"I didn't have my cell and Hannah was in the phone book," Tony mumbled without opening his eyes.

Hannah frowned at the lie. Her number was unlisted. "Tony, what's going on?"

"Gotta sleep," he replied, thick-tongued with exhaustion.

"Tony!" Hannah repeated.

Delores shushed her. "Can't you see he's worn out? He needs to rest."

"I'm calling Dresden," Hannah said.

Tony's lids fluttered open. He met her stare, and Hannah felt the air between them briefly charge. She looked away, breaking the connection.

I'm not going there, not anymore. Flirting with Tony was like eating candy—a sweet rush for the moment, but not something to live on. And now Hannah knew the wisdom of watching her sugar intake.

"Talk later…too tired…" Tony's eyes closed again.

"But the kidnappers—" Hannah said.

"I think I killed one of them…" he said into the pillow. Within moments, he was asleep.

Hannah looked at Delores. From the expression on the other woman's face, it was clear that she had heard it, too. Hannah reached into her purse for her cell phone.

"We've got to call the police."

But as she began to punch in the number, Delores clamped a hand onto her wrist.

"You can't," she said in a fierce whisper. "Not until he has a chance to explain. This is about more than Tony, Hannah. The real estate offering, the tribe's reputation—everything is on the line."

Hannah paused. Clearly Tony was in no condition to talk to the police. What he said could be true, or a hallucination born of exhaustion.

"Wait just a few hours," Delores pleaded.

Hannah looked at Tony. His chest rose and fell in a slow rhythm, while the circles under his eyes stood out like dark bruises.

She knew Dresden would be furious if she didn't call. Delay would give the kidnappers more time to disappear. Could she be held responsible for aiding their escape? Hannah thought back to law school, trying to remember the difference between obstruction of justice and accessory after the fact. *Five years in prison? Ten?*

Her hand hovered over her phone's keypad, ready to push buttons. She looked at Delores' anxious face, then closed the phone, knowing it was the wrong thing to do.

"I'll wait until he wakes up. Then we're going straight to the police."

Delores lay on the other side of the bed, her hand closed over Tony's. Hannah dozed uncomfortably in the chair. She would have preferred napping at her condo for a few hours, but wasn't altogether sure Tony and Delores would still be at the motel when she returned.

At quarter past nine, Tony pushed himself up to a sitting position and rubbed the stubble on his jaw.

"God, I needed that." He stretched his arms overhead. "Did you bring anything to eat?"

Delores sat up and reached for her shoes. "I'll

get you something. What would you like? Eggs? A burger? Coffee with two sugars, right?"

Hannah wrinkled her nose. If Delores' voice were any more saccharine, she would be at risk for diabetes. "I brought some fruit and energy bars," she offered.

"That'll be fine," Tony said.

Hannah took an orange and a bottle of water out of the bag and handed them to him. He uncapped the water and drank half the bottle in one swig, then dug a fingernail into the orange's skin. The scent of citrus burst into the air.

"This is great." He chewed on a section of orange, then drank the rest of the water. "Thanks."

Hannah had become fed up with delay. "When you were falling asleep, you said—"

"Shouldn't we be on the way to the hospital?" Delores interrupted. "You might be bleeding internally, or have something broken."

Tony poked around in the grocery bag and pulled out an energy bar. "I need food, not a doctor." He tore open the foil wrapper. "I'm fine."

"Tony, if you don't tell us right now what happened, I'm calling Dresden." Hannah ignored Delores' look of censure. "Who kidnapped you? Did they let you go? *What happened?*"

"Okay, I'll tell you. Let me get comfortable first. My ribs still hurt."

Tony propped the pillows against the headboard and leaned on them. Delores lay next to him on the bed, the tops of her feet pressed against his legs, her fingers on his torn sleeve. Hannah sat in the chair.

"After the three guys grabbed me, we rode to one of the abandoned houses nearby. I got the impression they had been surprised to see Hannah, and were worried that she might try to follow us. We waited there a little while, then they blindfolded me and we started riding again."

Tony paused to take another bite of energy bar.

"This time we went for several hours. When they finally stopped and took off the blindfold, we were somewhere in the desert. The only building around was an old mining shack. Two guys in ski masks came out of the shack, pulled me off the horse, and dragged me inside. They locked me in a room with a loaf of bread, a jar of peanut butter, and some bottles of water. I heard the first three guys ride away, and that was it."

Hannah stared at him. "What do you mean, *that was it?*"

"They just kept me locked in the room—never talked to me, never opened the door."

"Did you recognize any of them?"

Tony shook his head. "No. But I think I know who they're working for."

"Who?"

"That anti-Indian group, the same one that organized the boycott."

"You're saying Control Growth had you kidnapped?" Hannah asked.

"The walls in the shack were pretty thin. I heard Control Growth mentioned a few times. They talked about the Fantasmas Azules and Ge Oidag, too."

Control Growth? The local gang? Dresden had said kidnapping wasn't *White Power* man's style. From what Hannah had seen, she couldn't disagree. But the detective had also doubted that the kidnapping was gang-related.

"I still don't get why someone would want to kidnap you," Delores said.

A funny look came over Tony's face. "I think they were going to kill me."

Delores made a sound in the back of her throat.

"One of the guys had a cell phone. It rang at the same time every day. Whoever answered it would listen for about thirty seconds, then hang up. Afterward he would tell the other guy something like *Not yet* or *We still gotta wait.* But yesterday morning a call came in that got them both got excited. I heard them talking about *picking up a piece* and *doing the Indian*. Wasn't hard to figure out what was going to happen."

Tony rolled the empty water bottle back and forth between his hands. "After that, I heard one of them drive away, and figured it was now or never. I managed to pull one of the slats off the bed frame, and started banging it against the wall. When the guy who had been left behind opened the door to see what was going on, I hit him on the head with the piece of wood and got out of there."

Delores crossed herself. "*Dios mio!*"

"I walked through the desert for a while before I realized I was in that undeveloped area east of town, just this side of the rez. By then I thought the other guy might have come back to the shack and seen what had happened, so I stayed away from the roads and kept walking. When I hit town, there seemed to be a lot of Fantasmas Azules on the streets. They might just have been hanging—you know, usual Friday night stuff—but I was worried that they also might be looking for me. I decided to hide out in an old warehouse until it got dark." Tony looked sheepish. "I must have fallen asleep. When I woke up, I called you." His brown eyes met Hannah's.

"Your turn to rescue me."

The air in the room was cool, but it couldn't compare with the look Delores aimed Hannah's way—it was downright arctic. *You can have him,* Hannah was tempted to say. Instead, she stuck to the more pressing issue.

"You need to tell all this to the police," she said. To her surprise, Delores nodded in agreement.

"It'll look bad if you wait any longer. Hitting that man was self-defense. Anyway, he probably only has a bump on his head. If the Fantasmas Azules were looking for Tony, that means the *cholos* were behind the kidnapping. Bad press on gangbangers won't hurt the tribe."

Delores was beginning to sound like more of an Indian zealot than even Tony. *A ploy to spark his romantic interest?*

"I can't talk to the cops, at least not yet," Tony said.

Both women looked at him—Hannah with impatience, Delores fearful again.

"After I hit that guy, I pulled off his ski mask." Tony rubbed a hand across his chest as though it ached.

"He was very Tohono O'odham. And very dead."

Chapter Twenty-seven

"Impossible!" Delores cried. "No Indian would be involved in something like this. The man had to be Hispanic. You know a lot of them look Native."

"I know what my people look like, Delores. Just like I know not all of them support the casino expansion."

Tony and Delores stared fiercely at each other, and Hannah sensed there was an argument going on between them that she wasn't privy to. *Not my problem*, she reminded herself. Once Dresden was called, she would be in the clear and—

Hannah suddenly realized that Tony didn't know about the murder. "Tony, there's something you should know. About Baptisto." She glanced at Delores to see if she wanted to break the news, but the other woman was staring stonily at the floor.

"He was killed yesterday."

"*What?*"

"Someone shot him and dumped him in a ditch near the rez. They don't know who did it yet."

"The police questioned Hannah," Delores interjected, her tone laced with spite. "Lucky she was with me all afternoon."

Tony looked at Hannah. "*You* were a suspect?"

"Not really. It was just routine," Hannah said, throwing an annoyed glance at Delores.

"This is not good," Tony said. "Not good at all."

Delores let loose with a torrent of Spanish that Tony answered in kind before adding, "In English, please. There's no need to be rude."

Making a face, Delores switched languages. "Without Mr. Baptisto, the numbers won't work!"

Numbers? Was Delores talking about the two sets of projections in Tony's notebook? Maybe now she could find out what was going on. "Tony, I need to ask you about the private placement," Hannah said.

"This isn't really the time." Tony ran a hand through his hair. From his vacant eyes, Hannah could tell that he was still thinking about Baptisto. But she couldn't wait anymore.

"Just tell me the estimated rate of return to the investors."

"Five over prime."

"Are you sure it wasn't closer to half a point over?" Hannah watched him carefully.

He looked puzzled. "Of course not. Why would you think that?"

"I found your notebook."

Hannah heard Delores' sharp intake of breath. Tony shrugged.

"I didn't know it was missing, but that's good to hear. It'll come in handy when you do the deal documents," he said.

"There are two sets of numbers in it. The projections you gave me to use in the offering memorandum, plus another group of figures—one that shows a much lower rate of return."

Tony still appeared unconcerned. "Those were preliminary calculations, compiled before all the information was in."

Hannah paused, taken aback by his calm demeanor. She had expected an apology, perhaps a confession. Had Cooper been mistaken about what the numbers meant? The beginnings of a blush creeping up her neck, she decided to probe a little more.

"I don't see how the two are related. What information were you missing when you ran the first set of numbers?"

"It's a bit complicated," Tony said.

There it was—the too-casual tone, the stiff delivery. *Cooper had been right.* Hannah felt anger of the primal variety flood through her.

"Complicated? Most frauds are pretty simple," she snapped.

Tony's expression was one of outraged innocence. "I would never ask you to do something illegal!"

Unless you thought we wouldn't get caught? Hannah thought as Tony pushed himself off the bed. He reached into the grocery bag and took out the shampoo and razor, along with the change of clothes.

"We'll talk about this later. Right now I need to get cleaned up so we can leave." He walked into the bathroom and turned on the shower.

"You know, that notebook has a lot of confidential stuff in it," he said over the noise of the water. "Maybe we should stop by your place on the way and—"

"I gave it to your partners," Hannah said.

The sound of water abruptly stopped. A shirtless Tony reappeared and advanced on her while a wide-eyed Delores watched from the bed.

"Why did you do that?" he demanded.

"Because the other documents were stolen,

and I thought it was the only way your precious deal could go forward!" She braced herself for his sharp comeback, still feeling her own fury. After the stresses of the past week, part of her was looking forward to unleashing some of it.

But Tony didn't respond. Instead, the *if only* expression flitted across his face—the look that Hannah knew signaled the start of the refrain that hummed in the ears whenever one looked back at the small step taken that had led to comprehensive ruin.

"Well, shit," he finally said, and walked back into the bathroom. A moment later Hannah heard the shower start up again.

"Delores, tell her about the company while I get cleaned up," he called over the rush of sound, and then shut the door.

Mystified, Hannah looked at Delores, who had scooted into a sitting position on the edge of the bed. "You can't tell Peña or Moreno."

"Not tell them *what?*" Feeling her temper spark again, Hannah tried to cool it off with a sip of water from one of the bottles she had brought. *What exactly had Tony done?*

Delores' hands fluttered up to her mouth, as though to catch her words before they escaped.

"About the two sets of numbers."

"Peña and Moreno have the notebook. Don't you think they have already figured it out?"

"*You* didn't," Delores said with a touch of defiance.

But I'm not an expert in finance, like Cooper or Tony's employers. "I can't make any promises," she replied. "Not while I am the attorney on the offering."

Delores' face crumpled. "If you don't keep quiet, the offering will be dead and the casino expansion won't go through!" she wailed.

"Okay, okay—for now everything's confidential, unless it's something the law says I have to disclose."

Delores looked as though she were going to object. Hannah held up her hands.

"It's the best I can do. So spill."

"Tony knew it would be a while before the real estate project was profitable," Delores said, swinging a leg back and forth as she talked. "The first-round money went into Ge Oidag, Mr. Baptisto's company, to buy machinery and stuff like that. The funds raised in the second phase were supposed to pay for constructing the building."

Hannah heard the hesitation in her voice. "But?"

"But then Control Growth began the boycott, and Tony was afraid that not enough white investors would buy units. If the deal failed, Peña & Moreno would go down, too, and Tony didn't want that to happen. So…"

Delores' voice trailed off, and Hannah knew that she was going to regret hearing whatever the other woman said next.

"So Tony made a deal with the Investment Authority. It's the group that oversees the investment of casino profits. Mr. Baptisto's the chairman. The IA agreed to guarantee a minimum return on the project of seven over prime," Delores said.

That explains why Baptisto's development company got the contract to build the shopping center. "Seven over is a pretty phenomenal return."

"That's the point. The IA also agreed to buy any unsold units."

"Wouldn't that defeat your purpose of making the deal look like a success? Property ownership records are public." Comprehension dawned. "Unless the buyer was a shell company owned by another shell company?"

Delores didn't answer, her silence an admission.

Hannah couldn't believe what she was hearing.

"Is the Investment Authority usually in the business of guaranteeing investor returns?"

"It could be, if there was full committee approval. But Tony and Mr. Baptisto didn't think they had the votes. Most of the committee members are tribal elders, and a lot of them don't want the casino to expand. So Mr. Baptisto signed the guarantee in secret—no one else on the committee knows about it. The numbers you saw in Tony's notebook show the estimated shortfall in unit sales and the difference in the rate of return that the IA will have to make good on."

Hannah rubbed the space between her brows. "I need to get back."

Delores looked confused. "Back to where?"

"Back to normal! What were you and Tony thinking? The expected rate of return—the *real* one—is a material fact that has to be disclosed in the offering materials, and so is the guarantee!"

Tony emerged from the bathroom emanating a just-showered aura and the lemony scent of Hannah's shampoo. The hem of Cooper's sweatpants dragged on the carpet, but the crimson t-shirt, shrunken after many washings, fit him reasonably well. Tony pointed at the faded white *H* on the shirt's breast pocket.

"I always wanted to be a Harvard man. How about some fresh air?"

He pushed back the drapes and slid open the window. Outside, a *pasteleria* van was parked on the corner, dispensing coffee and twists of fried dough rolled in powdered sugar to a small crowd of brown-skinned men wearing gardener's overalls.

"Churros!" Tony exclaimed. "Delores, would you be a sweetie and get me some? Coffee, too. Hannah?"

"I'd prefer some answers," Hannah replied.

Tony plopped down on the bed. "What would you like to know?"

"For starters, did it ever occur to you that what you were doing was illegal?"

"I didn't think it was really a problem because of the guarantee—every dollar of investor money was protected. Any payout by the IA would be a drop in the bucket when compared with the casino's revenue stream."

"That's not the point. You could have been indicted and the tribe sued for fraud. Good intentions aren't a defense when it comes to securities law."

"Well, they should be. You live in reality, Hannah, but I'm from a faith-based world. In the Mexican view of life, ability takes a back seat to fate.

All I did was look out for my people—I just didn't let everyone know how I was doing it. You can't seriously think the IA committee wouldn't honor the guarantee after the fact if it were the only way to beat the Control Growth boycott and save the tribe from embarrassment."

"I'm not so sure. Why were you kidnapped and Baptisto murdered?"

"That had nothing to do with the guarantee," Tony declared.

"Oh? What if someone at the Investment Authority found out about the guarantee and thought it was a bad idea? Someone who wants the real estate project and the casino expansion to fail? Killing everyone involved is a pretty effective way to undo the deal."

Tony shook his head. "Killing me and Baptisto wouldn't affect the project. The guarantee's in writing, and only Delores and I know where it is."

"Then someone wants you dead for another reason."

Delores gave a little moan. Tony shot Hannah a look of annoyance, then made a show of patting his stomach. "I could really use those churros and coffee now."

After Delores had left, Hannah took a banana

from the grocery bag and began to eat it. She felt the fatigue radiate off of her, slowing her movements, even her sense of time. If she was this tired, Tony must be running on nerve alone. She didn't know how he did it.

Hannah tossed the empty banana peel into the bag. "I'm withdrawing as counsel for the project unless the guarantee is disclosed in the offering papers."

"It's moot," Tony said, becoming subdued. "Without Baptisto, there's no one to run the development company. We won't be able to find a replacement CEO before the second phase is supposed to close. Ge Oidag will have to be liquidated and the assets distributed to the investors. At least any shortfall will be covered by the guarantee."

Tony sat on the bed, a discouraged look on his face. A moment later, he snapped his fingers. "Nothing says I can't put together another deal!" He sprang to his feet. "I need to talk to Josef de Segura."

"Who?" Hannah asked.

"The vice-chair of the Investment Authority. Actually, I should say chair, now that Baptisto's gone. The guarantee is explicit—it applies to the piece of property where the shopping center will be located. Nothing limits its terms to this particular offering. If we put together another private placement, the provisions on covering shortfall and unsold units would still apply."

"What happened to the Mexican view of life? Accepting your fate and all that?"

Tony's eyes crinkled as he grinned. "My Latin self may believe in destiny, but the Indian half makes me fight until I can fight no more."

He reached for his cowboy boots and pulled them on under the too-long sweatpants. Hannah noticed a spattering of drops on the toe of one boot, dark against the light-tan leather. *Blood?* Not surprising, if he had hit the guard over the head—

Another thought occurred to her. Tony said he had escaped in the morning. Baptisto was dead by the afternoon. Could he possibly have...

Hannah couldn't help thinking how Tony would benefit from Baptisto's death. *A bigger share, if they were running a scam. Someone to take the blame if the guarantee failed. A chance to move up in the tribe hierarchy—*

"What did Delores tell you about Ge Oidag?" Tony asked, interrupting her musings.

"Baptisto's development company? Not much."

"Did she say anything about the money from the first phase?"

Hannah shook her head. "I know from the

documents that the three million dollars was used to fund the company."

"Well, it's gone."

"The three million?"

"Every penny, spent the first nine months. I inventoried the premises, looked at the equipment leases and purchase orders—doesn't even come close to one mil, let alone three. But the corporate account has less than a thousand dollars in it."

"What about company records?"

"Never received them. Baptisto kept promising, but all I ever saw were a few handwritten pages."

"And just exactly when were you going to tell me this? *After* the offering materials went out to investors?"

"I didn't even figure out how much was missing until last week, the day before you got the job. In fact, I was hoping that when you did the due diligence on the second phase, you'd be able to help me trace the funds."

Tony looked thoughtful and, to Hannah, a little sad. "What if the guys who kidnapped me were working for Baptisto? I'm positive the guard I saw was Tohono O'odham."

"Did you ask Delores about this?"

Tony tapped the toe of his boot against the chair leg.

"No. She was Baptisto's assistant—knew everything that went on in his office, handled all the paperwork. I wasn't sure…"

If Delores was involved with the disappearance of the money, too? Hannah thought. "And now?" she asked.

Tony shook his head. "I still don't know."

"We need to talk to Dresden. Do you want to bring Peña or Moreno into the loop? Do they know about the guarantee?"

Tony looked grim. "Not until you gave them that notebook. I'm guessing they're not going to be too happy to hear from me."

Chapter Twenty-eight

Delores returned with a white bag and a covered cardboard cup in a paper tray. Tony took a churro from the bag and hungrily bit into it. The smell of cooking grease filled the room.

"Mmm—real food." The pastry was gone in three bites, and he took out another.

"What do we do now?" Delores asked.

"Talk to de Segura," Tony replied through a mouthful of dough. "Tell him about the guarantee, then get to work on undoing this deal and starting another."

"*After* we talk to Dresden," Hannah said. She waited for an objection from Tony, but he merely popped the lid off his cup and took a long swallow.

"Fine," he said when he was finished drinking. "Let's go."

"I think I'll take a cab home," Delores said. At Hannah's surprised look, she added, "It's been a long night."

Hannah watched her raise up on her toes to kiss Tony good-bye. *Was Delores going home to rest—or to avoid talking to the police?*

After almost an hour of questions, Tony had had enough. He pushed back his chair.

"Detective, I've told you everything I know, several times. It's been a pretty bad three days. I need to go home and catch some sleep."

Everything he knew? Maybe about the kidnapping, but Hannah hadn't heard him say one word about the three million missing from the development company. Arguably, the money had nothing to do with his abduction, but it certainly could be relevant to Baptisto's murder. *Was he protecting the tribe—or Delores?*

Dresden had allowed Hannah to be present at Tony's insistence, even after she had made it clear she wasn't there as his attorney. Hannah thought Tony's lack of candor foolish. It was only a matter of time before the detective got wind of Ge Oidag's financial problems. Once that happened, Delores would come under scrutiny. And it wouldn't be much of a stretch for Dresden to conclude the missing money gave

Tony a motive to kill Baptisto—or have him killed. *Would being held hostage make for a sufficient alibi?*

Hannah and Tony walked out of the police station and to her car. "Do you want me to take you home? Or back to my place, so you can pick up your car?" Hannah leaned against the Subaru and let her eyes briefly close behind her sunglasses. She was exhausted.

"Neither. I called Mr. Moreno from the station and told him we'd come by once we were done here." Tony opened the passenger door. "Do you mind driving? I'm beat."

The sight of Tony rendered Moreno vocally incontinent, his words tumbling out without pause.

"Tony! Are you okay? Have you seen a doctor? No wait, tell me what happened first. My goodness, what are you wearing?"

"Alex, take it easy. I'm fine," Tony said.

Moreno's cheeks were flushed, and a rim of moisture rested on his upper lip. Hannah hoped the excitement wouldn't be too much for his heart.

Even Peña seemed happy to see Tony. "*Bienvenida, hermano,*" he said, following up with a complicated handshake that Hannah assumed was a Hispanic thing.

As Tony launched into a description of his three days in captivity, Hannah's cell phone rang. She moved out of earshot of the others and opened the phone.

"Hello?"

"Hannah? Detective Dresden. Wanted to give you and Mr. Soto some peace of mind. Looks like Baptisto's death was random, a *cholo* mugging gone bad."

"How do you know?"

"According to his secretary, Baptisto always carried a lot of cash, and didn't make a secret of it. His wallet was empty when we found him, and a witness saw a man in a blue jacket accost Baptisto shortly before he was killed. And so you know, Kawarshki alibis out."

Hannah was bewildered. *Kawarshki?* Then she remembered—*White Power* man.

"I have been trying to reach Mr. Soto, but he's not answering his cell phone. Do you have an alternative number?"

"He's here with me. I'll tell him."

"Thank you." Dresden hung up.

Hannah drifted back toward the others, thinking about what the detective had said. *A random mugging?*

"You were so fortunate that guard fell asleep!"

Moreno was saying as Hannah rejoined the group.

Grasping the meaning of Moreno's remark, Hannah looked at Tony. He met her gaze and subtly patted his chest.

Was Tony saving Moreno's heart from the shock of learning that he had killed the guard? Or the fact the man had been Indian?

Peña didn't say anything. To Hannah, he looked thoughtful—skeptical, too. She wondered if he also saw that his employee bent the truth as needed.

Tony clapped Moreno on the back. "It's like I told you, Alex—some people come into luck, and some are born lucky. Fortune's always been on my side."

Moreno hugged him one more time, then stepped back, a worried look on his face.

"I hate to bring this up, however the clock is ticking. What is going to happen with the real estate offering?"

"Let me tell you about my idea…" Tony outlined his plan, Moreno nodding as he spoke. By the time Tony had finished talking, the general partner's chin was dipping up and down like a bird on the edge of a fountain.

"That's a splendid idea, Anthony!"

A splendid idea? Hannah was astounded. What about the second set of numbers in Tony's notebook?

Could the two general partners have misunderstood what they'd read? Hannah considered saying something, then decided against it. The tribe was her client, not Peña & Moreno. It was Tony's responsibility to come clean with his employers.

Moreno's features furrowed with concern again. "How are we going to cover the three million that has to be paid back to the phase one investors? Liquidating the development company's assets won't bring anything near a hundred cents on the dollar."

Hannah resisted shaking her head. *If you only knew how true that was, your heart would stop for sure.*

"When I put together the first offering, I was concerned about the risk to the firm if the second phase didn't close. So I arranged for insurance to cover any shortfall," Tony said.

Moreno beamed. "Brilliant! Robert, I told you Anthony would have everything handled."

"Indeed." Peña walked to the nearest filing cabinet. Opening a drawer, he took out a familiar object, the embossed letters on its cover catching the light.

"No doubt you'll be needing this. We never had a chance to look at it. Once Baptisto turned up dead, we were certain the deal was, too." He handed Tony the burgundy notebook.

"Glad I'm here to prove you wrong," Tony said as he tucked the notebook under his arm, smiling broadly. Hannah knew that smile. It was the same one on the three-card-monte hustlers in *El Mercado* the moment after the pigeon had guessed which cup the ball was under.

Some people come into luck, and some are born lucky. She hoped she wouldn't be around if Tony's apparent good fortune ever ran out.

"You know, I'm feeling pretty beat." Tony yawned, a gesture Hannah doubted was genuine.

"Of course! We'll continue this later," Moreno said. "So glad you are back safe, Anthony."

Tony could barely control his ebullience as they walked down the stairs to the street. "How great was that? They still don't know about the guarantee!"

"You'll have to tell them, sooner or later."

"So I choose later. By then, I'll have everything worked out." Tony's face shone with enthusiasm. "We should meet with de Segura today. I'll call him from the car."

"Tony, I'm tired…"

"C'mon, Hannah. You know we should get on this."

As much as she wished it weren't so, Hannah knew he was right.

"Okay. Find out if de Segura's free this afternoon," she said.

Maybe it was her exhaustion, but the events that had led her to this point seemed to have taken place in the distant past, instead of just six days ago. More than ever, Hannah regretted taking the OTA job, in no small part because she still wasn't convinced that Tony had told her the whole story. If he played fast and loose with the truth to manage his partners, why not be less than honest with her, too? She unlocked the Subaru, her body so heavy with fatigue, she felt as though she were sleepwalking.

Tony squatted down next to the driver's door so that they were at eye level. "We're on with de Segura at five. First, though, we have to stop by the Ge Oidag offices."

"Why?"

"Because de Segura wants us to bring the original of the guarantee."

"You keep it at the development company? Why not some place like a safe deposit box?"

"I meant to, just never got around to it. I couldn't keep it at the OTA—too much chance someone would find it."

"It's Saturday. How are we going to get in?" As far as Hannah was concerned, she had done enough breaking and entering.

"Delores has a set of keys. I already called her. She'll meet us there at four thirty."

Hannah looked at her watch. It wasn't even noon yet. "So am I taking you home?"

"I need to get some papers from my office for de Segura. Why don't I catch a cab to the OTA? You can pick me up there around four and then we'll go meet Delores."

"Fine," Hannah said, too tired to argue.

"Can you lend me a twenty for cab fare? My wallet is still in my car."

Hannah shed her clothes as soon as she was inside her condo, dropping them in a pile next to the ones she'd worn to climb into the hospital. She stepped into the shower and turned the water as hot as she could stand it, letting it melt the tension in her neck and shoulders. Then she twisted the control to the cool setting, the iciness cascading over her until her teeth were chattering.

Relaxed but revived, Hannah wrapped herself in a towel and went foraging in the pantry. A box of cheddar bunnies and her cell phone in hand, she curled up on the sofa.

After eating a handful of crackers, she rang Cooper's cell. The voicemail came on immediately.

"It's me," she said after the beep. "Sorry I haven't called. It's been a crazy day—and night. You won't believe—"

Cooper's voice came on the line. "Hannah? I was on another call. Where have you been?"

"Things at work got a little…crazy. But don't worry, everything's okay."

"Where are you? What happened?"

Hannah hesitated, tempted to tell him about Elizabeth's medical records. With his computer skills and connections, Cooper could probably find out the particulars of the court proceeding, maybe even locate a clean copy of the blood tests.

No, she decided. When she had sought his assistance deciphering the notebook, Tony's life was at risk and time was of the essence. This was different. Her quest for her parents was pulling Hannah back into the past, at the expense of her future with Cooper. It wouldn't be right to ask him for help.

"Can we catch up later? I'm fine but I'm really tired."

"Call when you wake up, no matter what time

it is. Glad you're okay. Sleep well."

"Thanks. I love you."

Hannah hung up before realizing what she had said. She opened the phone to call Cooper back, then paused. *What was she going to say?*

About that I love you—*well, I might have meant it. And I might not have. I'll get back to you when I know, after I sort out some other stuff in my life first.*

Hannah closed the phone, then pressed the heels of her hands to her head and groaned. Elizabeth, Richard, Shelby, her birth father, Tony—somehow she had invited all these people into her life, and now their presence only made more acute the absence she felt. It wasn't the type that could be filled by a lover or family, but a gap in her identity.

Don't be afraid to climb. Lucky number is one.

Hannah glanced at her watch. She had three hours until she was supposed to pick up Tony. Brushing cracker crumbs off her lap, she opened her phone again. Scrolling through the listings under the letter D, Hannah chose the entry for his home number and tapped the green *Call* button.

Richard answered on the third ring.

"This is Hannah. We need to talk."

Chapter Twenty-nine

The turrets of the Mission-style house stood starkly against the wide swath of unsheltering sky. Bees buzzed among the cactus flowers edging the portico, and the air was pungent with sage. Purse clutched under her arm, Hannah rang the doorbell.

The wooden door swung inward, revealing a housekeeper dressed in black pants and a white shirt. Hannah couldn't remember her name, but then she only visited Richard's home a few times a year, usually for business parties.

"Good afternoon, Ms. Dain. Please come with me."

The interior of the house was cool and shadowed, filled with heavy furniture and muted colors. The housekeeper led Hannah through tall-ceilinged rooms to a patio off the kitchen where a wrought iron table and four chairs clustered under an umbrella. Two glasses and a sweating pitcher of orange juice were on a tray in the center of the table.

"Mr. Dain will be with you shortly," the house-keeper said, and went back into the house.

Hannah sat in one of the chairs. The paint was flaking off the tabletop, and she picked at a loose piece with her fingernail, stopping only when the door to the house opened again.

Richard walked onto the patio. "Hello, Hannah."

Even though it was the weekend, he looked immaculate—blue chinos and a crisply ironed white shirt topped with a yellow cashmere sweater tied with perfect symmetry around his shoulders. Hannah briefly regretted her choice of battered jeans and a shrunken polo shirt, then thought of the photo in his office. *I'm a long way from lace-collared dresses and flower barrettes.*

Richard took a seat and poured a glass of orange juice. By habit, Hannah eased her chair back from the table a bit. Whenever he came into a space, it always felt smaller to her.

"Would you like some juice?" he asked.

"No thanks." Hannah unzipped her purse, took out the copy of the court order, and handed it to him. "What I want is Elizabeth's medical records. *All* of them."

Richard's body tensed, as though he were ready to fight off something. He set down the glass of juice without drinking any.

"Where did you get this?"

"I broke into the records room at the hospital and stole it."

"Hannah, you're a licensed attorney. What if you'd been caught?"

"I'm sure you'd take care of it. After all, you're great at covering up things." Hannah heard the harshness in her voice but didn't care. "I want to know what's in that file. Starting with my father's name."

Richard leaned back in his chair and passed a hand over his face. For the first time Hannah saw his largeness wasn't just a product of his bulk, but also his energy, his voice, his volatility. Without them, he was human-sized.

With effort, he got up from the table. "I'm sorry this day is here." He walked into the house.

Was he retrieving the uncensored records? Or shutting her out—permanently? Hannah swallowed, her mouth suddenly dry.

A minute went by, then five, then ten. She debated whether to go after Richard or just leave. After fifteen minutes, Hannah snatched the order from the table. *Privacy be damned—I'm going to court.*

She jumped to her feet, bumping her hip against the table. Some of Richard's untouched orange juice sloshed onto the tray. Hannah grabbed the glass and drained it, the petty act of rudeness not doing much to make her feel better. She was wiping the stickiness from her mouth with the back of her hand when Richard walked onto the patio. He was carrying a large envelope.

"This should answer your questions."

Hannah took the envelope, holding it as though it might explode, and sank back into her chair.

The envelope once had been sealed, but over time the adhesive had lost its stickiness. Hannah lifted the flap and pulled out two sheets of paper.

The top one was a copy of Elizabeth Dain's blood test, minus any redacting. The entry under *Notes* was brief: *No sickle cells observed.*

Sickle cells?

She looked at the second page. Another blood test, again without any information blacked out. Hannah saw the notation *Patient is male parent of Baby Dain* and breathed deep into her chest. Her eyes went to the name printed across the top.

Moore, Tel. CBC w/DIFF.

A date of birth was listed, but the space for a Social Security number was blank. Next to *Address* was printed *East 72nd Street, NYC*, followed by a phone number. The *Notes* were brief: *Family history of sickle cell trait and sickle cell disease. Results: Numerous sickled RBCs seen. Diagnosis: Sickle Trait.*

Tel Moore was her birth father. And according to the blood test results, he carried the gene for sickle cell anemia.

Hannah's hand shook, rattling the paper. Although her knowledge on the subject had been gleaned from public service commercials and college science, she was pretty certain that it was accurate. *Sickle cell anemia was an African-American disease.* Confused, she looked up to find Richard watching her.

"I—I don't understand."

"If you were born today, your hemoglobin would be tested for the presence of the sickle cell gene. Thirty years ago, the only way to detect either the trait or the gene was by looking at a drop of your blood under a microscope. Both sickle cell anemia and the trait would show sickled cells—cells shaped like sickles or crescent moons, rather than round. A few sickled cells meant you had the gene. The presence of a lot meant you had the disease."

"I'm not talking about the test!" Hannah thrust the documents at him. "Does this mean I'm half-black?"

Richard's face was impassive. "I don't know."

"When you saw this, didn't you wonder?"

"It didn't matter. You were my daughter and I was going to take care of you."

"So how long was it before you changed your mind?"

Anguish welled up in Hannah. She raked a hand through her hair—wavy brown hair that, like her olive skin and dark eyes, she had been led to believe was the legacy of her mother's Italian background. *More lies.* She jerked her hand away. No wonder Richard had gotten the court order. How would he explain a biracial daughter to law firm clients, or the committee that recommended candidates for the federal bench?

"I know this may be hard to understand, but I sealed those records to protect you."

"Don't you mean to protect yourself?"

"Living with Elizabeth's betrayals was very… difficult. I didn't want you to have that burden, too. Perhaps it was a mistake not to tell you the truth."

Hannah could barely speak. "A *mistake?* I think the word you're looking for is *racist.*" Clutching the test results and the envelope, she rushed from the patio.

Hannah sped along the road that led north of town with the windows down, wanting to feel the wind against her face. The sign for the rock-climbing park loomed into view and impulsively she twisted the wheel. Spitting gravel, the Subaru raced up the gravel road. Barely slowing to fling a dollar bill at the gate attendant, Hannah pulled into the first empty canyon she could find and parked.

The ticking noise the engine made as it cooled mingled with the hum of insects through the open window. Vermillion cliffs threw claret shadows onto the desert floor as Hannah took out the test results and read them again.

Tel Moore. A name that might be incomplete or fake. A DOB and three-decades-old address and phone number, all of which could be phony, too. No SSN, no photo. Even aided by the wide reach of the Internet, it wasn't much to go on.

Hannah slumped in her seat, exhausted. She knew she should go home and rest, restore her depleted psyche. But when she opened the envelope to put away the papers, she glimpsed another document inside. With shaking fingers, she pulled it out.

Several typed sheets were stapled together. The top page was labeled *Trial Memorandum*, and bore the case caption for a New York civil action filed over twenty years ago. Hannah quickly skimmed its contents, finding *Tel Moore* listed under the section entitled *Defendant's Witnesses: Experts*. She didn't recognize any other names until she came to the last page, where *Counsel for Plaintiffs* was listed as Elizabeth Shelby Dain.

Her mother had slept with a witness for the other side?

Hannah checked the memorandum for the date that trial was scheduled to begin, then counted back from her birthday. There was only the slimmest of possibilities that Elizabeth had waited until after the trial was over to begin the affair.

Her overwhelmed mind tried to sort through the implications. Was sleeping with the defendant's expert an unethical trial tactic or simply to spite Richard? Was that why Elizabeth had chosen an African-American lover? Perhaps not used birth control?

The possibility of such calculated cruelty made Hannah realize that she had had enough. Enough unraveling of small and not so small secrets and lies, enough discoveries of hidden motives and private weaknesses. Hannah wanted to find her birth father, but not if it meant going down a road paved with malice and revenge, unhappiness and bad memories.

She would let someone else do it—hire a professional to slog through the muck and find Tel Moore. Let him spend the time on the search engines, let him track down witnesses from a trial thirty years ago, let him write/phone/email all the Moores in New York City or wherever the trail led.

And let him talk to Tel Moore. If Moore wanted to meet Hannah, fine. If he didn't, she would consider that aspect of her life closed. Hannah couldn't take any more painful revelations—or rejections.

Her cell phone rang. Hannah checked the Caller ID to make sure it wasn't Richard. *OTA* came up on the screen.

Tony! She had forgotten about picking him up. The dashboard clock read *4:05*. Opening the phone, she started the car.

"I'm on my way," she said and hung up. The phone rang again but Hannah ignored it.

How was she going to find a suitable PI? She didn't want to randomly choose a name off the Internet. But asking Cooper or even Tony for a reference would raise questions that she wasn't ready to answer. Maybe Dresden would know—

An idea popped into her head. *Last Monday at the hospital.* Hannah pulled over to the shoulder, threw the car into neutral, and took out her cell phone again. After finding the listing in her cell phone book, she hit the *Call* button, hoping he had forgotten about Borneo.

"You've reached the voicemail of—"

Hannah chewed on her lip as she waited for the greeting to finish playing. Why didn't people just say something like *Talk* or *Speak* so it wouldn't take so long to get to the beep?

"Hi Joe, this is Hannah Dain. Would you please call me with the name and number of that P.I., the guy who was with you at the hospital? Thanks." She rattled off her phone number and hung up. Shifting into first, she drove the car back onto the road again.

Unburying the past has its price. But then, so does ignoring it. Hannah pressed down on the gas pedal, thinking not for the first time that perhaps it would have been best to have never known it at all.

Chapter Thirty

Tony was waiting outside when Hannah pulled up to the OTA offices. She barely had a chance to brake before his hand was on the door handle.

He settled into the passenger seat. "Well, you obviously aren't late because you were sleeping. Check out those bags."

Hannah glanced in the rearview mirror at the black shadows under her eyes. She looked like a linebacker on game day.

"Something came up. Where are we going again?"

"Ge Oidag's offices. Get on the road to downtown. They're near *El Mercado*."

"They aren't on the rez?"

"Town is closer to the construction site. And Baptisto didn't want the workers picking up their paychecks near the casino. Looks bad to pay people and then have them lose their wages at the tables."

The *El Mercado* sidewalks were more crowded than usual. Tourists, generic in baseball hats and shorts, mingled with big-buckled cowboys and strutting Hispanics, the latter's hair as shiny as their patent-leather shoes. Mexican flags decorated nearly every storefront, while red, green, and white streamers hung from trees and lampposts. Somewhere a mariachi band played.

"What's going on?" Hannah asked, braking for a jaywalker in an oversized sombrero.

"Mexican Independence Day." Tony powered down his window and rested his elbow on the sill, obviously enjoying himself. "It's officially the sixteenth, but the parade and the rodeo are always held on the weekend." He pointed to a spot being vacated by a pickup with naked-lady mud flaps. "You should park here. The office is only a few blocks away."

Hannah jockeyed the Subaru into the space, and she and Tony joined the throng on the sidewalk.

"Check it out!" Tony bounded up to a food stall on the sidewalk. Behind the flour-dusted counter, a woman with high cheekbones and skin the color of reddish earth packed a handful of *masa* into a cornhusk, then topped it with chile sauce and shredded meat.

"Want a tamale? It's an Independence Day tradition."

Hannah was about to refuse when she caught a whiff of sweet roasted corn. Her stomach rumbled and she realized she was famished. Except for the orange juice at Richard's, she hadn't eaten since dinner last night.

"Chile please—*sin queso o carne.*"

"Vegetarian it is. Green chile or red?"

Hannah's stomach growled again. "One of each."

They ate as they walked, the neighborhood changing from shops and restaurants to two-story office complexes that stood mostly empty on the weekends. Although cars of parade-goers lined the streets, there weren't a lot people around. Hannah tossed most of her second tamale into a trash can. The corn and beans were making her feel sleepier.

They rounded the corner, and Hannah spied Delores halfway up the block. She was slumped against the side of a building, head down, arms wrapped around herself as though she were in pain.

"Tony—look!" Hannah cried, but he was already running.

They sprinted down the sidewalk, Tony's cowboy boots beating a tattoo on the concrete. Reaching Delores first, Tony crouched in front of her. Hannah stood alongside, gulping mouthfuls of air and hoping the tamales she had consumed would stay down.

"*Chica*, are you okay?"

Delores lifted a tear-stained face. "There were two men…" She began to weep.

Hannah curved an arm around the other woman's shoulders. "Did they hurt you?" she asked softly.

Delores choked back a sob. "No, I'm okay. They were coming down the stairs when I was unlocking the front door. They pushed past me and ran down the street. I went up to the office and—" Delores covered her face with her hands. "Oh Tony, it's gone!"

"*What's* gone?"

Hannah was surprised at the sharpness in his tone. "Let's get you inside," she said to Delores, helping her to her feet and into the lobby.

Tony took the stairs two at a time, Hannah following more slowly with Delores. At the top of the stairs were several doors. The one marked *Ge Oidag Construction* stood ajar. Tony pushed it open the rest of the way.

A supporting arm around Delores, Hannah stood inside the doorway and stared. The room had been thoroughly ransacked—drawers pulled out, furniture overturned, architectural drawings ripped to shreds. The only item left intact appeared to be a sketch of the Tohono O'odham Man in the Maze.

With a muttered curse, Tony dropped to one knee next to what once had been a model of the proposed project. The roof had been torn off and walls flattened. Miniature trees and miniature cars were scattered across the carpet.

"I don't know how they knew it was there! I didn't tell anybody!"

The anguish in Delores' voice pulled Hannah out of her spectator state. "What are you talking about?"

Tony set down a miniature lamppost he had been fingering and got to his feet.

"The guarantee. Delores hid it in the presentation model. Those guys probably found it by accident when they were smashing things."

Or maybe the vandalism was the result of searching for the guarantee. Hannah looked at the Man-in-the-Maze painting, untouched in its frame. *Baptisto's murder, Tony's kidnapping, and now the theft of the guarantee—the work of a tribe member opposed to casino expansion?*

"Delores, did you get a good look at the two men?" she asked.

"Not really. I was trying to fit my key into the front door when they barged by me. Dark hair, dark skin, maybe dark baseball hats. That's all I remember."

"What were they were wearing?"

Delores screwed up her face. "Jeans…long-sleeved shirts. Blue, I think."

Cholos—*or Indians dressed up like to look like them?* Hannah wondered.

"Tony, if they took the guarantee, what are we going to do?" Delores' voice quavered, and her eyes began to fill again.

The other woman's weepiness was starting to get on Hannah's nerves. "Look, I'm sorry the office was trashed, and that those men scared Delores, but what's the problem? You have a copy of the guarantee somewhere else, right?"

The edges of Tony's mouth went slack. "It's not so simple. De Segura's a traditionalist. That means he follows tribal law. Unless we have the original document signed by Baptisto, the committee won't honor the agreement."

"That's absurd!"

"Maybe so, but it's the rez, and I'm half-Indian."

As though that explained anything, Hannah thought, knowing it would be futile to argue the point.

Delores righted a chair and sat with her shoulders bowed, weighed down by the cloak of misery that had wrapped itself around her. Tony rocked back on the heels of his cowboy boots, his brow furrowed in thought.

"We need to call the police," Hannah said. "There might be fingerprints or other evidence that will tie whoever did this to the kidnapping or Baptisto's murder."

Tony barked out a laugh. "Don't hold your breath. You can bet those two guys are long gone. And whoever they're working for is counting his three mil, glad he doesn't have to cut Baptisto in for a share."

Delores raised her head. "What are you talking about?"

"This." Tony indicated the room with a sweep of his hand. "It's worth nothing. Ge Oidag is broke—the three million is gone. Without the guarantee, the first phase investors are going to be lucky to see a penny for every dollar they put in."

"And you think Mr. Baptisto had something to do with taking the money?" Delores said, the usual musicality of her voice replaced by a stilted cadence.

Tony pinned her with his gaze. "You sound surprised. I was pretty sure you knew all about it."

Delores sprang out of her chair and cracked Tony across the face with her open palm.

"How dare you! I would never do anything to hurt the tribe!" She raised her hand to strike him again, but Hannah grabbed her wrist.

"Stop it! If the guarantee's gone, the only thing left to do is find out where the money went. Delores, who had access to Ge Oidag's accounts?"

"Only Mr. Baptisto could sign checks," Delores said, glaring at Tony. Gone was the puffy, just-cried look, Hannah noticed.

"So we begin with the bank records and work backward to find out where the money went." Hannah looked at Tony. "Have you already asked for those documents?"

He shook his head. "The account is with the Tohono O'odham Nations Bank, OTA branch. I knew the gossip would start the moment I made the request."

"If I ask for the records, it'll raise less attention," Delores said.

"And I'll talk to de Segura." Tony had regained some of his usual optimism. "Maybe I can persuade him to honor the guarantee without the original. I've got a scan in my computer. If we leave now, I can probably still make our meeting this afternoon."

"And I can get to the bank before it closes. The rez branch stays open until six on Saturdays," Delores said.

"What about the police?" Hannah asked.

"Waiting around for the cops will be a waste of time. Delores didn't get a good look at the two men, and you and I didn't see them at all. Like you said, it's fingerprints and the other *CSI* stuff that's important, and that's nothing we can help with. We'll shut the door and call them from the car."

Tony shepherded them out of the room. As she followed the others down the stairs, Hannah grew more irritated with each step. Delores' role as victim was becoming irksome, and she was fed up with Tony, too—his half-truths, his empty flirting, his zeal for the tribe at the expense of everything else. She was also tired of giving in to Tony's reckless disregard for the rules.

"Where's your car?" she asked Delores once the three of them were on the sidewalk.

"Up that way, about four blocks."

"You guys can go to the OTA and the bank if you want. I'm calling Dresden, and I'm staying here until he comes."

Tony spread his hands. "Suit yourself. I'll let you know how it goes." He and Delores started walking up the sidewalk.

After going back into the building lobby to get out of the sun, Hannah took out her phone and tapped in Dresden's number. She was still waiting for the call to go through when the lowrider cruised past.

Windows tinted black, chassis inches off the ground, the car virtually growled along the asphalt. Chrome spinner wheels spattered droplets of light across its gleaming cobalt paint.

Something registered in Hannah's subconscious.

Blue. The car was dark blue.

A sharp sensation of fear rose up from her gut. She dashed out the door, shouting at Tony and Delores, but they were too far away to hear her. Transfixed, she watched the car close in on the two pedestrians.

The scene became more auditory than visual— four percussive *pops* in rapid succession, the roar of a car engine followed by a squeal of rubber, a strangled scream.

It was the scream that propelled Hannah into motion. Breath rasping, she sprinted toward the two bodies crumpled on the sidewalk.

Delores' thin arm lay outstretched, the wrist

exposed. Fighting nausea, Hannah made herself lean over and press the blue-veined skin for a pulse. There wasn't one.

Next to Delores, Tony was lying face-up on the sidewalk, his eyes open but unseeing. He looked as though he were sleeping, except for the two jagged holes in his chest that were leaking red and staining his shirt.

"No. Oh no," Hannah whispered.

She dropped to the ground, her eyes slightly out of focus and her balance uncertain, as though her body wanted to blur the scene before her. Even though she knew he was past caring, Hannah gently lifted Tony's head into her lap and cradled it.

As sirens started wailing from somewhere, the last of her self-control dissipated into the warm air, and Hannah began to sob. She stayed like that, hunched weeping over his body, until a paramedic's blunt fingers grasped her shoulders and half lifted, half dragged her away.

Chapter Thirty-one

Tuesday, September 22

Tony had been laid to rest two days after he died in a traditional Tohono O'odham burial ceremony. Although Michael Chiago had said she would be welcome, Hannah didn't attend.

"We bury our people with the things that were the most important to them, along with enough food and water for the four-day journey to the East," Chiago had explained. "It's quite a send-off—lots of wailing and carrying on. Instead of wearing black, mourners cut their hair."

"I think I'll pass," Hannah had said.

For someone she had known only a short while, Tony had managed to take up a lot of room in Hannah's life. His death had created a vacuum, and Hannah thought attending his funeral would only make his absence seem larger. She didn't know how long it would take for things to rearrange themselves to fill up the space he had occupied. Or, if Chiago were to be believed, whether Tony would ever truly be gone.

"Part of the reason we make a big deal out of saying good-bye is so the deceased stays in the afterworld, and doesn't come back to haunt us. According to the elders, you shouldn't even think about a dead person, because you might conjure up his ghost," he had said.

Hannah hadn't called Chiago to talk about Tony. It was another ghost she sought.

"I want to hire you to find someone. Here's what I know…"

Later that evening when Cooper was asleep, Hannah had slipped out of bed and gone into the bathroom. Using a pair of nail scissors, she had snipped off a piece of hair from the nape of her neck, then wrapped the strands around the slot machine token Tony had given her during their night at the casino. She had buried the token in the pot of dirt on the windowsill where her crocuses hibernated, waiting for spring.

"Go and never come back," Hannah had whispered, repeating the mourner's admonition Chiago had told her. Turning off the light, she had returned to bed, where sleep continued to elude her.

Now, a scant eight hours later, she steered the Subaru into the casino parking lot. De Segura's message on her voicemail earlier that morning had been brief but polite.

"Ms. Dain, I know this is a difficult time, but the real estate project requires immediate attention. Three million dollars must be refunded to the first phase investors, and your assistance would be most appreciated."

Hannah opened her car door, feeling the orange heat push against what the calendar proclaimed was the second day of fall. A monarch butterfly fluttered by, a shard of stained glass against the blue sky. Sunglasses in place, she walked briskly across the asphalt to the OTA building.

"Boss!" Clementine jumped up from her chair to envelop Hannah in a hug. The mushroom-shaped buttons on her secretary's sweater pressed painfully into Hannah's midsection. "What are you doing here?"

"De Segura asked me to come in," Hannah replied once she had her breath back.

"That's ridiculous! And aren't you supposed to be under some sort of police protection?"

"The sheriff's department is stretched to the limit, investigating…" Hannah's voice trailed off.

Seeing Clementine's sympathetic look, she added in what she hoped was a matter-of-fact tone, "It's not like someone couldn't get to me if they really wanted to."

"Even Cain evaded surveillance more potent than the cops to off his pain-in-the-ass brother," said the by-now-familiar voice.

"Zel!" Clementine frowned at the reporter, who had sauntered out of the coffee room.

"Hello, Mr. Kassif." Hannah wasn't that surprised to see him. Tony and Delores' deaths were front-page news. But that didn't mean she was ready to talk to the press.

"I'm not really in the mood to answer questions right now."

"Good, because I'm not asking any."

Hannah shot him a disbelieving look.

"Another reporter's covering the murders. I'm here to pick up Clementine for an early lunch."

Hannah's secretary smoothed the front of her skirt. Today's choice featured tiers of bright colors edged with contrasting ruffles.

"I didn't think you'd be in today, Boss, so I thought it would be okay if I…"

Hannah waved a hand. "Go ahead."

Clementine turned to Kassif. "I just have to

drop off these papers at Accounting and then we can go." She bustled off, the tops of her nylons making swishy noises.

Hannah regarded the reporter with something approaching distaste. Now that the real estate deal was no longer a potential story, Kassif was obviously pulling out all the stops to get the scoop on Clementine's father. Maybe it was the weekend's horrible events, or three nights of non-sleep, but she was sick of subterfuge.

"I know what you're doing," she said.

"Sorry?"

"You know what I'm talking about—dating Clementine just to get the story on her family."

Kassif looked confused. "What story?"

"You want me to believe the only reason you're here is because you like Clementine?"

"She's a better cook than my mother, loves watching horror movies, and drives a muscle car. What's not to like?"

Studying his guileless expression, Hannah began to wonder whether Kassif was telling the truth.

"Nothing," she mumbled as her secretary reappeared.

Clementine looked from Kassif to Hannah. "What are you guys talking about?"

Kassif helped her into her jacket, an orange number that clashed horribly with his paisley shirt. "The new vegetarian restaurant north of town. Hannah wasn't sure you'd like it."

Clementine slipped her arm through his. "I don't have a problem with vegetarians. They're all I eat."

"Have a good time," Hannah said faintly.

She retreated to her office, feeling terrible. Assuming Kassif wouldn't be romantically interested in Clementine because of her size was exactly the type of thinking Hannah abhorred in others. Just days ago she had scoffed at Baptisto's claim that all Indians helped each other. *So much for my intuition—or would that be intelligence?*

A dozen cartons had been stacked next to Hannah's desk. De Segura had arranged for the documents to be collected from the Ge Oidag office so that Hannah could inventory the company's assets and arrange for their sale. She hadn't talked to the tribe's new chairman about how the shortfall would be covered. As far as she knew, the original of the guarantee was still missing.

Hannah opened the first carton and started to put the documents back into their original order. It was like trying to organize sand. Even so, after thirty minutes of work Hannah could see how easy it would have been to siphon money from the development company through padded invoices, non-existent suppliers, and similar techniques. But who at Ge Oidag was running the fraud? *Baptisto? Delores? Someone with access to Ge Oidag's computer system?* Hannah thought about the men in blue. No reason they couldn't be *cyber-cholos.*

She rubbed her eyes tiredly. Perhaps the police had come across something that would help her narrow the search for the missing funds. She called Dresden's direct line. He answered after the first ring.

After identifying herself, Hannah said, "The tribe has asked me to sort through Ge Oidag's finances. I was wondering if you had found out anything new on Mr. Baptisto or the company."

"No." Hannah heard the hesitation in his voice. *What wasn't he telling her?*

"Do you know anything more about the kidnapping or the—" She couldn't say the word *murders* yet.

"We think we've located the mining shack where Soto was held captive. Won't know for sure until the fingerprints come back." Dresden paused. "There weren't any signs of a struggle. No broken bed, no body…"

No body? Had Tony's story of his escape been another of his untruths? Or was something else going on? Hannah's tired mind couldn't make sense of it.

"We're still not sure the Soto and Alvarez murders are related to the Baptisto killing. There have been four Las Fantasmas drive-bys in the last six months, and Soto was wearing red clothing in their neighborhood."

Hannah felt an urge to throw up. The Harvard t-shirt had been her choice. She forced a swallow.

"So now what happens?"

"We wait for the lab reports to come back and hope we get lucky with fingerprints or other trace evidence. Beyond that, we don't have much to go on."

Hannah could hear the finality in his tone. If the people working the crime scene came up empty, Dresden would write off Tony and Delores' murders to gang activity.

"Thanks for the update," she said, and hung up.

Why had Tony lied about killing the man in the shack? To protect someone else? A more disquieting thought occurred to her. *What if Tony had told the truth?*

Hannah knew these were questions for the

police to answer, not her. But part of her felt as though Tony were still only missing, and that her obligation to the tribe's project had become a duty to vindicate his name. Survivor's guilt, denial— whatever the reason, she couldn't walk away. At least not until she knew who was responsible for the murders. Maybe then Tony's ghost would let her sleep at night.

Her cell phone rang. It was Alexander Moreno.

"Ms. Dain? I'm sorry to bother you so soon after…" Moreno's voice broke. "Forgive me. I still can't believe he's gone."

Hannah could hear his labored breathing, and wondered how his heart was holding up.

"Me neither," she said gently.

He cleared his throat. "I'm calling about the insurance Tony mentioned. De Segura tells me you're reviewing the Ge Oidag documents. Have you found the policy, or the name of the company that issued it?"

"Not exactly. You see…" She started to explain about the guarantee. Moreno interrupted her.

"You mean Tony's insurance is that deal he cooked up with the chairman?" He gave a little moan. "That detective told us about it. But when I met with de Segura this morning, he said the committee won't honor any guarantee without the original document. And he didn't seem all that unhappy we couldn't produce it."

Just what Tony had been afraid of. Was de Segura one of the elders opposed to the casino expansion? Hannah wondered.

"We can't find even a copy of the guarantee. Do you have one?"

"No. Tony said he had a scan of it on his computer, so you may want to ask the police. I understand they picked up Tony's laptop on Monday."

"They've reviewed the hard drive. It wasn't there." Moreno made another sound of distress. "I don't know what we're going to do! When the investors find out about the two sets of numbers, they'll claim the entire deal was a scam and sue. Because Tony was our employee, Robert and I will be responsible for any judgment against him."

"What about your E&O policy?" Most financial firms carried errors and omission insurance to cover negligence or fraud by their employees.

"We don't have one—there was no point. Under the terms of our fund, a finding of fraud triggers the redemption option. Any limited partner can ask for the return of his investment."

Investors in private equity funds were known

as limited partners, *limited* because they had no authority over investment decisions and their potential loss couldn't exceed the amount they put into the fund. They also were bound by restrictions when it came to cashing out—money was typically tied up for five to ten years. Hannah knew that once the news got out an employee had stolen client assets, investors would liquidate their holdings in the P&M fund like Depression-era depositors during a bank run.

Clearly Moreno knew this, too. "Most of our net worth is tied up in the fund. If it goes under, we'll be left with nothing. That's why we can't risk a judgment for fraud, and why the three million will have to be paid. But without the guarantee, it comes out of our pockets!"

Moreno's voice had lost its modulated tone. "If Tony weren't already dead, I'd be tempted to kill him myself!" He banged down the phone.

Chapter Thirty-two

Clementine strolled into Hannah's office a little after two o'clock.

"Lunch was divine! But never let anyone tell you that rattlesnake meat tastes like chicken. Unless he's talking about a chicken that works out every day and can bench press forty pounds. Snake's about as tough as meat gets."

Clementine set an aluminum-foiled container and plastic utensils on the edge of Hannah's desk. "Here. I knew you'd forget to eat."

Hannah eyed the container suspiciously.

"Don't worry—it's rigatoni with tomato sauce. Not as good as mine, of course."

"Thanks," Hannah said, then cleared her throat. She disliked making apologies almost as much as she hated receiving them.

"Clementine, I'm sorry I looked in Kassif's notebook, and that I told you what it said. I was just—"

"Looking out for me. And I appreciate it. But you don't have anything to worry about. I'm a big girl"—Clementine cracked a grin—"in more ways than one. Besides, I showed Zel my Corsican vendetta. He knows I can take care of myself."

"You showed him your what?"

Clementine opened her purse and extracted a leather sheath from which she pulled a triangular blade about four inches long. Hannah gaped at the knife.

"It was my brother Enzo's. He gave it to me when I moved to Arizona. Under the vendetta code, if someone disrespects you, they get three choices: *schioppo*, *stiletto*, or *strada*. The gun, the knife, or the street, which means they leave." Clementine held up the blade so it caught the light. "Look, it's engraved. *Che la mia ferita sia mortale.* May the wound be fatal."

Kassif is the one I should be worrying about, Hannah said to herself.

Clementine re-sheathed the weapon. "You know what I think?"

"I try not to."

"I think you should go somewhere with Cooper. I know some incredibly bad things happened this year, but it's time for you to move on. We're done here. Why not take a few weeks off?"

It was time for her to move on? Hannah nearly laughed. If Clementine only knew.

"I have some other stuff to take care of." *Like find my father and figure out who's responsible for killing Tony.*

"Are you sure it's more important than spending time with the guy you're crazy in love with? Remember, I'm the woman who had to watch you pant after him for two years."

Hannah flushed. "And this is your business because…"

"Friends don't let friends live stupid. Just like you making sure Zel was the real deal."

"Are we done here?"

"Not yet." Clementine pulled out two message slips from her pocket. "This guy's called twice to set up a lunch appointment. Who is he?"

Hannah squinted at the name on the pieces of paper. *Osborne Hepworth.* It took her a moment to remember who he was. *The immigration lawyer.* Why would he want to have lunch with her? With a pending indictment, maybe he was looking for a referral to a criminal attorney. More likely, Hepworth had heard about Tony and wanted gossip on the murders, or information on the status of Peña & Moreno. No matter—after his fraudulent visa proposal, he was someone she intended to steer clear of.

"I don't want to see him." Seeing Clementine's questioning look, she added, "Trust me, he's trouble."

"You're the boss—I just run things. Speaking of which, I sent flowers to Delores' memorial service yesterday. Signed your name on the card."

Hannah felt a prickle of shame. Three people had died, but only Tony's murder was uppermost in her thoughts.

"Thanks. Was it local? I haven't been reading the newspaper lately."

Clementine shook her head. "LA. One of the receptionists told me her dad owns a supermarket chain and is big in SoCal politics."

"Delores' family is wealthy?" *Hadn't she said otherwise during their dinner together?*

"Buckets of money."

Why would Delores lie about being poor? To fit in with her fellow activists? To avoid the burdens associated with a well-known last name? Hannah could certainly sympathize with the latter.

Her cell phone rang, and Hannah checked the Caller ID. When she saw the name on the screen, she opened the phone so quickly, the hinge on the cover almost broke.

"This is Hannah. Would you hold for a moment?"

She depressed the *Mute* button and looked at Clementine. "I've got this."

Clementine feigned ignorance. "Okay."

Hannah pointed at the door. With an exaggerated pout, Clementine turned on her heel and left.

Once she was alone, Hannah raised the phone back to her ear.

"Go ahead, Mr. Chiago." She listened, a look of wonder spreading over her face. "*You have?*"

The PI had located Tel Moore. Something fluttered in Hannah's chest as she kept listening.

"Yes, your first contact must still be in person." she said. "No phone calls or emails first. It doesn't matter where he is—I'll cover your expenses to get there."

Hannah figured Chiago would have a better chance of realizing a mistake or unmasking an imposter if his initial encounter with Moore were face-to-face. And while she wouldn't admit it to anyone, part of Hannah feared her father would run once he heard that a daughter was searching for him.

"Don't call until after you've talked to him."

Hannah didn't want to have her expectations raised by what would turn out to be reports on missed connections or wrong addresses.

Chiago rang off. Feeling unexpectedly dizzy, Hannah steadied herself in the chair. *I need more sleep. And food.*

Peeling back a corner of the foil container from Clementine, Hannah forked up a clump of pasta. It was cold, but she wasn't eating for pleasure. After swallowing another mouthful, she picked up her cell phone and hit the first number on her speed dial. The voicemail came on.

"Hey, it's me. Hope you're coming over tonight. There's something I need to tell you."

Hannah sat on the sofa with her feet tucked under her. She had traded her work clothes for a pair of gray sweats and a ratty t-shirt from a bike race held two years ago. The glass of red wine beside her was half full, premium stuff from California. Hannah didn't imbibe that often. When she did, she was considerate of her palate.

Cooper lay on the floor, his head propped against the wall, hands folded across his stomach. He wore a frayed polo shirt over a pair of cargo shorts. Next to him was an empty bottle of beer and a plate with some bits of egg left on it.

"So I told Chiago not to call until after he talks with him face-to-face," Hannah said.

"Are you sure you want to do this? After what you've gone through with Richard and Shelby—"

"I'm sure. I used to think it was my fault things weren't right between me and them. Now I know that whatever I do, we'll never be close."

"I'm not so sure about that. Blood or not, nobody's family is as connected as it could be."

Hannah felt the weight of her hope pressing down on her shoulders. "This gives me another chance. I can't not take it."

"If you want company for the meeting, I'm happy to be there."

Hannah smiled at him. "Thanks, but I think I'll go solo." She wanted this to be a personal quest—or, failing that, an impersonal one. If she had to face rejection again, Hannah wanted to do it privately, or at least in the presence of strangers.

"You seem to be doing that a lot lately."

So he *had* noticed her aloofness. Hannah was about to respond when he nodded at the plate next to him.

"By the way, those were decent scrambled eggs.

You may become a cook yet."

Hannah poked him in the side with her foot. "That was supposed to be an omelet, thank you very much."

Cooper grabbed her ankle and held on to it, then began to rub his thumbs in slow circles on the bottom of her foot. Watching him, Hannah suddenly felt as lonely as she ever had. Perhaps it was the bleakness of the condo. Rooms denuded of furniture and art-empty walls, the abode of someone who was neither here nor there. Or maybe it was because Cooper so indisputably lived in the present, while she was mired in the past. At any rate, the expanse between them had never seemed greater.

And it was into that gap that she had dropped *I love you.* Hannah knew she had to retrieve it, to have for when the time was right to put it out there again.

"There's something else we need to talk about. What I said on the phone over the weekend… It's not that I don't… I mean, I was really tired, and…"

"Your words got ahead of your heart?"

Hannah looked into his clear green eyes and saw the faith behind them. "Actually, it's my brain—it's too full up there. Sometimes things get pushed out before they're supposed to."

Cooper laughed, releasing her foot, then picked up their dishes and carried them to the kitchen. He turned on the tap and raised his voice over the sound of the water.

"So the police are nowhere on any of the murders."

Hannah had told him about her conversations with Dresden. "Looks that way."

"Where are you with your Indian job?"

Hannah let her head drop back against the sofa cushion and looked up at the ceiling. "Your guess is as good as mine. They want me to unravel the first phase—oversee refunds to the investors, maybe put the development company into bankruptcy. I don't know what the council is going to decide to do about the guarantee."

"How long will that take? A week? A month?"

Hannah understood what he was really asking. *When are you going to quit so you can look for a real job?*

"I don't know," she said.

I don't know how to explain that Tony is one of those things taking up space in my head. He's not alive, yet he's not really dead, either. He's someplace in-between, trying to find his way like the Man in the Maze. And I have to help him.

Cooper came back into the living room and lay down on the floor again. "I can't believe Baptisto and Soto thought they'd get away with it. I take that back—Baptisto might be that dumb. But Soto? The guy was with a top investment bank in LA. He knows what the securities laws say about disclosure."

"It wasn't like Tony was benefiting personally." Now that he was gone, Hannah couldn't bring herself to call him *Mr. Soto* anymore. "He didn't do anything wrong, other than keep the guarantee secret from the investors and his employers."

"Isn't that enough? Those first phase investors won't see their money for months, maybe never. And Peña and Moreno will lose their reputations and probably their firm in the process."

"But everything would have been fine if the guarantee hadn't been stolen! Then the tribe's IO committee would just pay off the investors."

Cooper steepled his fingers across his chest. "Are you sure there is a guarantee?"

"What do you mean?" Hannah said.

"The original is missing, the police couldn't find a scan on Soto's computer, and no other copies have turned up. Who's to say it even exists?"

"Three people, and they're all dead. Doesn't

that tell you something?"

"What it tells me is either there's such a thing as coincidence, or someone didn't want that guarantee to surface. But assume for a minute there is no guarantee. You have to wonder if the kidnapping was real, too. It gives Soto an awfully convenient alibi for both the theft of the deal documents from your office and Baptisto's murder."

Hannah crossed her arms. "You're saying that I'm completely off the mark with this guy."

"Welcome to the human condition, Hannah. Everyone gets people wrong—before we meet them, when we're with them, when we go home and tell someone else about them. No matter how hard we try, we never get it right. A big part of life is making adjustments to our mistaken perceptions."

Like with Elizabeth…Richard…Kassif… Hannah breathed deep into her chest. *But not Tony.*

She thought back to the afternoon in the desert—the hard eyes of the men in blue, the rifle shot that had barely cleared their heads, the terror rolling through her.

"That kidnapping felt *real*, Cooper. Tony was truly angry, and as scared as I was—he wasn't faking. And he seemed genuinely upset that the original guarantee was missing."

"But if someone else took the three million, why would they kill Soto and Baptisto, or take the deal documents from your office, or steal the guarantee?"

"You're right, it doesn't make sense." Hannah fingered the freshly cut piece of hair near the nape of her neck.

Cooper stood and held out his hands to her. "I guess it wouldn't take very much time to check out the development company, as well as gang activity in the area. Maybe I'll come across something the police missed."

Hannah grasped his wrists and let him pull her up. "You'd do that for me?"

"You can't imagine what I would do for you." Cooper wrapped his arms around her. His bare feet were under hers, his toes curled under and a little cold. "We're assuming the same person is responsible for all three murders, as well as the thefts. What if that isn't true?"

Cooper had a point. Perhaps they had been looking at things too narrowly. Hannah thought about Delores. As Baptisto's assistant, she had access to Ge Oidag's files as well as the company's bank accounts—easy enough for her to discover that three million dollars was missing. Clementine's gossip notwithstanding, Delores had said that she'd grown up poor. Would she have engineered the document theft from Hannah's office, perhaps with extortion in mind?

Hannah let her imagination shift into high gear, knowing she wasn't waiting to see if plausibility was along for the ride. Had the Ge Oidag office really been ransacked? Maybe Delores had done it to cover her theft of the guarantee? Had the two men in blue helped her? Were they even there at all?

The police—and Hannah—had assumed Tony was the target of the drive-by shooting, with Delores unfortunate collateral damage. What if *Delores* had been the intended victim?

When Tony questioned whether Delores knew about the missing money, Hannah had given his suspicions short shrift. Would he still be alive if she had taken his misgivings more seriously?

Chapter Thirty-three

Wednesday, September 23

The voicemail from Moreno was short and to the point.

"Our lawyers obtained an emergency order from the bankruptcy court this morning. As chief creditor of Ge Oidag, we'll be overseeing its liquidation. A messenger will come by your office later today to pick up the documentation pertaining to the company and the first phase of the real estate offering." Moreno cleared his throat, the sound harsh over the speakerphone. "I'm sure you would have done a fine job of handling the situation. But given our personal exposure, our counsel thought it best if we began investor reimbursements as soon as possible."

Hannah deleted the message. She had to agree. The sooner investors received money, or the promise of money, the less likely they would be to sue.

Trouble was, that meant she was out of a job—and left with a lot of *nos*. No word yet from Chiago. No idea where her next job would be. No leads on the three murders.

Clementine appeared in the doorway. Her generous chest was caught in the embrace of a bead-trimmed sweater, while the rest of her was wrapped in a tight ankle-length skirt beneath which could be seen a pair of lace-up boots.

"Does this mean what I think it means, Boss?"

Hannah was no longer surprised by her secretary's eavesdropping. In fact, she presumed it.

"Looks that way."

Clementine handed Hannah a message slip. "You should call this guy then. He's the one hot for a lunch meeting. When you're unemployed, you don't pass up free food."

Hannah suddenly was conscious how self-centered she had been. So caught up with the impact of recent events on her interests, she had overlooked their effect on her secretary.

"Clementine, I'm sorry. I promised you six weeks of work. If you need help—"

Her secretary looked at her in astonishment. "You're kidding, right? If it weren't for you, I would still be on the sofa watching *Passion Beach*—not that

that's a bad thing. But I would have never met Zel. *I owe you*, sister."

Sister? Hannah had thought it couldn't get more annoying than *Boss*. She glanced at the message slip Clementine had given her. *Osborne Hepworth*. She crumpled up the piece of paper and tossed it in the trash.

"I do *not* want to talk to that man."

"Suit yourself. But when I see you in the dollar line at Mickey D's, I'm going to say *I told you so*."

"I look forward to your empathy and kindness. In the meantime, would you please find me some cartons so I can pack up all this stuff?"

"Will do. Oh, I almost forgot." Clementine reached into a pocket in her skirt and extracted an envelope. "Somebody left this for you at the front desk."

Hannah recognized Richard's bold writing. "Thanks," she said brusquely.

Under Clementine's curious gaze, she put the envelope into her purse without opening it. *What a coward.* As far as she was concerned, Richard's behavior warranted an apology in person. Not that she would accept it.

Hannah looked at her watch. She had to get moving if she were going to have the Ge Oidag documents ready for P&M's messenger. Pulling the closest stack of papers toward her, she dug in.

As she worked, her mind kept going back to the murders. From Dresden's comments, it sounded as though he was ready to write off the killings to random crime. Without new evidence, it was unlikely he would change his mind.

Maybe Cooper had uncovered something on Baptisto's company or the gang situation. He had logged a lot of hours on the computer, staying up so late he had slept through his alarm that morning. When Hannah had left for work, he was still in bed.

She took out her cell phone and called the condo.

"Hello?"

Cooper's voice sounded thick and loamy, like ore through a sluice box. Hannah imagined him lying in bed with the sheets wrapped around him, his hair going every which way. The muscles in the pit of her stomach contracted.

"It's me. Any news?"

"Not really." He stifled a yawn. "I was up until four. Managed to get into some databases I don't think even the local cops can access. But I couldn't find anything hinky on Baptisto or Ge Oidag. No big debts, no unusual transactions. I still can't figure out where the three mil went. And I didn't turn up anything new on Las Fantasmas. They're pretty much how Dresden described them."

"Darn!" Hannah's shoulders drooped. *Dead end.*

Cooper's voice was soft in her ear. "By the way, I might have been too hard on Soto last night. I did some checking—prior employment, deals he's done. He came back absolutely clean. Maybe he did just get in over his head, trying to do a good thing for his tribe."

And someone killed him for it. Cooper's words only made Hannah more determined to see Tony's death avenged.

The phone on her desk rang.

"Thanks for the info. I've got another call—talk to you later." Hannah closed her cell phone on Cooper's sleepy *Good-bye* and picked up the handset. It was Moreno again.

"Are the papers ready?" he asked without preamble.

"I'm just finishing up. Have you found out anything more?"

"If by that you mean more bad news, the answer is *yes.* Our lawyers confirmed the Ge Oidag accounts were emptied. And they say an action against Anthony's estate won't recover much. Apparently he was a generous donor to Indian causes."

Hannah was puzzled. Surely any money Tony gave to the tribe would be insignificant compared with what the casino brought in. Had he just acted out of principle? Not sure what response Moreno expected—*I'm sorry* or *Too bad* seemed woefully inadequate—Hannah finally settled for "Wow."

"Wow, indeed. At any rate, it appears Robert and I will have to cover most of the loss ourselves. The lawyers are trying to broker a settlement, persuade the investors to accept a reduced refund in return for immediate payment."

"I hope that works out for you." Hannah knew that after their initial outrage cooled, wronged investors often saw the wisdom of fewer dollars in hand immediately versus the chance at more much later.

"Right now we're preparing for the outside auditors. They have to review every client account—firm policy in the case of an irregularity of this magnitude." Moreno sighed. "As much as it pains me to say this, I am beginning to suspect Anthony was involved in taking the money."

Hannah couldn't help herself. "But that doesn't make sense. You know as well as I do Tony wanted the real estate project to succeed to build political support for the casino expansion. For that to happen, Ge Oidag had to stay in business. Sure, he let his nationalism go too far—the guarantee was a dumb thing to do. But only *investors* would have benefited from the arrangement, not Tony. Why go to all that trouble if he were planning to steal the money?"

"You're saying that while Anthony may have been stupid, he wasn't a thief."

"Exactly."

"If the three million was already gone, then why would someone kill Mr. Baptisto, or Anthony and Ms. Alvarez?"

It was the question Hannah couldn't answer. If the victims had been embezzling money from the development company, it might be reasonable to assume they were killed by a coconspirator. But three million dollars split three ways wasn't serious money, not to Indians whose share of casino revenues were worth many times more. On the other hand, a million bucks was an unattainable dream to a *cholo* from the barrio.

Hannah had a sudden idea. Tony had been acting out of concern for his people. What if the murders didn't have anything to do with personal gain either?

"Maybe we're looking at this wrong. Tony was willing to violate the securities laws and risk being sued, even prison, to make sure the real estate project succeeded. To him, the casino expansion and the resulting wealth for the tribe were worth it. What if someone was just as strongly opposed to the project?"

"Like someone with Control Growth?" Moreno asked.

"Maybe. Or even a tribe member. The casino brings in money—a *lot* of money—but it brings a lot of problems, too. Tony told me some of the tribal elders thought that additional revenues weren't worth the social cost when it came to expansion. Did you get a sense of this when you spoke to de Segura or the rest of the IA committee?"

"All anyone talked about was how much Anthony had done for the tribe, and how much they missed him. The IO committee's main concern seemed to be making sure custom was being followed, not whether the guarantee should be honored. A tribe member responsible for the murders? I don't know, it seems pretty thin."

Pretty thin is all I have. Hannah knew the idea of an O'odham committing murder to stop the casino expansion seemed farfetched. There were easier ways to torpedo the real estate offering than killing three people—leak the second set of projections and the guarantee to the *Express*, for example.

"I'm afraid we're back to pointing the finger at Anthony," Moreno said. He ended the call with a promise to let Hannah know if the auditors turned up anything unusual that might be connected to the murders.

Hannah finished boxing the documents Moreno had asked for just as the messenger arrived. After he had carted everything into his van, she walked over to the Trading Post and bought lunch to go. By the time Clementine knocked on her office door, Hannah was halfway through a pizza topped with tomatoes, onions, and *nopale*—skinned and dethorned paddles of the prickly pear cactus grilled until tender.

Clementine stared at Hannah's plate. "What the heck is that?"

"Cactus pizza. Want a slice?"

Her secretary screwed her face into an expression of disgust. "That's like eating tofu—something you do only when the only other choice is starvation. And even then, you think about it." She handed Hannah another message slip.

"You probably won't want to call this guy back either. He was screaming into the phone, demanding to talk to you. Claimed it was a matter of life or death."

Moreno's name and the P&M phone number were printed on the message. Hannah picked up the phone. The general partner answered on the first ring.

"It's millions!"

Hannah thumbed the handset's volume control, turning it down. "What's millions?"

"The amount that bastard stole from our client accounts! Forty to be exact, according to the auditors. Anthony and those two other Indians siphoned the funds through the development company."

"*What?*"

"The auditors are still working out the details. They have some questions about the private placement. Can you meet with them today around four?"

Hannah felt numb. "Of course."

After Moreno had hung up, she sat at her desk, gnawing at the edge of her bottom lip. A share of three million may not have been sufficient incentive, but one-third of forty would be temptation enough for even a tribalism fanatic like Tony.

But was he really that interested in money and the things it could buy? If so, why trade a Los

Angeles condo for a cinderblock house on the rez? His passion was Ge Oidag, the offering, the casino expansion, and ultimately, the tribe's prosperity. Mounting evidence to the contrary, Hannah nevertheless wasn't yet ready to concede Tony had chosen personal gain over the good of his people.

Clementine stood in the doorway. "Boss?"

"Mmm?" Hannah's mind was still on Moreno's phone call.

"That guy Hepworth called again when I was at lunch. One of the girls on the lobby desk took the message, and she told me something you might want to know."

Hannah recognized her secretary's gossipy tone. "Clementine, I don't really have time—"

"Did you know Delores used to work for Hepworth? The receptionist saw them having lunch together a few weeks ago."

Hannah blinked. Delores and Hepworth? She considered the implications. Had former employee and boss conspired to steal the three million, with Hepworth then killing off his partner-in-crime?

"Thanks, Clementine," Hannah said, reaching for the phone. But instead of returning Hepworth's call, she tapped in Cooper's number.

"I think I know who killed Delores and

Tony, and maybe Baptisto," she said as soon as he answered.

"Hi to you, too. Now what are you talking about?"

Quickly Hannah related what Clementine had told her.

"Even if it's true—and when we're talking about Clementine and gossip, that's a big *if*—that doesn't mean Hepworth killed anyone. Could just be coincidence."

Hannah was annoyed at his tepid response. "You don't believe in coincidence any more than I do."

"Let's talk about it over dinner. I'm knocking off early today. How about meeting me at the Saguaro Grill around six?"

"Can't. I've got a late afternoon meeting at Peña & Moreno." Still feeling peeved, Hannah decided not to tell him about the money that was missing from the P&M client accounts. She wasn't in the mood for another anti-Tony harangue. "I'll call you when I'm done."

"If I'm not on my cell, I'll be at the condo."

Hannah hung up, unable to shake her suspicion that Hepworth was somehow involved in the missing money and the three killings, maybe even the millions looted from P&M.

Just because you don't like the guy, don't go over-board, she told herself. *Still…*

She thought about Hepworth's comments to Tony at the Trading Post, his visa-fraud proposition, his subsequent indictment, then the courtyard meeting two days later with Delores and the other woman's description of her job with the tribe. Finally, there was the latest question—*Why would Hepworth be calling her?*

It was one of those moments, one of those rare occasions when the puzzle pieces fell into place, the forest was visible through the trees, and the big picture came into view. *Late,* Hannah thought, *but definitely better than never.* She felt foolish to have missed it for so long.

Hepworth and Delores, the immigration lawyer and his former employee—they had been using the Tohono O'odham visa program as a way to sneak workers from Mexico and other Central American countries into the States. When Delores became Baptisto's assistant and gained access to the development company's account, the three million dollars must have been too much of a temptation. She and Hepworth stole the money, probably killing Baptisto when he tumbled onto their scheme. But after the funds were safely stashed, Hepworth had gotten greedy and eliminated his partner in crime. Tony had been killed because he had happened to be there, too.

Hannah tapped a finger on the desk, impatient to act but unsure what to do next. She thought about calling Cooper, then decided against it. For whatever reason, Tony's death had become personal, and she wanted to be there for the end—something Cooper would never agree to.

Briefly, she was tempted to circumvent the law and ask Enzo, Clementine's oldest brother, for assistance. But then an image of her secretary's Corsican vendetta came to mind, and she decided against it. There had been too much violence already.

Hannah could think of only one way for her to be part of things without adding to the mayhem quotient. But she couldn't do it without help. If she had learned anything from the events of last month, *Don't go after bad guys alone* topped the list. She opened her phone and keyed in the number.

I should have him on speed dial, she thought as the call went through. He answered on the second ring.

"Detective Dresden? This is Hannah Dain. I have an idea…"

Chapter Thirty-four

While waiting for Dresden in the police station lobby, Hannah unzipped her purse to turn off her cell phone. *Better to miss Cooper's call than to lie to him. Marginally.*

Her hand brushed against a stiff rectangle of paper. She glanced down and saw the envelope from Richard. Feeling a flash of her earlier anger, she started to zip up her purse, then stopped.

You know Richard isn't much for talking. Or writing, either. And how can you complain about his pride if you're acting the same way?

Hannah took out the envelope and tore it open. Inside was a note wrapped around a business card.

She read the note first. Written in Richard's oversized cursive, its message was brief:

I hope you are interested—R.

Puzzled, Hannah turned over the business card.

Engraved black letters stood out starkly against white vellum. In the lower right corner was Hannah's name, along with the law firm's address and phone number. But it was the center of the card that had caught her attention.

Dain & Daughters
Attorneys at Law

The words blurred through the wetness in her eyes as Cooper's words came back to her. *Welcome to the human condition, Hannah. Everyone gets people wrong...*

Could she have completely misread Richard's motives? Had he kept Elizabeth's secrets not to save himself, but because he worried the truth would harm her? Hannah's internal compass was spinning. She felt as though she had crossed over an interior meridian into an unknown area, forsaken the boundaries of her previous life.

Tony had chosen to become Indian, turning his back on his Hispanic heritage. Maybe Richard had wanted to protect her from having to make a similar choice, saving her from labels—mixed-race, illegitimate, absentee birth father—that weren't of her making. Maybe he feared she wouldn't have a choice at all in an America where *part black* usually meant *all black*.

True, he had been emotionally distant, yet he could have treated her much worse—no private school tuition, no job at the firm. Indeed, Richard didn't have to make room for her in his life at all. *Nature* wasn't optional, but *nurture* was. While Tel Moore may have fathered her, Richard had chosen to raise her.

Hannah ran a finger over the word *Daughters*, lingering on the final *s*. She still thought Richard had been wrong to hide the truth about Elizabeth. But perhaps his motive wasn't bigotry or pride. Maybe it was care, even love.

For a moment Hannah wished the clock could be turned back, to before she had uncovered so many family secrets, to a time when bad choices and misunderstandings had yet to intervene. But part of her suspected that even if she and Richard could start over, they'd probably make the same mistakes again.

If I can't go back, then what about forward? Impulsively she took her phone out of her purse and punched in the number for the law firm.

"Put me through to his voicemail, please," she told the receptionist. Richard wasn't the only one not ready for an in-person conversation.

"It's Hannah," she said after the beep. "I read

your note. Um, thanks. I'd like to talk about it." She took a gulp of air, then let her words out in a rush. "I'm sorry about that...word I called you. Anyway...I was wondering...if the ballet is performing this weekend, maybe we could catch the matinee and—"

"Ms. Dain?"

At the sound of Dresden's voice, Hannah closed the phone.

"Sorry to keep you waiting," he said.

Hannah slid the note and business card back into the envelope and put them in her purse.

"No problem. Gave me a chance to do some catching up."

The meeting with Dresden went well, the detective surprisingly quick to buy into Hannah's theory.

"We have to move quickly," he declared. Because Hannah had dodged his calls for the past two days, the immigration lawyer—out on bail— could be getting antsy. If Hepworth ran for it and managed to get south of the border, it was unlikely he would ever be found.

Only one thing troubled Dresden. "Why do you think he's calling you?"

Hannah was still wondering about that, too. "Delores and I went out to dinner, and she did some stuff for me on the real estate offering. Maybe Hepworth wants to make sure she didn't say anything about the money or Mr. Baptisto's murder." The explanation was flimsy, but it was the best she could come up with.

"Well, I don't like it. But right now you're the only person who can draw him out. If we go looking for him, word will be out on the street before my deputies leave the station and he'll be gone."

At Dresden's direction, Hannah called Hepworth to set up lunch for the next day. But the immigration lawyer declined, asking her to meet him for dinner that evening instead.

"I'm afraid my schedule's quite full tomorrow."

Travel plans? Per Dresden's coaching, Hannah arranged to meet the lawyer at a small restaurant on the outskirts of town—a restaurant where cops posing as patrons would arrest him as soon as he arrived.

"I'll see you at seven-thirty, my dear. Looking forward to a *delightful* evening." His smarmy tone made Hannah want to wash her hands.

"Stay here until it's time to go to the restaurant," Dresden ordered after she had hung up. "I don't want to take any chances."

"That's fine. I just need to cancel an appointment."

But when Hannah tried to postpone her four o'clock at P&M with the auditors, Moreno dug in his heels.

"These guys are in from LA, and they have to catch the evening flight back. We're talking about forty million dollars, Hannah. You *have* to speak with them!"

Hannah pressed the *Mute* button. "I've got a problem. Mr. Moreno is insisting that I meet with the auditors."

"Then go. If Hepworth used to do P&M's immigration work, we don't want him talking to Moreno and finding out that you canceled. It could tip him off that something is up."

"I'll be there," Hannah told Moreno.

"Someone will be posted at the building. I don't expect any problems, but be quick about giving those auditors what they want, then get back here," Dresden said when Moreno was off the line.

"No problem," Hannah said.

Three hours later she stood in front of Peña & Moreno's building. The shadows stretched long and distinct across the sidewalk and the late afternoon air was unseasonably cool. For a moment she remained still, mesmerized by the motionless cityscape. No wannabe *cholos* loitered on the corner, no cars cruised by. Even with a light breeze, not even the scraps of paper in the gutter moved. Hannah wiped suddenly damp palms on the front of her pants. *Where was the deputy?*

She pushed open the lobby door. *That's why they call it undercover,* she told herself.

Hannah climbed the interior staircase, the musty odor stronger than before. The smell reminded her of the attic in Olivia's house, with its dust and spiders and echoes of lives past. She thought about what Chiago had said about restless spirits straying from the afterworld.

I hope catching Hepworth will bring you peace, Tony. She stopped in front of the office with the brass nameplate.

Moreno opened the door so quickly after her knock, Hannah half-thought he had been standing on the other side waiting for her.

"Hannah! Come in, come in." He gestured at one of the chairs in the reception area. "May I offer you a beverage?"

Hannah chose a seat. "No, thank you."

Moreno remained standing, clasping and unclasping his hands. "I can't tell you what a horrendous situation this is! According to the auditors, about twenty percent of our clients' funds are missing. They traced the money to an account in the Cayman Islands, which means the chance of recovery is essentially zero."

"I'm very sorry, Mr. Moreno. But I still can't believe Tony was responsible," Hannah said, wanting to blurt out the news about Hepworth. Instead, she pulled back her cuff and looked at her watch. "I have another meeting after this. Are the auditors ready?"

Moreno's eyes slid away from hers. "I'm afraid they caught an earlier flight back to LA. But they left a list of questions. One of our lawyers is here to go over them with you." Moreno raised his voice. "Robert?"

His face more funereal than ever, Roberto Peña appeared in the hallway that led to the office interior. Behind him was Osborne Hepworth. At the sight of the immigration lawyer, Hannah's palms went damp again. *Now what was she supposed to do?*

"Hello, Hannah." While appearing as austere and just this side of affected, as before, Hepworth was paler than Hannah had remembered, like a man without enough blood to push around his body.

"Hello, Mr. Hepworth. I didn't expect to see you here," Hannah said, trying to keep her voice even.

"When my clients told me about Tony's heinous crime, I could not help but offer assistance. The last several hours reviewing the documents with the auditors have been most illuminating."

Several hours? That meant he arrived at P&M well before the deputy had been posted outside. Nervousness knotted Hannah's stomach.

Moreno produced a file folder. "Shall we get started? We want to look at everything Tony said or did the last six months in the hopes that it will shed some light on what happened."

The questions were pretty much what Hannah had expected. She answered in the negative to nearly every one.

Had Tony talked to her about the Ge Oidag account? How about the money raised through the first phase of the real estate project? Did he ever mention any financial problems? Wire transfers? The Cayman Islands? P&M's client funds? Did he gamble? Use drugs? Did he mention any travel plans?

"No…no…no…no…no…" Hannah shook her head back and forth so much, her neck became sore. Her indignation mounted with every question, as Hepworth's tone made obvious his belief in Tony's guilt.

Be cool. Dresden's deputy will arrest him as soon

as he leaves the building.

"Is there anything else you can think of that we should know?" Moreno said after Hepworth had asked his last question.

Hannah couldn't restrain herself any longer. The words burst from her lips.

"Money, drugs, gambling—Tony didn't care about any of these things. Helping the tribe—and that meant making sure the casino expansion went through—was what mattered to him. He was even talking about moving onto the rez. And I was there when he discovered the original guarantee was gone—he was devastated!"

"Maybe not for the reason that you think," Hepworth said. Before Hannah could ask what he meant, Moreno spoke up.

"I'm afraid you've been fooled by Anthony's charm. We all were."

Hannah's mind flitted back to the kiss in the desert. *Had he just been playing her?*

"Robert, Anthony, and I are each responsible for our own book of business," Moreno continued. "The results are tallied monthly and circulated. Apparently Anthony altered his sheets, as well as the firm's monthly bank statements."

Hannah stared at him, unbelieving. "Tony

altered *bank* statements? How could he do that?"

"It wasn't that hard. He picked up the mail from our post office box every day on his way to work. When a statement arrived, he would steam open the envelope, scan the statement into his computer, change the figures, print out the altered document, put it in the original envelope, and seal it up again. We wouldn't have found out about the fraud until next year, when the accountants prepared the firm's tax returns. Unless, of course, a midyear audit was ordered for some reason."

"Which would explain why Tony was so upset about the disappearance of the three million dollars from the development company and the missing guarantee," Hepworth said smugly. "He knew the auditors would be brought in, therefore prematurely exposing his greater theft."

Hannah tried to sort it all through. The only reason Tony had cared about finding the missing Ge Oidag money—or, in the alternative, having the loss covered by the guarantee—was to delay the discovery of his embezzlement of the P&M client funds? Hannah thought back to four nights ago in the motel room. Tony hadn't acted like someone with forty million dollars on the line. Part of her—admittedly, now a very small part—still resisted the idea that he was a thief.

"Anyone could have altered the statements," she said weakly.

Moreno extracted a piece of paper from a file folder on the receptionist's counter.

"Would they have done this, too? We found it hidden in Tony's desk." He handed the document to Hannah.

The imprint across the top read *Second Caribbean Bank*, followed by an address in Grand Cayman, Cayman Islands. Halfway down the page, under last Friday's date, CONFIRMATION OF DEPOSIT VIA WIRE TRANSFER was printed in block letters next to an amount: $25,000,000.00. At the bottom of the page was the number of the recipient account and the name of the account holder: *Anthony Soto.*

Hannah felt sick.

Hepworth's smile was ugly as he got to his feet. "What would you do for forty million dollars, Ms. Dain? Steal? Alter documents? Kill?"

"No!" The only thing that kept Hannah from slapping him was the thought of his pending arrest.

Moreno stood as well, kneading his chest. "Osborne, that was unnecessary."

"As has been this entire pretense," Peña said.

He was leaning on the wall beside the office's main door. Hannah had almost forgotten he was there. "I told you this would be a waste of time."

Hepworth's mouth pulled downward. "We had to find out what she knew. It's not my fault the bitch wouldn't call me back before today."

"But now *we* have to deal with her." Any pleasantness in Peña's voice had burned off, exposing something cold and hard. "Osborne, go downstairs and make sure no one comes up to the second floor. Don't worry about the cleaning crew. They aren't due for another five hours."

Bitch? Deal with her? Fear ran through Hannah like a river.

"Rafael!" Peña called.

The door to the outside corridor swung open and a man walked into the room. Over six feet tall, his massive head appeared to melt into his shoulders. A navy bandana tied low around his forehead hooded his eyes. Blue work shirt, blue denims, and black leather boots with thick rubber soles all screamed *cholo*, as did the tattoos on his knuckles—*SUERTE* across the left hand, *MUERTE* on the right.

Luck or death. Hannah felt her stomach fall away.

Moreno looked alarmed. "Robert, what is this?"

Peña ignored his partner, instead jerking his chin in Hepworth's direction. "Get out of here."

With a sardonic smile, the lawyer left, taking care to close the door firmly behind him.

Stunned, Hannah watched him go. *Hepworth and Delores are supposed to be the bad guys*, she thought stupidly, at the same time knowing they weren't. And now Dresden was miles away, waiting to arrest Hepworth. In less than a minute, she had gone from being the hunter to the hunted. Hannah heard herself swallow.

"Ms. Dain, allow me to present Rafael. He is one of my associates in the import business," Peña said.

Import business? Did he mean drugs?

"People, not *drogas*," Peña said as though reading her mind. "Where would we be without the Mexican *braseros*? They do the work no one else wants to do. Indian visas make it easy to cross over, and when it's time for them to go back…" He shrugged. "Illegals disappear—it's a fact of life. Who can track mercury?"

Hannah understood that she had been wrong about the criminals but right about the crime—illegal aliens were using the Tohono O'odham visa program to enter the United States, through the efforts of Hepworth and Delores. But how was that connected to the money missing from the Ge Oidag or P&M accounts?

"Robert—" Moreno began.

"*Silencio!* This is that idiot lawyer's fault. We should have had Rafael's people take care of him when he was in jail."

Hannah's pulse reverberated in her ears. She had a pretty good idea what Peña meant by *take care of him.*

"Osborne wouldn't have been indicted if we had stuck to bringing over laborers. I told you *narcotraficantes* would be too risky," Moreno said, petulance in his voice.

"I didn't see you turning down the fee," Peña retorted. "Everything would have been fine if he hadn't tried to bribe a rookie agent. Delores was supposed to make sure he tapped the right people. Instead the stupid slut was chasing after Tony."

"Robert, must you use such language?" Moreno rubbed his hands together. "At least it is all over now. And with such extraordinary results!"

"Thanks to Tony and Ms. Dain." Peña gestured at Hannah. She flinched at the sudden movement and he laughed.

"It was all laid out in the notebook—Baptisto

looting his own company, he and Tony cutting a deal to guarantee the revenues from the real estate project. Who wouldn't believe they also embezzled forty million dollars from our clients?" Peña gave a malevolent chuckle. "Especially if they aren't around to say otherwise."

Through her terror, Hannah's mind grasped what he was saying. Peña and Moreno had read Tony's notebook after all—and realized that Baptisto's dishonesty and Tony's secret guarantee made the duo perfect fall guys for a much larger crime. Bile rose in the back of her throat. *If she hadn't turned over the notebook, would Tony and Delores, even Baptisto, still be alive?*

"Alejandro, it's time to leave. The jet is scheduled to take off in forty-five minutes." Peña picked up two duffel bags from the floor. "You know, I won't miss this country. So many little indignities. If you're white, you can fill your car with gas, then pay. If you're non-white, you have to pay first. Same at the take-out counter, the dry cleaners. I'm looking forward to living in a place where I'm a first-class citizen."

Moreno glanced nervously at Hannah. "Aren't we going to tie her up or something?"

"Don't worry about it," Peña said.

"But she'll call the police as soon as we leave!"

Peña's face darkened with anger. "You think I am stupid? *I'm* not the one who let Tony escape. If he and Baptisto had been found together, those Control Growth people would have been blamed. At least the drive-by got rid of Delores. This one's the only problem left." He looked at Rafael.

"You know what to do. Just make sure it burns to the ground."

The *cholo*'s eyes locked onto Hannah's and she started in recognition. The lifeless pools of black had last stared at her over the barrel of a rifle in the desert.

"*No problema.*" Rafael drew out the syllables. Hannah could feel the anticipation of pleasure emanating from him, and her heart began to beat faster. After the events of last summer, Hannah had promised herself no more deer-in-headlights moments. If she were ever in physical peril again, she was going to fight back or try to get away.

She sprang from her chair and bolted for the corridor door. Her hand was on the knob when Rafael grabbed her around the waist and dragged her back into the room. Hannah kicked at his shins and flailed with her arms, subsiding only after he pressed what felt like a knife against her throat.

A very sharp knife. The metal point dug into Hannah's neck. Her stomach roiled, the nauseating smell of his cheap aftershave unable to mask the stink of violence that rose from his skin.

Moreno threw up his hands in horror.

"Robert, what are you doing? We agreed—no more killing. Hepworth was supposed to find out what she knew, then keep her out of the way until the plane left. Another body will raise too many questions!" Moreno's face was pale and sweaty, and Hannah could hear his breathing.

Peña's face twisted into a sneer. "I doubt it. Everyone knows bad things happen to white girls in the *barrio.* And we'll be in Mexico before they know she's dead."

Rubbing his left arm, Moreno took a step in Hannah's direction. Briefly she thought he was coming to her aid. Instead, he staggered forward another step, then fell to his knees. Gasping for breath, he pressed both hands to his chest, eyes wide, clearly scared of something far more frightening than his partner.

Hannah felt Rafael's hold on her slacken as Moreno began to topple to the floor. Taking advantage of the moment, she whirled out of his grip and darted behind the low counter in front of the receptionist's desk. Seeing a pair of scissors in a cup next to the blotter, she grabbed them and turned, expecting Rafael to come after her.

Instead, he and Peña gazed down at Moreno, now crumpled on the floor. He was ghost-white, and appeared to have stopped breathing.

Peña prodded his partner's ribs with the toe of his shoe. There was no response. He slung the duffel bags over one shoulder.

"I told him he needed to eat more *maiz con frijoles.*"

Hannah took advantage of their momentary inattention to scan the desktop for other weapons. *Stapler…paper clips…phone…*

Phone! Her eyes on the two men, she carefully lifted the receiver off the hook. But the system had been set to Auto-Answer, and a dial tone buzzed through the instrument's speaker, clearly audible throughout the room.

Despite his size, the *cholo* was cat-quick. Rafael reached over the counter and ripped the phone wire from its connection before Hannah could finish punching in 911.

Not without a fight. Hannah swung the scissors in a downward arc, feeling the blades vibrate in her hand as they plunged into Rafael's shoulder. With a roar, the *cholo* grabbed her by the throat.

"*Puta!*" He started to squeeze.

Little pinwheels danced in front of Hannah's eyes as she fought to suck in air. She clawed at Rafael's arms, and he tightened his grip.

Unaccountably, a memory of Cooper swam into her head. It was last spring, and she had been watching him rope stock on the ranch. He had thrown his lariat at a calf, the loop about to settle over the animal's head, when the calf ducked at the last minute and avoided capture.

Blackness began to edge her vision. *Do what the calf did.* Hannah tucked her chin as best she could and dropped to the ground, the unexpectedness of her fall breaking Rafael's hold. Throat aching, she scrabbled into the desk's footwell and waited for the *cholo*'s next attack.

It never came. Instead, Hannah heard the sound of a door crashing open.

"Everyone on the floor, hands behind your head!" a voice shouted. "Get down! Now!"

"We need the paramedics!" another voice yelled.

Hannah tried to call out, but her throat went into spasm. Blood ran down her neck from the knife cut, warm against her skin. Resting her cheek against the carpet, she waited for a few seconds, then tried to speak again. But all she could manage was a cough.

"You, under the desk—come out of there now!"

Still coughing, Hannah crawled from her hiding place, coming to a shaky halt in front of two highly polished black shoes. She looked up to see Deputy Frampton with his gun pointed at her.

Hannah blinked several times, not quite believing the scene before her. Directly behind Frampton, a pair of deputies stood guard over Peña and Rafael, who lay prone on the floor with their hands cuffed behind their backs. Another deputy assisted the paramedics loading Moreno onto a gurney, while still another removed what looked like stacks of cash and documents from the two duffel bags Peña had been carrying.

"Officer Frampton, put up your weapon," ordered the familiar baritone. "And get the paramedics over here pronto."

Detective Dresden squatted down next to Hannah. His smile was small, but it was there.

"Believe it or not, this one's on our side."

Chapter Thirty-five

Friday, September 25

Hannah rubbed at the gauze strip on her neck. "You guys could have gotten there a little bit sooner." She and Cooper were in Dresden's office, completing Hannah's follow-up interview.

Cooper's arm around her shoulders tightened, the usual calm in his eyes briefly replaced by a rage Hannah hadn't seen there before.

"We rolled as soon as we had Hepworth. The deputy watching the building picked him up the minute he hit the street," Dresden said.

"Did he tell you about Peña and Moreno?" Hannah asked.

The detective nodded. "Hepworth's not stupid—he knew it was over. He also knew what Rafael's being there meant. Called his lawyer, cut a deal with the DA to take the death penalty off the table, and started talking."

Hannah grimaced. "Talk about being off-base—I was sure one of the council members opposed to the casino expansion was behind the murders. My second choice was Hepworth, because his visa fraud business with Delores was falling apart."

Cooper gave Hannah's shoulder another squeeze. "I was so convinced Soto had taken the P&M money, I overlooked the fact that if he weren't involved, the thief was probably someone else at his firm."

"Baptisto's skimming and the secret guarantee made Soto an easy fall guy," Dresden said. "After Peña and Moreno saw what was going on, it didn't take much for them to figure out they could blame Soto for any money missing from their client accounts, too."

For the umpteenth time, Hannah wondered whether she would have seen the greed driving Peña and Moreno if she hadn't been so caught up in proving Tony's innocence. If she hadn't turned over that notebook…

Her climbing instructor had talked to her about the nature of risk after another student suffered a brain injury in a bouldering fall. "Occasionally, there's a price to be paid."

"But by more than the climber!" Hannah had said, thinking of the man's wife, whose spouse now required constant care.

"That's part of the largeness of the price," her instructor had replied. "You can't achieve big without risking big."

I don't mind taking risks, but only when the stakes are big and the odds are in my favor. Hannah blinked away tears—of rage or sorrow, she wasn't sure. Tony's ambition to help his tribe had spurred him to take great risks—risks that, no matter how well-intentioned, would have caught up with him eventually, whether she had been involved or not. The realization didn't make her feel better, or any less culpable.

"So it was just about the money?" Cooper said.

"Looks that way," Dresden agreed. "Moreno had already had two heart attacks. He just wanted to enjoy the time he had left in style. Peña, though, is one angry Hispanic. He grew up envying white success. Then the Indians began to thrive. When he saw a chance for financial freedom, along with an opportunity to burn those he saw prospering at his expense, he took it."

Hannah couldn't get the image of Peña standing over his fallen partner out of her head. "Why was he going to let Moreno die? Hadn't they been friends for a long time?"

"Apparently Moreno wasn't as committed to the plan as much as Peña was, especially after the killing started. And I'm not sure Peña liked his partner that much anymore. According to the people we've interviewed, the more Moreno aspired to the white world, the more Peña despised him."

"Wiring the forty mil to the Soto account was pretty smart," Cooper said.

Hannah hadn't been able to figure out that part of the scheme. "If Tony wasn't involved, how come he had that account? And if the account was in his name, how could Peña and Moreno take money out of it?"

"Soto didn't open the account—Peña and Moreno did. They formed a corporation called Anthony Soto, Inc. and opened an account in its name at a bank known for playing fast and loose with the rules.

"Even though the wire instructions named *Anthony Soto*—no *Inc.*—as the recipient, the bank still accepted the transfer. To anyone looking at it from this end, it would appear as though the money had gone to Soto. And bank secrecy laws would make it difficult, if not impossible, to find out that Peña and Moreno were the real account beneficiaries."

Hannah rubbed the bandage on her neck again. "How did Hepworth fit into all this?"

"Peña knew about Hepworth's fraudulent visa scam and *cholo* connections. When he and Moreno came up with their plan to embezzle the money and kill Baptisto and Soto, they promised Hepworth a share if he would arrange the murders."

"What happened to the man at the shack? The one Tony thought he had killed?"

"We found him buried nearby. Hepworth was worried another death would bring the feds out in force, so he got rid of the body."

Hannah realized that she was discussing multimillion-dollar crimes and dead bodies as though it were an ordinary thing. Had she become that hardened by the events of the past few months?

Before moving back to Arizona, Hannah would have guessed if anything could inure her to violence, it would be living in an urban environment. But the city had nothing on the desert. Camus was right—amoral urges are emboldened under a blinding sun. Eat or be eaten, kill or become roadkill. No wonder bleached skulls and barbed plants were the icons of the Southwest.

"Delores' only involvement was providing visas for Mexican illegals?" Cooper asked.

Dresden nodded. "Looks that way. Because of her attachment to Soto, Peña and Hepworth were worried what she might do after he turned up dead, so they decided to kill her, too."

"I feel sorry for Delores," Hannah said. "She probably thought she was helping poor workers, not drug traffickers. And then she fell in love with Tony. Hepworth must have let something slip about the kidnapping, or she found out about it from the *cholos*. Even after it was clear Tony wasn't interested in her, she tried to protect him and his dream for the tribe."

"The things we do for love," Cooper said.

Like Richard's decision to conceal the truth about Elizabeth? Hannah unconsciously pressed her hands together. Would Cooper see the conclusion she had arrived at yesterday in the same light?

Dresden pushed back his chair. "I think we're finished here. Thank you again for your cooperation, Ms. Dain. And I hope you stay out of police work for a while."

Hannah pulled a face. "Gladly."

As Dresden opened the door, Hannah had a sense of something going out of the room, something beyond the losses already sustained. *Tony's ghost?* Its departure felt like a good thing.

"Safe journey to the East," she whispered.

The wind slapped at Hannah and Cooper as they descended the steps of the police station. Cooper's shirttail billowed and luffed like a spinnaker, and bougainvillea blossoms scudded along the pavement.

They walked along the sidewalk, fingers interlaced. The late afternoon light cast violet shadows on the hills close to town, while the mountains beyond were an ever-darkening succession of purples.

Hannah broke the silence. "One good thing came out of all this."

"What's that?"

"Clementine and Zel. I think she's taking him to meet her dad next weekend."

Cooper grinned and shook his head. "Wait until Zel sees where Dad lives. Not your usual gated community."

His red truck came into view, angled into a space on the corner. Hannah had parked the Subaru one block over. She was picking up Shelby at the rehab center in half an hour and, knowing the reunion should be sisters only, had suggested to Cooper they take separate cars to the appointment with Dresden.

Earlier that afternoon, Hannah had cleared out her office at the OTA. There wasn't anything she was going to miss about the job, except for maybe the Chief. The wooden Indian had disappeared as mysteriously as he had arrived, and she half-regretted not saying good-bye.

Hannah slowed her pace and tugged on Cooper's hand.

"Wait up a minute."

He stopped walking and turned to face her. Hannah could sense the emotion coming off of him, low-wattage but steady. The feeling was back, the one in her chest, as though air couldn't get all the way in.

Yesterday she had driven alone to the rock-climbing park. Leaving her climbing gear in the car, she had hiked along the path that skirted the base of El Piniculo, taking advantage of the solitude to think—about Tony and Cooper, Shelby and Richard, Elizabeth and Tel. Now she had to tell Cooper her decision.

She liked having Cooper in her life. Liked it very much, actually—the sharing of a home, the physicality, the knowing there was someone who would listen and care. But she also knew that wasn't enough to protect their relationship from ruin.

Hannah tightened her grip on his hand. "Things are kinda messy in my life right now. Dealing with what happened to Tony and Delores...finding out about my parents...looking for a new job." She forced a laugh. "If you can believe it, I'm thinking about going back to Dain & Dain."

The wind had settled into a steady blow, and Hannah pushed a strand of hair out of her face. "Anyway, all this *stuff* is taking up most of my head space. Heart space, too. It's not fair to you. And if we're not starting in the same place, there's no way this...this feeling that's between us will have a chance to succeed."

Part of Hannah wondered if every relationship didn't have its own DNA, a unique essential nature. Maybe someday it would be possible to examine a thin slice under a microscope and know whether the structure was likely to withstand the pressures of the long haul. *Sure would save a lot of heartache.*

"Are you saying you want us to take a step back for a while?" The drawl had disappeared from Cooper's speech. Hannah imagined the long vowels vaporizing into the bright blue heat. She nodded.

He reached out and briefly touched her cheek. "There's usually a gap between what we know and what we do. And people spend a lot of time and energy trying to close that gap. I think you're going to do better than most."

A hawk floated overhead, a dark speck against the faded denim sky. Cooper dug his car keys out of his pocket and pressed a button on the remote. The doors on the pickup chirped open. Still holding his hand, Hannah walked with him to the driver's side.

"Oh hell," she blurted when she looked into the truck cab.

The vehicle's seat was piled high with clothes spilling out of garbage bags, a desk lamp, a jumbo-sized pasta pot—all of Cooper's things that had been in her condo that morning.

"How did you—?"

"Now and then I know what you're thinking, sometimes before you even do. It can be pretty scary." Behind his humor, Hannah could hear grief, too.

"I haven't been blind to what's been going on, Hannah. You're being pulled in a lot of directions. I just hope you head my way again. Soon."

Hannah hugged him. She felt time stretch out, the moment suspended like a hammock between them.

"I better go," Cooper finally said, his voice husky.

"I know." Hannah unwrapped her arms from around his waist. She felt a moment of hesitation, a kicking-in of the reflex to ask him to stay. Biting her lower lip, she backed away, telling herself *not now* wasn't the same as *never*.

Cooper paused with his hand on the truck's door handle. "Give me a call when you're in the mood for some plantains."

She nodded, not trusting herself to speak.

He climbed into the cab and backed the truck out of the parking slot. Squinting against the harsh light, Hannah watched him go. Already she missed him.

But as the red pickup merged into the traffic, Hannah felt the tightness in her chest start to ease. She took in a deep breath, letting her ribs expand, feeling both better and worse as the realization sank in just how badly she had wanted it, how much that surprised her, and how relieved she was to be done with it for a while. She inhaled again, and the tourniquet that had encircled her heart loosened and slid away.

Her cell phone rang. *Cooper already?* Hannah fished it out of her purse. The letters on the screen spelled out *Chiago*.

Shock rippled through her. *Did this mean...* She opened the phone.

"This is Hannah."

"Chiago," he replied with his usual bluntness. "Your father's full name is Othello Moore." *Othello?* Hannah rolled the name around in her mind. "So you've spoken with him?" Nervousness trickled through her.

"There's been a complication."

Hannah stiffened with anger. "You weren't supposed to call until—"

"I'm at the cemetery. He's dead."

Hannah stared at the phone in disbelief. A feeling of loss came down on her like hard rain— piercing, sharp, chilling her to the core. She stood there dumbly until she realized Chiago was still talking, his voice tinny through the small speaker. Hannah raised the phone to her ear again.

"What?" she asked dully.

Half a block away, the light at the intersection changed, and she glimpsed the flash of Cooper's brake lights before the pickup turned the corner and disappeared.

"There's someone here who wants to talk to you. Says she's your half sister."

Shelby was in New York? And she knew about Tel Moore? Hannah's mind reeled. She felt disoriented, in another world.

"I don't understand. How did—"

"Hi," said a voice Hannah had never heard before. "I'm Anuja, Tel's daughter. Or I guess I should say, *one* of his daughters." The woman's tone was warm, like caramel melting over ice cream. "It's good to finally talk to you."

To receive a free catalog of Poisoned Pen Press titles, please contact us in one of the following ways:

Phone: 1-800-421-3976
Facsimile: 1-480-949-1707
Email: info@poisonedpenpress.com
Website: www.poisonedpenpress.com

Poisoned Pen Press
6962 E. First Ave. Ste 103
Scottsdale, AZ 85251